Wakefield Press

The Girl with the Gold Bikini

Lisa Walker writes novels for adults and young adults. She has also written an ABC Radio National play and been published in the *Age, Griffith Review, The Big Issue* and the *Review of Australian Fiction*. Her recent novels include a young adult coming-of-age story, *Paris Syndrome* (HarperCollins, 2018), and a climate change comedy, *Melt* (Lacuna, 2018). She has worked in environmental communication and as a wilderness guide and recently spent six months in a Kmart tent in outback Australia. Lisa lives, surfs and writes on the north coast of New South Wales. *The Girl with the Gold Bikini* is her sixth novel.

You can visit Lisa at www.lisawalker.com.au.

The Girl with the Gold Bikini

LISA WALKER

Wakefield
Press

Wakefield Press
16 Rose Street
Mile End
South Australia 5031
www.wakefieldpress.com.au

First published 2020

Cover designed by Liz Nicholson, Wakefield Press
Edited by Margot Lloyd, Wakefield Press
Typeset by Michael Deves, Wakefield Press

ISBN 978 1 74305 687 5

A catalogue record for this
book is available from the
National Library of Australia

Wakefield Press thanks
Coriole Vineyards for
continued support

For my sister, Sue,
a keen early reader of my work.

Whenever I see a girl in a gold bikini, I think of Princess Leia. Here on the Gold Coast, gold bikinis are common, so I think of Princess Leia a lot.

Princess Leia doesn't stand for any nonsense. When the giant slug made her wear that ridiculous bikini, she whipped out her chain and gave it a thrashing. Then she changed quick smart into something more sensible.

'Dance with the hottest crowd in town, our stunning waitresses will ensure ...'

Punching the radio 'off' button, I squeeze my car into a metered spot near Cavill Avenue and glance at my watch. Late again. The good thing about working in Surfers Paradise is that the meter maids will be along soon to stick money in the meter. That's if they don't recognise my parents' bombed-out Daihatsu, in which case they'll know I'm no tourist, but a shameless leech on the system.

I jog up the street, jumping sideways to avoid getting wiped out by a guy with a nine-foot surfboard on his head. A tout calls out from a doorway, gesturing towards his shop. *Get your stuffed koalas, didgeridoos and Akubra hats here, folks.* Or that's what I imagine he's saying. As I don't speak Japanese it's hard to be sure.

I nod at the tout. He nods back. Seiji's All Australian Souvenir Shop and Outback Bar is my regular lunchtime haunt. I don't buy much but it's always quiet in there, compared to the hustle bustle of the street. Seiji is nice. He never seems to mind if my ice-cream drips. He's a good salesman, too.

As I push through the door of Gold Star Investigations I pause to savour the thrill it gives me. Here I am. Straight out of school and already a private investigator in training. It's funny, though, how when dreams come true they're never quite what you expect.

I hadn't thought it would be so hard to work with Rosco. He and I are no strangers. We grew up on the same street in Southport. He was one year ahead of me in school, but we hung out together after hours. Rosco was Luke Skywalker and Han Solo to my Leia. We took turns to play Yoda, and very accomplished in Yoda-speak we were. The force was with us. I misheard this phrase the first time he said it, before I watched the movies, and *the horse is with you* became our little in-joke.

Rosco ditched me as a playmate when he turned ten and I didn't see much of him for a while. It soon became clear that he hadn't ditched me to hang out in the skate park with the other boys, though. Rosco had his eyes on broader horizons. He started his first business when he was eleven, selling funky caps online. At fourteen he switched to designing apps for businesses and made some serious money. Now he's thrown all this capital into opening Gold Star Investigations. The Gold Coast, he says, is crying out for PIs. He's changed a lot since we were playmates, but I suppose I have, too.

Rosco's been in business for six months and I am his first

employee. My relationship with him as a CEO is different to when he was Han Solo. From the moment I started, a week ago, he's treated me like an IQ-challenged sidekick. My role is clear. I am not Princess Leia, Nancy Drew, or even Batgirl. No, I am Watson to his Sherlock, Hastings to his Poirot, Robin to his Batman.

Rosco has now become something of an enigma to me. He makes out like he's a typical Aussie surfer boy, but he's never been that. How many nineteen-year-old surfers start their own PI business? I know why I'm in the game, but as for him ... no idea. He says it's purely business but I'm not buying it. If he was trying to make money, he'd have stuck with IT.

As I sprint up the grey-carpeted stairs, my glasses fog up from the effort. I burst into the office and, even through the haze on my lenses, I can see that Rosco doesn't look happy. 'Sorry, Rosco. You wouldn't believe the traffic.'

'Hudson rang, asking after his background check.'

'Yeah, sorry. I'll be right onto it.' I slink off to my corner. My work to date has revolved around two things – internet searches spiced up with a bit of surveillance. This involves sitting in bushes taking shots of men doing things they don't want you to see. Crouching in bushes is the assistant's job. Exactly what the manager's job is, I haven't yet worked out. Fast-talking and hustling, perhaps. Rosco's good at that.

I press the power button, polish my glasses on my T-shirt, and hum the theme music from *Star Wars* as I wait for my computer to boot up. Everyone has their morning routines.

'Earth to Tatooine. Look out the window and tell me what's wrong with this picture.' Rosco is behind me. It's been ten years since we played *Star Wars*, but he still knows the theme song when he hears it.

The music dries up in my throat and I slide my glasses back on. This is Rosco's form of on-the-job training. I might be earning less than minimum wage, but I'm getting the benefit of his vast experience, he says. When he tells me this I resist the urge to point out he only trained as a PI last year.

A few times a day he pops up beside me and gives me a grilling. *You're doing surveillance in a suburban street; how do you avoid getting noticed?* he'll bark. Or, *Name three good ways to get information out of a reluctant witness.*

I feel like he'll keep me in after work if I give the wrong answer. Or maybe boot me out for good. Rosco can't expect a super sleuth on my salary, but a girl who's learned all she knows from Nancy Drew and Veronica Mars might not be what he had in mind either. He's having second thoughts about me, I can tell, and he's not the type of guy to let a childhood friendship cloud his judgement. Business is business. As much as I try to stay cool, I want to keep this job.

My pulse races as I peer out the window. It's a typical Gold Coast street scene. Two blonde teenage girls in short shorts. Two blond teenage boys in baggy board shorts with surfboards. One couple – an older man with a girl around my age. A yellow bus with red and blue surfboards painted on the side, stopping to pick up passengers.

'Nothing. It's a trick question.' He's done that to me before. *Just keeping you on your toes,* he says.

'Look again.'

I look again. The teenage boys have turned to watch the girls go past. The bus is making its way up the street. *Nothing abnormal – code green.* There must be something about the couple.

The man is middle-aged and dressed in what passes for casual on the Gold Coast: ironed polo shirt, tailored slacks and white leather shoes. He looks ready for a round of golf at Sanctuary Cove.

The girl is one of those sleek beauties who look like they don't even need to try. Her glossy hair hangs to the belt of her simple, but probably designer, little white dress. Gorgeous for sure, but her type isn't exactly unusual on the Gold Coast. *Code green, or ...*

'No suntan!' I yell like a contestant on *Quiz of the Century*.

Rosco smiles – a proud teacher. 'You're getting there.'

The couple pause beneath our sign, glance up and down the street, then open the door.

I look at Rosco and he nods. 'They're coming our way.'

This is a momentous event. It's the first time since I've started that a potential client has visited the office. Now, the theme from James Bond, *The Man with the Golden Gun*, starts in my head; *Olivia Grace and the case of the—*

There's a sharp knock. Rosco acts cool. Straightening the collar on his blue cotton shirt he opens the door.

The couple take off their sunglasses, as if on cue. 'Good morning, Mr Ledger.' Their accent is American. If they are surprised to find the office staffed by teenagers, they don't show it. Rosco has never let his youth affect his confidence.

The girl is even more beautiful close-up. She's almost geisha-like with her pale, oval face and brilliant red lips.

'Let me introduce you to my assistant, Olivia Grace,' says Rosco.

I bound from my chair, tugging my too-short T-shirt over my cargo pants. I need to make a good impression. *How? How? How?* Cogs whir in my head. Steam practically comes out my ears, I'm thinking so hard.

Rosco raises his eyebrows. I'm taking too long. I should say hello, but it's so boring, so unimpressive. I can do better than that. The couple's faces are impassive. They think I'm shy.

I've got it. I open my mouth. 'Howdy,' I say in a hearty voice.

It doesn't go down as well as I'd hoped. They look puzzled.

Perhaps they didn't hear me. I try again with a different emphasis and a more encouraging expression. 'Howdy partner!'

The girl smiles and I breathe again.

'Oh, you mean *howdy pardner.*' She sounds like she's walked out of a movie set in New York. One filled with yellow taxis and smart-talking street vendors. 'Your pronunciation is very,' she purses her shiny, red lips, 'Australian.'

The man gives me a small nod. 'Can we speak somewhere private, Mr Ledger?'

Rosco ushers them towards his glass-walled office, flinging me a *what the hell?* look over his shoulder.

Deflated, I sink back to my seat.

Rosco is ensconced with the Americans for some time. I complete the Hudson check in a fury of efficiency, print it out and arrange it in a folder. Glancing over at Rosco, I see he is putting everything he has into this pitch. His suntanned face is animated and he doesn't pause to flick his blond hair out of his eyes. He looks like Han Solo trying to convince Chewbacca to break out of prison.

I pretend to work until I hear Rosco's door open. The American couple walk straight to the door. I can't let them go like that. This is a big job, I can sense it. It's an American job, a New York job, and jobs don't come bigger than that. I want in.

I'm well qualified to liaise with American clients. I lead an exciting multicultural life. Watching Hollywood blockbusters and eating hamburgers is my favourite weekend activity.

'Bye guys, can't wait to ride shotgun with you,' I call. That's what they always say in the movies – *ride shotgun*. It means to help someone out, I think.

The Americans swivel at the door. They stare at me, their faces blank, then the girl murmurs something to Rosco. He taps the side of his head with his index finger. I strain my ears but can't catch what he says. It doesn't look good.

Code orange. Code orange. Faster beats my pulse. In times of stress I find Yoda-speak calming.

As their steps recede down the staircase Rosco turns on me. 'Ride shotgun? What the hell? I had to tell them you were a few spanners short of a picnic.'

'Did they know what that meant?'

'They got the idea.'

'I was just trying to be friendly. It's nice to talk to people in their own dialect. It makes them feel at home.'

He folds his arms and looks stern. The fact that I've seen him dressed in his mother's white dressing gown brandishing an umbrella as a lightsaber should be helpful right now, but it is not.

Code red. Code red. I've seen that look before, he's about to ditch me. I decide to get in first. 'Okay, sorry. It's not working out, is it? If you want me to leave, I'll go.' I stand; stuffing the snow-dome surfer I bought from Seiji yesterday into my shoulder bag.

The corner of Rosco's mouth quivers.

I pick up my Surfers Paradise drink coasters and drop them in my bag too. I can't believe it; he's really going to let me go.

Rosco laughs. 'Don't be such a drama queen. Everyone makes mistakes. Go get some lunch; I'll see you back here in half an hour.'

I pull my souvenirs back out and sit them on my desk. Disaster averted. My pulse settles. *Code green.*

Rosco leans against the door frame watching me, his face unreadable. 'Olivia?'

'Yes?' I have no idea what he is going to say next. It's so weird how someone you've known since childhood can turn into a stranger.

He puts his hand in his pocket and jingles his change. 'Get me a salad roll while you're out, will you?'

Nancy Drew and Princess Leia put up with this would not, but I want the job so I put out my hand. 'White or wholemeal?'

'Excitement is found in all corners of the Gold Coast. Bungee jump in the middle of Surfers Paradise, skydive, paraglide, parasail, hangglide, abseil, hot air balloon or ...'

The loudspeaker blasts across the mall. Cavill Avenue is bustling as always. Seiji eyes me under his black hair and nods as I reach his souvenir shop and outback bar. You might think this is a strange combination, but in Surfers it's normal.

I nod back. This nod is something I've been working on. *I am a tough and resourceful PI on her lunch break*, it says. *You don't want to mess with me.* I'm pretty sure Seiji gets it, but as I don't speak Japanese and he speaks very little English it's hard to be sure.

Seiji holds out a mug with a picture of a kangaroo on it. 'Special. Five dorrars.'

A kangaroo mug for five dollars! How could you go past it? Seiji knows how to exploit my weakness. I started collecting Australiana many years ago and have a large collection of trinkets at home. Here in Surfers, I'm constantly tempted.

Our transaction complete, I put the mug in my bag and wander over to order a sushi lunch box from McSushi. You never have to go far on the Gold Coast to find one these days. The McSushi ambassador's face is plastered across the shiny white walls of the food franchise. It's Ajay, yoga guru to the stars and founder of the Bikini Beach Body Speed Yoga Boot Camp franchise. At least, I think that's what it's called. It's some combination of those words. Like McSushi, he is everywhere too. In the last week I've seen him on the cover of *GQ*, talking on *Sunrise* and guest-starring in a panel show. Ajay is like Madonna – he's so famous he only needs one name.

Yoga is my life. McSushi is my food, reads the caption on the poster. Dressed in red hotpants, Ajay sits on a rock in lotus pose with a nori roll in his hand. It's not a look many could pull off, but he does.

Picking up a copy of the free daily rag, the *Gold Coast Times*, I wander to the wall lining the beach. Sunbathing hasn't gone out of style on the Gold Coast. A stiff wind is blowing sand over all the roasting bodies. A clubbie sits watch on the tower. Flags flutter and swimmers frolic in the twin mirrors of his sunglasses.

I hold onto my floppy hat with one hand and stuff the nori roll in my mouth with the other, while attempting a lotus pose. I don't pull it off, but I Instagram it anyway, tagging *#bikinibodyspeedyogabootcamp #livingmybestlife.* Irony can be tricky on social media, but I've never let that stop me.

Putting my phone in my pocket, I survey the scene. I can't believe I've ended up working in Surfers Paradise. I grew up on the Gold Coast and it does have some good parts, but I've never warmed to Surfers. I eye the seething mass of tourists on the beach and the high-rise towers – Horizons, Mariner Shores, Pelican Sands, Chamonix. I'm like an anthropologist, studying an exotic tribe. Why do people come here? I wouldn't if I had a better offer.

Basically, I'm here for the job. The PI thing has been my dream for years. I blame my grandmother. She's the one who gave me my first Nancy Drew book when I was ten and followed up with more volumes at every birthday and Christmas thereafter. Ever since, I've imagined myself roaming the streets, helping out the good guys, bringing down the bad guys. Wiggling out of scary moments with some girl-power ingenuity. Nancy Drew has style and chutzpah, not to mention a snazzy sports car. I have none of these, but what the hell. There's nothing to stop me trying.

Mum and Dad aren't too keen on the PI thing. They want me to go to uni. I applied for law to keep them happy and the offer from the university's still there. It's only January and uni doesn't start until March, so I've got a few months to try this out. 'I'm keeping my options open,' I told them. I can't see myself as a lawyer though. I've always been a 'colour outside the lines' kind of girl and law strikes me as an inside-the-box profession.

I have another reason for wanting to be a PI. It's because of what happened in Byron Bay a couple of years ago. I need to find my mojo again and I figure being a PI is a good way to start. So far though, it hasn't quite worked out that way.

January is a funny time around here. A lot of the locals clear out. My friends Abbey and Frannie have gone backpacking in South-East Asia to celebrate the end of Year Twelve. I was going too, but once I saw Rosco's job advertised, that was it, I had to have it. Jobs like that don't come along every day.

Also absent are my mum and dad, who have gone trekking in Nepal for a month and rented out our house on Airbnb. For them, the words holidays and hiking are interchangeable. They live to hike. Usually my six-year-old sister Jacq and I tag along, but this year, seeing as I'm tied up, they've decided to go without us.

So, one week ago, Jacq and I moved into my grandmother's two-bedroom unit south of Surfers. Our neighbours include a constantly stoned white-haired surfie and a quiet woman who is on the mend from a face-lift. I wouldn't say it's my spiritual home, but Nan does have over two hundred Nancy Drew books, so it's not all bad.

I swallow the last of my nori roll and flick through the *Gold Coast Times*. The editorial bleats its dismay at the way a Sydney football event portrayed the Gold Coast. It was a closing ceremony where the baton passes on to the next host; in this case, the Gold Coast. Bikini-clad dancers featured prominently.

It's a mixed message from the editor. Firstly, doesn't Sydney realise the Gold Coast has two universities and leads the nation in biotechnology? Secondly, the dancers were supposed to represent the Gold Coast but they weren't suntanned and their bikinis didn't fit.

In front of me, a meter maid in a snug gold bikini, high heels and cowboy hat poses for a photo with a hairy, barrel-chested man. It seems like feminism has passed the Gold Coast by. No one questions the idea that paying bikini girls to roam the streets is a good thing.

As I sip my orange juice, I imagine how the meter maid concept might have started.

Surfers Paradise, 1965. Surfies cruise the streets in EH Holdens whistling at girls in that great new look – the mini skirt. The sun shines, the Gold Coast booms. But a cloud looms on the horizon. A lone stranger gallops into town. 'Parking meters are coming! Parking meters are coming!' Panic hits the streets. Men in suits huddle around a table. 'It's a disaster.' 'We're ruined.' 'No one will shop here anymore.' A light bulb comes on. 'I'm thinking, girls in bikinis.' 'Girls in bikinis?' 'Bikini girls who put money in meters.' 'Brilliant – great concept.' Back slapping all around.

Girls in bikinis can solve any marketing problem. They are like fairy dust – sprinkle them around and *poof*, problem solved. Even when I used to wear bikinis, I still found it strange. Bringing in pay-and-display machines instead of coin meters a few years ago hasn't changed things. The bikini girls just buy the tickets and place them on cars now.

The editorial concludes with what sounds like a threat from Doctor Evil. *There will come a time, in the not-too-distant future, when the capital cities will recognise the Gold Coast for what it is.* I imagine a bikini-clad takeover of Sydney. That'll teach 'em.

I pick up Rosco's salad roll and trot back to the office.

3

A blonde ponytail is flowing down the back of the chair opposite Rosco when I get back in. Two client visits in one day – our social media marketing must be paying off.

Rosco has instructed me to tweet and 'gram as much as possible *#privateinvestigator #privateeye*. Promoting yourself on social media while protecting client confidentiality is tricky. My work-related Instagrams feature blurry shots of windows with bushes in front of them. Despite my conscientious hash-tagging they haven't been a big hit.

Rosco waves me over. 'Olivia, this is Rochelle Randall.'

The ponytail-woman swivels and I put out my hand. Hers is warm and damp in mine. I spot a wedding ring. 'It's a pleasure to meet you, Mrs Randall.' Straight down the line. I'm not taking any chances this time.

'Rochelle.' A tight smile pulls up her suntanned cheeks. She's a Gold Coast girl all right. She must only be in her twenties, but her forehead is already less mobile than nature intended. Getting botox is like brushing your teeth around here. Her look is hippie chic, but a diamond ring and heavy gold necklace hint at serious money.

'Take a seat, Olivia,' Rosco says.

Yes! I might have been cut out of the American operation, but it looks like I'm in on this one.

'It's all right, Rochelle. You can rely on us,' he says.

'I hope so.' Her suntanned bosom almost bursts out of her off-the-shoulder gypsy top as she leans forward to push a flyer across the table. 'Felicity Knight spoke highly of the way you handled her divorce case.'

My stomach sinks. *Damn.* It's another *#matrimonial.* Rosco's been doing a brisk trade in rich but lonely Gold Coast wives whose hubbies cheat.

Meeting concluded, Rochelle stands and minces to the door in her high-heeled sandals.

I eye the thin gold chain around her ankle. Ankle chains are big on the Gold Coast. I'd consider getting one, but it would clash with the second-hand store look I'm currently rocking. My style is best described as utilitarian. But what I lack in grooming, I make up for in personality.

Rosco shows her out. 'We'll be in touch,' he says. As her footsteps recede down the stairs, he sits again. 'She thinks her husband's cheating on her. She found this in his pocket.'

I glance at the flyer he's given me. *Allure Speed Dating: Meet thousands of local singles.* 'Not looking good.'

'I want you on it straight away.'

'Me?' I moan. 'I'm still pulling prickles out of my bum from my last stint in the shrubbery.'

'That's your job. Besides, I'm pretty tied up.'

With the exciting American operation, no doubt. Typical.

He pushes a file across the desk towards me. 'Have a look through this. Go undercover. Join his yoga class. I want a progress report on Friday.'

'Yoga?'

'Didn't I say? Her husband's that yoga guy. You know, the one who trains Georgia Hansen?' He pulls a poster out of the file.

It's him, the hotpants-wearing bikini-yoga-boot-camp sushi-eater. I sigh, but I suppose I'm in no position to take a stand. All I can do is prove my ability to undertake more demanding assignments. Nancy Drew is constantly faced with sceptics, but she always proves them wrong.

'You'll need to go down to Byron Bay. You can claim back your petrol. No need to stay the night. It's only about forty minutes drive.'

'Byron Bay?' My heart beats faster.

Rosco's phone rings. 'Hi, Kenny. Yes, sorry. Didn't realise it was that time of the month already.' He pulls at his hair.

'Right, better get on with it,' I mutter, retreating to my desk. *Byron Bay.* I tap my fingers on the table. It's been two years since I was last there and I hadn't planned to go back anytime soon. But ... open to negotiation on this one, I don't think Rosco is.

Spreading the file out on the desk, I flick through it. Ajay, or Guruji as his pupils know him, has a distinguished career as a yoga guru. He's practised yoga practically since birth and spent many years in India studying under the yoga masters. The unique and profitable form of bikini speed yoga boot camp he now teaches was bestowed on him by some cave-dwelling hermit.

Inspired by his Gold Coast-born wife, Rochelle, he recently arrived from the States. His all-star devotees followed him all the way from LA to his new retreat in Byron Bay. The couple now divide their time between a multi-million-dollar 'beach shack' at Wategos Beach in Byron Bay and a luxury condo at Kirra on the Gold Coast. *Tough life.*

I pull a brochure out of the file. *Lighthouse Bliss: The newest place to replenish your bikini body and your soul.* On the front cover a woman with long, sun-bleached hair imitates a piece of spaghetti, leaning over backwards on the sand.

I flip the brochure over. The back cover is a shot of Ajay standing one-legged, the other leg held beside his head. His body is a testament to the power of yoga. His stern expression suggests a man with no room for slackers in his life. I don't think we're going to get along. Right now, though, that's not my main issue.

Byron Bay.

It was Abbey who first introduced me to the Bay.

My parents aren't into beach holidays. It's bad enough to live on the beach, they figure we don't need to holiday there as well. Our holidays have always revolved around forests and bushwalks. So, by the age of sixteen I'd been to a vast variety of national parks, but never over the border to Byron Bay.

At the end of Year Ten, with unbearable excitement, I set out with Abbey's family for a two-week holiday in Byron Bay. I had no idea what to expect. People said it was originally a hippie town, now filled with backpackers. It sounded exciting. It wasn't far, but it was uncharted territory. They could have scrawled *here be dragons* on the map south of Coolangatta as far as I was concerned.

We took the scenic route. As we wound down the leafy horseshoe bends of the Burringbar Range, Abbey and I stuck our heads out the window and smelt the rainforest. It seemed like we were in another world already.

Byron Bay, I soon discovered, was a place to conjure dreams.

The sweep of the bay to the base of the mountains; the dolphins leaping from water so clear it was barely there. For us, it was nirvana.

At my desk, I pull out my phone and find the photo from two years ago.

Two tousle-haired girls peer into the camera. Abbey took it one morning after we surfed at Wategos Beach. She held the phone out in front of us as we leaned our heads together, arms around each other.

I put my fingers to the screen and enlarge myself. Out of the phone smiles a girl with tanned skin and a white singlet top over her bikini. My hair is a tangled mess and even back then I didn't have a traditional bikini beach body. I look radiantly happy though. As if nothing could touch me. I'm holding a surfboard under one arm.

I still have that board, but it's gathering dust in the garage at home. *Byron.* Maybe it's time to brush the cobwebs off that surfboard.

If nothing else, a board on the roof will help with my undercover disguise.

South-American panpipes warble through a speaker on the ceiling. A whip bird calls outside. I peer through the middle of an autographed 'Ajay' organic yoga mat, observing the studio. Today Ajay's hot pants are green. His muscular and almost hairless body shines under the studio downlights. His voice drifts through the door, the American twang giving it extra carrying power. The microphone clipped to his head ensures his disciples don't miss a word of his teachings. At forty dollars a class, they wouldn't want to. Still, the students are jammed in tighter than a yogi's abs.

'Bring your feet inside your hands, cross them and lift off the ground.' Ajay pauses, his body dangling between his hands, then swings forward into a headstand. The whole class, bar one, follows his moves. I sympathise with the man in the sweat-soaked shorts who topples forward onto his nose. I've been there.

This is my second day following Ajay. Yesterday he led five yoga classes, jogged on the beach and paddled his surf ski out to Julian Rocks. It was like trying to keep track of a kangaroo on speed.

As well as the public classes, Ajay also took a private session in a room out the back. I was thrilled to see Hollywood superstar,

Georgia Hansen, sashay up the corridor. Huge sunglasses covered her face but you couldn't mistake those lips, that wiggle, and the thick blonde hair peeking out from her billowing scarf. *Who* magazine is calling Georgia the new Marilyn Monroe and it's not hard to see why. An hour later she emerged, dishevelled, and jumped into a chauffeured sports car.

I would have liked to stay in the juice bar, rather than face Ajay's classes, but the cost of wheatgrass juice was ridiculous. The only way I could justify hanging around Lighthouse Bliss was to join in.

As a result, yesterday I learned more about yoga than I ever wanted to. For a start, I soon caught on that there's no excuse for anything less than one hundred per cent effort in Ajay's classes. In one class he slapped a girl on the leg when she failed to execute a perfect handstand. I was shocked, but no one else reacted. From the corner of my eye I saw a red flush spread over her face.

Ajay's Bikini Beach Body Boot Camp Speed Yoga is powerful stuff. Each two-hour class covers all the moves other yoga teachers would take two weeks to fit in. As the brochure said, he learnt this form of yoga from an Indian guru, who granted him sole worldwide rights. I guess gurus aren't what they used to be back in the day.

For that matter, yoga isn't what it used to be, either. I did yoga for school sport in Year Ten. It was a popular option for those who didn't care to exert themselves. We lay around stretching as chimes tinkled. It was relaxing.

Ajay's classes are nothing like that. They're a kick-butt workout with a dollop of 'oms' thrown in. After almost two hours of gymnastics you lie down for a few seconds, sit up and stagger out. It's like a hardcore version of Twister.

I wasn't the star of the class. Obviously. Ajay blew a gasket as I attempted triangle pose. 'Stop; stop right there.' Stalking over, he circled me, barking commands while the whole class watched. 'Point your back foot forwards, rotate your right thigh, shoulders back, buttocks forward.' At last I forced my body into a painful state that was as close as I could get to his expectations. He snorted and returned to the front of the class.

When I rolled out of bed this morning, I felt like I'd survived a plane crash. Muscles I'd never noticed before were screaming in protest. My stomach is the worst, but even my chin is sore, which I can't explain at all.

Most of what Ajay does is so far beyond me it may as well be a circus show. Fling your legs to the side while holding your weight on your hands? Bend your feet over to touch your head while resting on your forearms? *I don't think so.* There is one move, though, that calls to me and, what's more, it may be within my grasp – the headstand.

Headstands are big on Instagram. People do the craziest things. I have no wish to breastfeed a baby while doing a headstand, though I totally support women who want to do that. Nor do I want to smoke a joint in a headstand like Miley Cyrus. But, all power to Miley. I would, however, enjoy posing in a headstand in exotic locations as so many seem to do. Visiting the Eiffel Tower? Why not do a headstand while you're there? The Taj Mahal? Likewise. The Sydney Opera House? Naturally. The headstand, like bikini shots, turbocharges your Insta posts. I've ruled out bikinis, so if I want to be an Insta star I'm left with headstands.

To be honest, I couldn't care less about being an Insta star, but still ... I'd like to do a headstand. I've only tried the practice version so far – head off the ground with the weight on my elbows – but I'm on a mission.

Today though, despite the lure of more headstand practice, my body demands I give yoga a miss. So, I'm browsing in the Lighthouse Bliss shop. The cheapest thing here is a sixty-dollar *Om* singlet. I pass.

'Lift the perineum.' Ajay's command echoes through the shop.

I'm not completely sure what the perineum is, or how to lift it. *Pass.* As I return my eye to the mat roll, I see Ajay's class lie down for their token few seconds of relaxation. Soon after, he lopes out of the building, a pair of loose trousers over his hotpants.

I straighten my white cowboy hat and follow him to his car. Disguises are one of Rosco's pet private eye techniques. *Keep a range of outfits handy to change your appearance. You need to be able to go from beach to disco without losing your target.* It's one of the more fun aspects of the job. In the first few days at work, I'd organised myself a collection of plastic bags labelled *surf chick, bikie, Norwegian backpacker* and *femme fatale*. Right now, I am modelling *Norwegian backpacker.* My white cowboy hat comes with long blonde plaits attached. I've teamed this with fetching pastel shorts and singlet and applied fake tan to complete the effect.

'Beach, beach, beach,' I mutter as Ajay zooms off in his sporty red car. I have a craving for the sea.

5

'Budgie, you are a soul surfer and wave wizard extraordinaire – tell us about your spiritual quest for the ultimate wave ...'

If the radio announcer spoke any slower you'd be able to fit a quick news break between each word. I hit the brakes as a guy in a mohair boob tube skateboards across the road in front of me. Byron fashions are so *whatever.* I like that. My fashion style is pretty much *whatever* as well.

I've been too busy to reflect on how I feel about being back in the Bay. And I guess I haven't wanted to. I need to focus on my work. Winding down my window, I sniff the air as I follow Ajay's car down the main drag. A light south-easterly is blowing – I bet there'll be a perfect off-shore wave.

I found my old board in the garage at Southport before I left for Byron. It looked desolate there, among the abandoned golf clubs and bicycles. 'There you are, old bluey,' I said. 'Waiting patiently for my return.' The fibreglass felt smooth under my fingertips and a faint memory of happiness ran through me as I pulled it out.

Yesterday, when Ajay paddled his surf ski out to Julian Rocks, I sat on the beach watching glassy little waves that looked perfect for an out-of-practice surfer like me. 'Ride me, ride me,' they screamed. It was painful. I wanted to, but I couldn't. Maybe today will be different.

As I wind past the cabbage tree palms to Wategos, Abbey's voice is in my head. *How good is this place, Ol? Surf and rainforest. It's paradise.* Abbey was right. Byron Bay is still paradise. Seems like the whole world thinks so too, though.

Outside Ajay's beach house, I park my car where I can keep an eye on both his entrance and the surf. His house reeks of money. A steep driveway winds up to a grey, two-storey mansion with wrap-around glass windows. He must have awesome views. In front, a waterfall washes down a stone wall from an infinity pool. I suppose I'd live there if you twisted my arm.

Wategos is exactly as I remember it; a sheltered half-moon facing the jagged pinnacle of Julian Rocks. A dive boat bobs, toy-like, in the deep water off the rocks. At the end of the beach near the rocky point, a woman in a red bikini is doing yoga. As I watch, she bends over, places her palms on the sand and flicks her legs into an effortless handstand. As if that isn't enough, she lowers her legs over her head, dropping into a back-bend. She must be made of rubber.

As I suspected, the surf is perfect; a two- to three-foot wave pushing all the way from the point to the beach. The waves are peeling in like cars on a highway, not one without a surfer gliding across its face. A mass of bodies waits in the water. Was it always this crowded?

A girl in a long-sleeved wetsuit top and green bikini bottom takes off on a wave out the back. She does a bottom turn, pulls up to the top of the wave and walks to the front of her board. Curling her toes over the edge, she leans back and rides the lip of the wave for a few moments, then, as if she's strolling down the street, she walks back to the middle of her board and drops into the splits. I pick my jaw back off the dashboard. *How did she do that?*

I'm so engrossed I almost miss Ajay jogging past me, surf ski under his arm. He's going to Julian Rocks again.

I look out at the surf, at the sparkle of the water, and listen to the siren call of the waves. It's been too long. I'm going to do it. This time I'm going to do it. It's time to surf.

The salty, fresh air sends a charge of electricity through me as I leap out of the car. Glancing around to make sure no one's watching, I whip off my hat and plaits and pull my faded old wetsuit out of the boot. The currents can still be cold at this time of year.

Getting into the wetsuit is a struggle. I've got bigger since I last had it on. I'm not sure if I'll be able to move.

'Filthy little pearlers out there,' calls a dripping wet surfer to a guy who's pulled up in an old Kombi. *Surf talk.* I've heard Inuits have forty-two words to describe ice. I reckon Australians would have at least as many words for surf. It could be interesting to keep track.

My stomach contracts as I head out. Ajay is paddling into the distance as I push my board into the waves. Then the salt spray dashes at my face and my body loosens. Why didn't I do this ages ago? It's not like there aren't waves on the Gold Coast; it's just that I haven't been catching them.

Letting go of my board I dive, dolphin-like, under a wave. The water fizzes like champagne against my skin. I burst out from under the wave, collide with a body board above me, and tip a small, freckled boy into the water. Dumbstruck, he crawls back on and paddles away as fast as he can.

My elation dented, I pull myself onto my board. A shimmering lattice of sunlight dances beneath me as I paddle out to the break. In a few moments, I'm lined up with the pack, ready and waiting.

Twenty minutes later, I'm still ready and waiting. I'd forgotten how cutthroat it is out here. One of the men in the line-up is a kind of man-fish thing. His hands are the size of flippers and he gets onto the waves with about two strokes.

The pack takes my measure quickly. Every time I paddle for a wave someone else comes in from in front or behind or materialises out of nowhere. I get psyched out and pull back while they take off. It's depressing.

My lack of action surf-wise gives me plenty of time to observe the line-up. It looks like a typical surf pack. As always there are:

(a) The old crusties – weather-beaten dudes who remember Byron Bay when you had to go looking for someone to surf with;

(b) The grommets – school-age kids with no respect for their elders;

(c) The surfing lawyers – distinguished by their name-brand clothing, shiny surfboards and superior attitude; and

(d) Backpackers – these are the most annoying.

All around me backpackers, who have probably never even *seen* a wave before, are jumping to their feet. Whoops and hollers in Swedish and German trail behind them as they ride into shore, legs stretched wide and arms out for balance.

I'm almost convinced to call it a day and head in when a voice behind me calls, 'Come on, it's yours.'

Craning my neck, I peer down the length of my board. The girl in the green bikini bottom is surfing towards me.

'Get on; party wave,' she yells.

I paddle hard, my arms straining against the constraints of my wetsuit. My yoga-weary muscles ache, but I ignore them. As a drop opens beneath me the wave picks me up. Using movements I've almost forgotten, I struggle to my feet. The girl whoops, surfing beside me.

But the enjoyment is short-lived. The wave curls and white-wash whooshes next to me. The wave sucks up and with a shriek I tumble down the vertical face. Water spins me head over tail, my leg rope dragging on my ankle. I pop up, holding my hands over my head to avoid getting conked by my fin.

Wiping water from my eyes, I see the girl doing some fancy footwork as she rides on ahead of me. As the wave dies she flicks her board around to face the horizon and lowers herself onto it. It's beautiful to watch – like a dance. She paddles back out to me, motoring across the water.

'Thanks for that,' I call as she comes near. 'First wave of the day for me. First wave for two years, actually.'

Close-up, she looks younger than she did at a distance, about my age. She is muscular and her short blonde hair clings in wet wisps across her face. There's not a lot to her, but what there is sure packs a punch.

She sits on her board next to me. 'Two years! You must have been hanging out for it. Great wipe-out by the way. Good effort.'

'Yeah. I know I can surf better than this.' I pause. 'Although I never have yet.'

She giggles, exposing a gap between her two front teeth. 'There're lots of things I know I can do better too, but never have.'

'Well, clearly surfing isn't one of them. You must have started at birth, right?'

'Yep, my dad whisked me straight from the delivery room into the break.'

Something in her tone suggests she's not exactly joking.

'That's him out there.' She points at a man leaping to his feet out the back.

It's the man-fish. That makes sense: like father, like daughter. He rides the wave towards us as if the board is an extension of his body. With a powerful thrust he flicks off next to us.

His weather-beaten face scans mine and moves on. 'Keep at it, Maya.'

'Yeah, I'll be right behind you.' She lies on her board again. Her father paddles back out, his shoulders rippling under a black lycra shirt. A wave washes over us, pushing me towards shore. 'Don't let them psyche you out,' she calls back to me. 'You've got as much right to the waves as anyone; and get further forward on your board when you're paddling for a wave. You have to commit more. Ask yourself: what's the worst that can happen?'

Another wave rushes over the top of us. Maya pushes her board under it, while I tumble off. 'I might get pounded on the head and killed,' I yell, scrambling back on my board.

'Right,' calls Maya. 'Hardly worth worrying about, is it? You know, in the scheme of things.'

I suppose I see her point.

Maya glances out at the break, where her father has taken off on another wave. 'I'd better make a move.' She gives him a mock salute as he nears us.

'See you 'round,' I call. I'm about to try for another wave when I spot Ajay paddling towards shore. *Damn, back to work.* I catch a friendly sweep of white wash into the beach, lying on my stomach. I'm smiling as I plod up the sand. I didn't exactly carve it up, but it's good to be back. It's really good. Two years out of the surf is way too long. I've forgotten the pleasure of tired muscles and salt-coated skin.

As I towel off next to my car, a girl with golden skin presses a pamphlet into my hand. 'Ten per cent discount on Bikini Beach Body Boot Camp Speed Yoga classes with this brochure,' she says in an unidentifiable European accent. Her tight orange T-shirt reads, *Want Bliss?* As she walks past I read the back; *Get it here.* Sexual innuendo never goes out of fashion as a marketing tool. I glance at the brochure. Ajay's on a heavy sales push.

Throwing the brochure in the car, I do a rapid under-towel shimmy and resume my position outside his house. As I do so my watch alarm goes off. I grimace at the condensation under the face. I know no one wears watches these days, but I like them. I'm too lazy to pull out my phone every time I want to check the time. Why I keep buying cheap digital watches though, I don't know. Last year I went through four. Each developed annoying habits. There was the beep-on-the-hour-every-hour watch, the stop-start watch, the faster and faster watch, and now, it seems, the watch with a random alarm function. I press the off button and it stops. I can only hope it's a one-off quirk.

The sun is low in the sky now and the surfers skim across a sea of melted gold. Maya is out the back with her father. They're a long way away, but something about their postures makes me think they're arguing. Maya's father waves his arm.

I don't have long to think about it as Ajay's car comes down the driveway and takes off at his usual break-neck speed. Turning my key in the ignition, I follow. He weaves through town, out onto the highway and then turns north.

A knot in my chest relaxes as I drive away from Byron Bay.

The surfing was fun, but I'm glad to leave. *Baby steps.*

To ease the boredom of the highway, I flick on the local radio station, Lighthouse FM. The announcer is a chirpy young woman. 'To wind up, what do you think of the commercialisation of yoga, as seen at Ajay's Lighthouse Bliss, Luna?'

My ears prick up at the mention of Ajay's name.

'Well, I think it's a bad thing for yoga generally. I mean, not only will Ajay put smaller operators like me out of business with his hard-sell tactics, but now he's going for us legally, too.' The interviewee, also a young woman, has a high-pitched voice and a broad Aussie accent.

'I understand Ajay has trademarked Bikini Beach Body Boot Camp Speed Yoga, is that right?'

'That's right. I mean, yoga is thousands of years old, you can't trademark it. Yoga is a gift.'

'So, you're still teaching speed yoga in your classes?'

'Well, I've got to watch what I say. I've been served a notice by Ajay's lawyers. Let's just say it's pretty fast.'

'You and Ajay go back a way, don't you, Luna?'

'Yes, I did my advanced teacher training with him. I don't know where his head's at now, though.'

'Well, that's it for the Spiritual Hour. If you want to catch one of Luna Nakamura's classes, she's at the Pink House.'

'Thank you, Gaia. Namaste, everyone.'

The Pink House. Holding the steering wheel in one hand, I flip open my notebook and scribble down the name, as well as hers, *Luna Nakamura.* Yes, I have a blue notebook, like Nancy Drew. I don't have a magnifying glass though. That would be weird.

The station fades as I near the Queensland border. It's a Friday night and it looks like Ajay has a date on the Gold Coast.

6

'*Go crazy in Surfers Paradise; fun party games all night and more …*'

I turn the radio off as I follow Ajay into a Surfers Paradise rat run and watch him vanish inside the Starburst Nightclub. A sandwich board outside reads, *Allure Under-Thirties Speed Dating: Tonight – Fully Booked.* I eye the flashing fluorescent lights. A man with a buzz cut, his solid body straining at his suit jacket, stands guard outside.

It looks like Rochelle's suspicions about Ajay were correct. The speed yoga guru is now at speed dating. First, exercise for those with attention deficit disorder, and now, romance. Maybe it's no coincidence? I make a quick note.

So, Ajay's doing something suspicious at last, but … I can't get in. Rochelle won't be impressed. Rosco should have covered this situation in his training.

First things first. Parking my car in a dark side lane, I rummage around in my bag. This situation calls for the debut of a new outfit – the femme fatale. Considering my usual look is T-shirts and cargos, femme fatale is a stretch. Second-hand shops though, I've discovered, are great for slinky dresses. I have two femme fatale outfits, and I decide to go for the eighties-style figure-hugging purple wrap dress with a silver clasp on the hip. It's like something Joan Collins might have rocked in *Dynasty*.

Fluffing up my blonde wig, I pull the rear-view mirror towards me and, taking off my glasses, slip in the blue contact lenses. I catch a glimpse of my chest as I climb out of the car. *Wow.* Push-up bras really work. My reflection in a shop window gives me a peculiar feeling. I look like a stranger.

So now I look the part, but I still need to get past that buzz-cut bouncer. He eyes me suspiciously as I sashay up the street and tuck myself into a doorway, down from the entrance.

Speed daters trickle past, easily identifiable by their eager nervous look. I can relate. Dating is hell. I've gone out with a few boys but none of them worked out. There were various problems – too pushy, no conversation, drunkenness. In the end, though – with one Notable Exception – it boiled down to one thing: their kisses left me cold. Having someone's tongue in your mouth is disagreeable when there's no chemistry.

I'm hanging on to the idea that when I meet the right person it will happen. Our lips will meet and *zing pow zap*. It will be like Han and Leia's first kiss in *The Empire Strikes Back*.

Having Han and Leia as my romantic role models sets the bar pretty high. Let's face it: their romance carried multiple *Star Wars* movies. That's a big ask. I adore the way Leia brings out the soft side in Han, even though he's such a vagabond. I love how she stays so feisty and independent, even when she falls for him. Their kisses seem so ... transcendent.

And the Notable Exception to the disagreeable kisses? Well, that's one more reason why working with Rosco is difficult.

I peek out at the door of the nightclub. The bouncer is still there. Maybe I could create a distraction and slip past him? That's what Nancy Drew would do. I should add firecrackers to my kit.

A girl with bleached blonde hair, wearing a gold boob tube and tight black pants, strides towards me. She has a grim look, like she's going into battle. I bet my push-up bra she's going in there. How can I convince her to give me her place? *My sick mother is in there? No, my boyfriend's in there and I want to spring him? Better.*

Sometimes I get so carried away with this private eye stuff I forget honesty can be the best policy.

'Excuse me,' I whisper as she walks past.

She jumps and gasps but her alarm fades as she sees I'm a girl. 'What? You scared the hell out of me.' Her accent is broad North Queensland.

I pull out my private investigator's card. 'I'm a PI and I need to get into that club. How much is it worth to you to give me your booking?'

She laughs. 'You're really a PI?'

I nod.

'That's pretty cool.' She glances towards the bouncer. 'To be honest, I'd pay you to stop me going in there. I've been trying to psyche myself up, but it's not me. I just don't know how to meet guys around here. It's not like Townsville. I know everyone there.'

'So, you'll give me your booking?'

Her face relaxes. 'Yeah, I'll take it as a sign that I'm not meant to do it. I'll go home and watch a movie. Take this stupid boob tube off.' Her hands pull at her top. 'My booking's in the name of Anna Smith. I haven't paid yet.'

I pull a twenty dollar note out of my bag. 'Here, get yourself something to go with the movie.'

She takes the note, tucking it in her purse. 'Cheers. Knock 'em dead, ay?' She looks ready to kick up her heels now she's escaped from the horrors of speed dating.

'You could try surfing,' I call as she walks down the street.

She turns, her face puzzled. 'Huh?'

'There's lots of guys out there.' I flick my head in the direction of the sea.

'Yeah, I hadn't thought of that. Hot tip, thanks.'

I watch her go, then glide up to the doorman. 'Anna Smith. I have a booking.'

Inside the nightclub, the air buzzes with conversation. Waiters in black and white shuffle here and there like penguins while customers mill about under blue downlights. I shiver. The air-conditioning is at Antarctic temperatures. Blinking in the blue glare, I scan the crowd for Ajay.

'Looks like *Happy Feet*, doesn't it?'

I know that voice. I turn. 'What are *you* doing here? I thought this was my job.'

Rosco takes a sip of beer. He speaks in a low voice. 'I got a tip-off from Rochelle Randall. She's been checking his email. I wasn't sure if you were going to make it. I tried your mobile, but you didn't answer.'

I detect a note of criticism. 'Of course I made it,' I hiss. 'You want me to answer calls while I'm driving?'

'You're not driving now.' Rosco's voice is neutral.

I reach into my bag and pull out my phone. It's ancient and the battery goes flat so quickly I've got in the habit of putting it in aeroplane mode when I'm not using it. I turn off aeroplane mode and it rings to let me know I've got a missed call. *Oops.*

'Almost didn't recognise you. Not your usual look.' Rosco's

eyes are carefully focused on my forehead but I'm sure my preposterous cleavage hasn't escaped him.

My cheeks turn warm. 'Femme fatale.'

'Good job.' He turns to survey the bar. 'Our man is over there.'

I follow his gaze. Alone at the bar, Ajay is nursing what appears to be a glass of mineral water. His shoulder-length brown hair is held back in a ponytail and his white silk shirt is buttoned up to the top.

I take out my phone and discreetly snap a few photos for our report. 'He doesn't look real keen.' He looks like a man dragged to the ballet by his wife.

The microphone squeals and a soft voice coos. 'Welcome to tonight's speed dating. I'm your facilitator, Maxine.' A spotlight zooms in on a woman on a blue-carpeted podium.

I'm glad to see my choice of fluffy blonde hair and push-up bra affirmed by an expert in the field. She's outdone me, though; her dress is covered in sparkles that shine in the light, drawing attention to her curves.

'We have fifteen couples and five minutes each to get those sparks flying. Try to relax and have fun. If you run out of things to talk about there's a laminated list of questions on each table.'

Is she joking? Laminated questions are not sexy. This is more like an exam than a date.

'If you could all take a seat we'll start. I hope Cupid's got his arrows pointed your way tonight,' she chirps.

Oh puke. I don't want Cupid shooting any arrows at me. Not in the Starburst Nightclub anyway. In the sudden lull I hear the background music; James Blunt singing 'You're Beautiful'. It's all way too desperado-ville.

'You suss out the guys, I'll suss out the girls,' says Rosco.

'Yeah, I bet.'

His brow wrinkles. 'Professionally, I mean.'

'Right. Of course.'

'Try and find out if any of them know Ajay,' he murmurs. 'Remember, he might not be here for the obvious reasons.'

'Got it. Nancy Drew 101: how to draw information out of a suspect.'

Rosco smiles, gives me a quick salute and saunters to his seat.

I reach my seat and inspect the guy sitting opposite. As the starting bell rings, all I can think of is high school biology case studies.

'Biologists got it wrong for a long time,' my teacher Mrs Sanderson used to say. 'They over-emphasised the role of the male in the courting process. The flashy peacock, the industrious bower bird, the eagle's tumbling cartwheels all illustrate one point: those males have to try hard to attract attention. It's the female of the species who does the choosing.' *Sperm is cheap,* she wrote on the board, prompting giggles. *Case Study One: The fiddler crab.* 'The female fiddler crab will scrutinise up to fifty males, including a thorough burrow inspection of at least fifteen, before she makes her selection.' It sounded gruelling.

I feel like a female fiddler crab beginning a long shift.

My first crab is a hippie who works in advertising. The contradiction between advertising, dreadlocks, a Greenpeace wristband and the state-of-the-art iPhone he makes a point of placing on the table gets me. Yep, he knows how to keep his idealism in a box.

On the other side of the room, Rosco leans towards a pretty brunette and laughs more enthusiastically than I believe professionalism requires. Spurred on by his example, I flick back my fake blonde locks and lick my lips. 'Are you interested in yoga?'

Of course he is. I hear all about it.

The bell rings at last and I advance to a graphic design student. He's fun, in a one-year-old labrador kind of way. He even looks like a labrador, with his big brown eyes and shaggy blonde hair. Mr Bouncy, I nickname him on my speed dating card – ten out of ten for vitality. He does kickboxing instead of yoga, but on a whim I place a tick next to his name. There's no rule against mixing business with pleasure, is there?

After that it all becomes a simpering, hair-flicking, banal-questioning blur. I'm like a wind-up speed-dating Barbie doll. Eventually I look up and find Ajay seated opposite me. I should have been mentally prepared for this, but I'm not. My mind goes blank. 'Ah, hello, are you into yoga?' I stutter.

Ajay shakes his head. 'Never done it in my life.'

Clearly he doesn't recognise me from his yoga class.

His eyes flicker over me as he reaches for his mineral water. I expect I fail the beach-body-readiness inspection. I notice a small tattoo on his wrist – an outline of a man cross-legged in lotus pose. I hadn't got close enough to him in his classes to see it before.

What's that on your wrist if you're not into yoga? I let it pass. 'Ah, so what brings you here?'

Ajay shrugs and glances around the room. 'Same as everyone else.' His eyes come back to me. 'And you?'

'Um. Same.'

He yawns. It must take it out of you, being a yoga guru.

My professionalism asserts itself. I must attempt to find out what he's up to. 'You seem distracted, is there something bothering you?'

He yawns again and sips his water. 'I'm not really into this,' he mutters.

'Well, I guess it's a big no then,' I cross the *no* box on my card.

His face flushes – I've probably spoilt his perfect speed-dating record. I'm relieved the bell goes at that moment. He gets up and walks stiffly to the next table. I glance over at Rosco and see him clink a champagne glass with his date. He isn't wasting his time checking on me.

The next few dates are hazy, although I come into focus for a guy I nickname the American Bloke. He's maybe a few years older than me and says he's into dancing.

'I'm into dancing too.' I don't mention it's more of a spectator sport for me. *Dancing with the Stars* is one of my favourite shows. I decide to give him a tick.

Throughout all this, James Blunt is on auto replay. *Unbelievable.* Maxine scurries around like a gym teacher encouraging us all to 'Give it our best shot' and reminding us of the laminated questions if we run out of conversation. It's about as sexy as a school athletics carnival. I'm surprised they don't hand out oranges at half-time.

Each time I'm asked a question from the laminated list, I give a different answer. 'What do you do for fun?' *I drink/go to church/ square dance.* 'Why did your last relationship end?' *He was on the run from the police/fell in love with my mother/drank too much* and 'If you could be any animal, what would it be?' *A pit bull terrier/ racoon/dolphin.*

I glance up from reviewing my dating card to find Rosco sitting opposite. Ajay is at the bar nursing a mineral water again. I hope Rosco's not going to make me keep following him. I'm ready for bed.

His eyes are on my card. 'Got a couple you liked, did you?'

I feel my cheeks colour. 'Just trying to look the part. Have you found out anything re our target?' I say in my best crisp PI tone.

Rosco shakes his head. 'Negative.'

'Did you learn that in PI school?'

'What?'

'To say negative instead of no.'

'Clear communication is good practice,' says Rosco. 'You should learn some communication protocols, too.'

'Roger. I observed that our target seemed tense. He said he's never done yoga, which is a weird thing to say, considering how recognisable he is. Over.'

Rosco is silent for a moment. 'Just because we played together as kids doesn't mean you can pay me out, Olivia.' He looks unamused.

I always push things too far.

The evening is drawing to a close. The microphone makes squawking noises and chairs are dragged out around us.

'Hello there, Ross,' says a loud, New York voice.

I swivel.

Rosco is on his feet already. 'Brooklyn.'

It's the American girl who came to our office. I didn't catch her name at the time. *Brooklyn*. It's like calling me Southport. It must be an American thing, naming your children after the place they're born.

Brooklyn is wearing a clinging black cocktail dress and looks like she's stepped out of a style magazine. I feel big and ungainly in my op-shop dress. She's the real femme fatale; I'm just a pretender.

'Am I early?' Her eyes flicker to me. The scent of something exotic drifts towards me.

'No, no,' says Rosco. 'Olivia and I were debriefing an operation. We'd pretty much finished, hadn't we, Olivia?' Rosco appears to suddenly remember why we're here. He scans the room.

I do the same. There's no sign of Ajay.

For a moment I think he's going to tell me to chase him. I see him weigh up the desire to find Ajay against the need to avoid drawing attention to the fact that we've lost our target. A flash of understanding passes between us. 'Take the rest of the evening off, Olivia.'

I glance at my watch. The face is barely visible through the water droplets, but it appears to be midnight. 'Gee, thanks. See you at work.'

Twirling my clutch bag, I head for the door.

Maxine is standing next to it. 'Your card?' she says.

After a moment's hesitation I pull my dating card out of my purse and hand it over.

'Your results will be there tomorrow morning,' she trills after me.

I glance through the window as I walk back to my car. Rosco is smiling as he and Brooklyn head for the door. A breeze from the street makes her long black hair waft behind her like a silken cloud. If this was a movie, they would be in slow motion. She gives a loud, honking laugh, which only adds to the effect. I've heard people laugh like that in New York movies.

I grind my teeth. Rosco appears to have a date with a beautiful American. Sure why I care I'm not, but it seems that I do.

Thousands of red-sided garter snakes slither together in a large den, a hundred males vying for the affections of each female. The nesting balls grow and grow. I am crushed beneath the heavy mound …

Eeoow. Where did that come from?

My dream fades. It isn't randy snakes, but my sister Jacq who is crushing me. Garter snakes were another biology case study. Those dates last night have triggered something.

The bedroom door hangs open and loud clattering drifts in. This is my grandmother's Morse code for 'time to get up'. Jacq wriggles on top of the sheets and I squeeze her, breathing in the smell of shampoo.

'What's this?' Jacq picks up my blonde wig from the bedside table. She sits up and pulls it on, shaking her head about, rock-star style. 'Yeah, yeah, yeah.'

'How've you been going here with Nan?'

'Good.' Jacq sounds dubious, still swishing her blonde hair to and fro. 'I've got soccer today,' she announces, jumping out of bed and tossing the wig back on the table. 'I'm very busy,' she calls out as she leaves the room.

I struggle into sitting position. I know I have weekend family responsibilities, but I ignore the pointed hoovering outside my door. Instead, I pull my laptop from the bedside table. *Let's see what kind of impact I made last night.* A faint ting tells me my results have arrived.

The subject heading of the email reads 'Congratulations, you are now an Allure Speed Dating Elite Member.' I practically swoon with excitement as I read on. Thirteen of the fifteen guys from last night want to see me again. I suspect Ajay and Rosco were the two I failed to impress, but never mind them. Thirteen out of fifteen is pretty damn good. *I am the Marilyn Monroe of 9 Seabreeze Crescent!* It does cross my mind that it is not me, but my push-up bra, blue contact lenses and blonde wig they want to see again. I dismiss the thought. *Let me revel in my moment of glory.*

The email continues, 'You are now entitled to attend events where all daters have a rating of seventy per cent or more in a prior event.' *Yeah, cop that Denise Maxwell and the rest of the high school hot chicks. I'm an elite dater.* Immature, I know, but isn't everyone scarred for life by high school? I seldom have anything to brag about, so I seize the day, sharing a screenshot of the email to Instagram – *A typical day in my fabulous life #elitedater.*

Jumping out of bed, I wrap myself in a dressing-gown and run a comb through my hair. In the kitchen, Jacq is pulling a tray of biscuits out of the oven. She already has her soccer uniform on. Nan enrolled her in a school holiday program and she's thriving on it. Jacq is the kind of kid who likes to have her days filled up with activities.

Nan, not unusually, looks ready for a garden party with the queen. Every time I see her she looks younger. She's pushing sixty-five, but today she looks no more than forty. Her blonde-streaked bob brushes the shoulders of her lace dress and I suspect she's been getting some work done on her face. She's ditched her heavy glasses too. She's blind as a bat without them so she must be wearing contacts. It can't be long before people start thinking I'm her sister.

Kevin, her terrier, is not so stylish. He's wearing a jacket I knitted him last year. Knitting was trendy at school for a while and I jumped on the bandwagon. I haven't seen the jacket on him before. It looks like it was made for a dog with more legs than Kevin. I take a photo and Instagram it *#knittingfail*.

'Good morning, Olivia.' Nan glances at her watch. 'It *is* still morning, isn't it?'

'Olivia,' Jacq squeals. 'It's my turn to do morning tea and I've made Anzac biscuits for the team.'

'Yummo, they smell great. You're so clever.' My stomach growls and I stretch my hand towards the biscuits.

'Olivia,' says Nan.

I know that tone. Nan has many annoying habits, but her obsession with weight-watching is the worst. Not being bikini-beach-body-ready doesn't bother me. I am what I am. This bikini-beach-body-ready thing drives me crazy. It's a multi-purpose expression around here. It may be used as a greeting:

Hi Olivia, are you bikini-beach-body-ready?
Hell yeah!

I figure if there's a beach and I've got a body, I fit the bill. Apart from the bikini, obviously. I don't wear bikinis. Not anymore.

It may also be used as an excuse for almost anything:

Want to go to the beach?
No, I'm not bikini-beach-body-ready yet.
Have you been studying for English?

No, I'm busy getting bikini-beach-body-ready.

If people on the Gold Coast didn't spend so much time getting bikini-beach-body-ready they'd have found a cure for cancer by now.

I tighten the string on my dressing gown. 'I've been doing a lot of yoga lately. It makes you hungry.' I know this will impress. Nan is a recent convert to the 'amazing benefits' of yoga and tends to drop 'My yoga teacher says' into discussions in a very creative way.

The red or the blue T-shirt? My yoga teacher says blue is a good colour for enhancing communication. Is the mince out of the freezer? My yoga teacher says red meat is bad for your chi. Are The Simpsons *on tonight? My yoga teacher says* The Simpsons *are the root of all evil.* Okay, I made the last one up, but, seriously, it's like living with a kid with a crush on their school teacher. The only positive side is, like all Nan's fixations, it will pass. Last year, she toyed with the paleo diet, tango dancing and stand-up paddle-boarding.

'Yoga?' Nan raises her eyebrows. 'Since when do *you* do yoga?'

'I've been tailing that guy from the McSushi ad for work, you know ...'

'Ajay? The bikini-boot-camp-speed-yoga man?' Nan couldn't have sounded any more impressed if I'd told her I'd won the Nobel Prize.

I use her excitement as cover to swipe a biscuit. 'I've almost mastered the headstand.'

The downstairs doorbell rings. 'Must go,' breathes Nan, picking up her overnight bag. 'Reggie's taking me to Springbrook. I'll be back tomorrow. You can tell me more about Ajay then.' She gives Jacq a big kiss and turns to me. 'Her game's at eleven o'clock;

Southport. The coach rang to make sure she's coming. They're a few down so they'll have to forfeit if she's late.'

I glance at my watch. Ten o'clock, better get my skates on.

I get changed, brush my teeth and grab my shoulder bag – five past – excellent result. 'Right. Let's go, Jacq.'

Her eyes fixed on the TV screen, Jacq stands at a speed that would make a sloth look hyperactive. It's ten past by the time we get to the door. At the bottom of the stairs Jacq remembers her Anzac biscuits.

'It doesn't matter. No one will mind if you don't bring biscuits. We need to get going.'

Jacq's lip trembles. 'But I made them specially.'

'Okay. Run up, fast as you can. I'll put my board on the car in case the surf's good up there.' I want to keep up my surfing roll.

I'm running towards the car with my surfboard, aware that the clock is ticking, when Jacq calls out behind me. I swing around, hitting her plate of biscuits with my board. They fall and break into a million pieces.

'No! Oh, Jacq, I'm so sorry.'

A red-eyed girl and her guilt-stricken sister finally hit the road at twenty past ten. The universe must have decided I've already paid for my sins as the roads are only moderately bad. We make it to the game by five to eleven.

While Jacq does a quick warm-up with her team, I dash over the road to pick up the *Gold Coast Times* and buy some lamingtons as a replacement morning tea.

Now, I have to confess to something worse than breaking Jacq's biscuits: I can't stand to watch her play soccer. It bores me to tears. I would lay down my life for hers in an instant; fight off sharks or gun-wielding robbers; anything like that. Just not watch her play soccer.

Oh, I *pretend* to watch. I'm there at the sideline, my face turned in more or less the right direction. But my mind won't engage, no matter how hard I try. Maybe it would be more interesting if she kicked the ball every now and then. However, if there are two kids standing in a quiet corner of the field having a chat while their teammates chase the ball, you can guarantee one of them is Jacq.

Hence, the *Gold Coast Times.*

As Jacq's team runs onto the field I flick to the letters section. In it is a well-argued letter from a regular correspondent – one Olivia Grace.

Re last week's demand that Sydney recognise the Gold Coast as a cutting-edge city; how can you expect respect when your streets are lined with meter maids in bikinis? In what other city does this happen ...

A roar from the side-lines interrupts my reading. For a split second I think they're applauding my sentiments. My head comes up, hands clapping as Jacq glances across at me. I give her a wave and a thumbs up, then look back at the paper. I flick to the front page and stop in shock.

How did I miss this?

Candid Yoga Shock Photos screams the headline. The picture shows superstar Georgia Hansen in downward-facing dog, her famous bottom towards the camera. It's not the most flattering angle, even for her. Another photo shows Ajay in black hotpants, slapping Georgia's leg as she struggles to execute a backbend. *Teacher or Tyrant?* reads the caption for this one. I bet they worked hard on that line. I can see the journalist poring over the thesaurus. *Guru or – nah, can't think of anything; Yogi or – nah, no good. I've got it: Teacher or Tyrant. Excellent.*

Ajay must be livid. Georgia Hansen won't be coming back to Lighthouse Bliss now and neither will her high-profile friends. I scan for a photographer's name, but of course there is none. *Photo supplied*, says the caption.

This begs the question of how these photos were taken. Where was I at the time? Did the private yoga room where Georgia Hansen worked out have windows? A trilling in my shoulder bag alerts me to an incoming call. I'm pretty sure I know who it is.

'I've seen it, Rosco. No, I don't know how they got those photos. No, I can't do surveillance today; I'm at a soccer match. I'm looking after Jacq.' I lower the phone as he protests. Something's caught my eye: Jacq has the ball. She's running down the field; steering around the opposition. She's opposite the goal. 'Go, Jacq,' I hear someone yell. It's me. What's happening? I'm turning into a soccer fan.

She kicks – she misses – it doesn't matter. I jump up and down. 'Way to go!' She turns, looking sheepish. I wave.

The whistle blows for the end of the game and, defeated but cheerful, Jacq's team races off and scoff their lamingtons. It's only when every last shred of coconut is gone I remember the phone hanging in my hand.

I put it to my ear. 'Hello?' The line is dead, of course, and my phone is almost flat. I put it in aeroplane mode and toss it back in my bag. Surely I deserve a weekend off. Besides, I have Jacq to think about. Rosco can do some surveillance himself if he's so keen.

Jacq and I have a relaxed afternoon at the beach; lots of tunnel digging and squealing among the waves. I left my board behind after the Anzac Incident, so it's lucky the surf is bad. A couple of surfers are mucking around on choppy little waves, but the swell's far from enticing.

A surfer in the car park shakes his head at his mate. 'Blown-out anklesnappers – can't believe I got out of bed for this.'

I take out my phone and, opening a new note, start a surfing vocabulary. Those Inuits need to watch their backs.

Back at the flat, it's time for homemade hamburgers and a Hollywood blockbuster. I do like to theme my fabulous dinner parties. By eight thirty Jacq is ready for bed.

I tuck her in. 'Good game today; pretty exciting.'

Jacq nods. 'Yeah; I might be a Matilda when I grow up.'

I believe it's an older sister's job to encourage their sibling, no matter how unlikely their aspirations. 'You might. Anything's possible if you try hard.' I stroke the thick, brown hair off her forehead and kiss her freckled nose. 'I'm sorry about your biscuits.'

'It's okay,' Jacq murmurs. 'We can make more next week.'

She's a good kid. Turning off her light, I go out to the kitchen. My mobile phone lies on the bench, accusing me with its blank screen. I switch off aeroplane mode – three missed calls from Rosco. He's not going to be happy. I should return his calls but it's probably too late now anyway. How can I make this up to him?

I ponder. If someone has it in for Ajay some research won't go astray. It will show Rosco I'm on top of the game mentally, if not physically. I type Ajay's name into Google and scan the results. The official Ajay website is unlikely to be interesting. The fan site is a possibility. I'm looking for dirt.

The fan site is packed with reports of amazing transformations after Ajay's classes but there is one lone voice of dissent. *I felt a bit weird about the way Ajay humiliated some of his teachers at the demonstration*, says Vanessa from Beverley Hills. She is howled down by a dozen others who insist this is an essential part of his strict yoga teachings. *How else can you strive for perfection?* says Bass from San Francisco. It's an interesting world, that of the yoga guru.

As I close the site I have a great idea. I'll take Jacq to Byron Bay tomorrow. I can talk to a few people; establish the feeling in the community about Ajay. Be ready to wow Rosco on Monday morning with my insights. Show him what a dedicated team player I am. *Go surfing.* Yes, that's what I'll do.

I check my emails. There are two new messages. Mr Bouncy and the American Bloke are both keen to set up a date with me. I use the term 'me' in the loosest possible sense. They want a date with the blue-eyed blonde who laughed at their jokes. Is it worth continuing any relationship begun on such fraudulent grounds?

Probably not, but I'm not beating off any other offers and I need dating practice, so I fire off two replies. If things ever progress beyond first date stage, I'll tackle the problem of how to reveal the not-so-fatale femme within.

Before I go to bed I practise my signature move against the wall. I manage a proper headstand, with the wall for support. It's pretty cool. I position myself opposite the body-length mirror, do another headstand and take a photo. *Feeling powerful and empowered #headstand*, I caption it and post to Instagram. This headstand thing has become a quest. I guess my logic is: if I can get this one simple thing under control everything else will follow.

A magpie bursts into a long, warbling song as Jacq and I drag ourselves into the Lighthouse Café. The place is bustling with famished beach goers. Toned bodies sporting suntans and little else laze at every table. I'm wearing faded Speedos paired with a threadbare towel around my waist. I've heard it's what all the beautiful people are wearing this season. *Ha.* I hope I'm not bringing down the tone too much.

A bush turkey roams around underfoot while the magpie cocks its greedy eye at a muffin. In Byron, the rainforest, with all its wildlife, comes right to the beach. Jacq and I claim a table with a view of that show-off, the sea. The lapping waves are the perfect accompaniment to our meal. Byron really is beautiful, I'm glad Rosco forced me to come back.

'Cool idea coming here,' says Jacq.

We've been having so much fun I've almost forgotten I'm supposed to be gathering gossip to impress Rosco in the morning. Jacq and I have surfed until we dropped. The conditions are perfect; waves so tiny the proper surfers have gone elsewhere, leaving us gumbies to have fun. Jacq's only been surfing a few times – she got a beginner's foam board for Christmas – but already she's showing some of that unique Grace style.

'Two hamburgers with the lot and two chocolate milkshakes, please,' I say to the waitress. Surfing sure makes you hungry. Jacq runs over to climb on a nearby pandanus tree while we wait. I snatch up a copy of the local paper someone's left on the table and turn straight to the classifieds.

I love the *Lighthouse News* classifieds; they give me such a sense of possibility. Someday I'm going to try the goddess dance or undertake a quest for the Holy Grail.

After the classies, I flick through the rest of the paper. Halfway through I stop at a picture of a brown-skinned girl wearing a floaty beige dress. A gold ring dangles from one nostril and her thick brown hair is tucked behind her ears. She's holding a sign – *No McSushi for Byron Bay*. I read the headline.

McSushi Moves in on Byron Bay

Skimming the article, I discover McSushi has applied to open a new outlet here. This is not a popular move. Spokeswoman for WAM (Women Against McSushi), Luna Nakamura says; 'I love sushi, but we don't need big faceless franchises in Byron Bay. We need to support our small, local sushi-makers.'

Interesting. This must be the same Luna I heard discussing yoga on the radio. She certainly has all sorts of reasons not to like Ajay. Could Luna have taken the Georgia Hansen yoga photos?

My eyes travel back to the photo. Luna looks feisty and ready for anything. And it seems she has Japanese heritage. Maybe she is a local sushi-maker herself. The plot thickens. I turn the page.

In the sports section, I see a familiar face; the girl I'd chatted to in the surf. ***Is Maya Our Next World Champ?*** reads the headline. It turns out she's already the Australian women's longboarding champion and tipped to win the world titles in Waikiki this year. How about that? I've had a brush with fame.

Satisfied with my research, I fold the paper and, waving Jacq over, tuck into my hamburger and milkshake. At least I'll have something to tell Rosco tomorrow.

'Did they have hamburgers when you were a girl?' Jacq wipes sauce off her face with the back of her hand.

'I like to think I'm still a girl, but maybe I'm kidding myself.'

She giggles. 'You know what I mean.'

'No, when I was a girl we used to eat raw meat and leaves torn off trees.'

'Did you wear animal furs?'

'Only in the winter, in summer we went naked.'

'Oo.' Jacq's horror makes her forget her food. 'You're joking. Aren't you?'

'Yeah, there's no tricking you. We went naked all year round.' I take a big slurp of my milkshake. 'Those were the days.'

With bellies full it's time to think about getting home but the beach is too perfect to leave. A sun-speckled sea beckons beyond the trees. The tide is low and transparent tongues of water lick at the sand. Some surfers are carving up waves off the rocky point. Out past the rocks, a few dolphins cruise northward.

'How about we check out the rockpools before we go?'

Jacq doesn't need persuading; she's already rushing towards the rocky platform at the end of the beach. Climbing up the rock, we put our toes in a pool and bend to stroke some tightly clenched anemones.

'They feel like the inside of my mouth.' Jacq pokes the inside of her cheek with a finger.

We follow a narrow walking track through the pandanus onto the top of the headland. The banksias are in bloom and a powerful honey smell wafts from their yellow flowers.

As we round the headland, Jacq drops my hand. 'There's Rosco,' she yells.

Jacq hero-worships Rosco. They used to shoot hoops together in the local park before he moved out of home. I think she just accosted him on the court one day and joined in. 'He looks like Prince Phillip from *Sleeping Beauty*,' she said to me once.

To be honest, put him in a pair of tights and it would be hard to pick between them.

I follow her pointing finger. At the other end of the beach a blond-haired guy is crossing the road, away from us. His broad shoulders push against a faded surf T-shirt. It could be Rosco, but it's hard to be certain. 'Did you see his face?' I ask Jacq.

'Yeah, it was Rosco.'

Cupping my hands to my face I call across the road. 'Hey, Rosco.'

The guy doesn't respond. If anything, he walks faster. 'Maybe it isn't Rosco,' I say to Jacq.

'It's Rosco. He's barring you out.'

'What do you mean?'

Jacq shrugs. 'It happens at school.'

I search her eyes. 'To you?'

'To everyone.' Jacq's voice is matter-of-fact.

I pick up her hand again. Jacq's just finished Year Two. I don't like to think of her alone in the playground jungle. 'I'll ask him tomorrow.'

On our way out of town I see a new McSushi billboard on the side of the road. Under the image of Ajay and his nori roll is written, 'Coming soon to Byron Bay.'

I wake early to the roar of surf. Jacq and Nan are still asleep. Turning on my radio, I catch the surf report. 'It's pumping – double-overhead at Snapper.' *Two more words – watch out Inuits.* I add them to my notes file.

As it turns out, the seas are rough and stormy in the office as well. Rosco is on the phone when I get in and he doesn't look up.

I write up a report on Ajay, inserting some photos – Georgia Hansen wrapped in her scarf; the speed dating bar. *Happy times.*

I'd managed to get both my potential dates – Mr Bouncy and the American Bloke – in the background of the speed dating photos. I appraise them in the cold light of day. Yes, they're still cute. It's a little weird that they think I'm a slinky-dress-wearing, cleavage-baring blonde, when I'm a cargo-pants-and-crew-neck-T-shirt-wearing brunette, but whatever. I'll sort that out on an 'as needs' basis. When I finish the report, I look up. Rosco is still on the phone.

He contrives to stay out of my way until midday – quite a feat considering the size of the office. Finally, I send him an email; 'Did I see you in Byron Bay yesterday?'

He looks up a few seconds later, shakes his head, and picks up the phone again.

That's strange. Jacq was sure it was him.

Pulling a piece of paper off my pad I write on it in big letters, 'I might have a lead on the Georgia Hansen photographs.'

I walk over to Rosco's office and hold my note against the glass. He's still on the phone, but his eyes scan it. I press my nose to the window and breathe heavily on it. In mirror writing, I trace 'Sorry' into the mist.

At last he puts the phone down. Pushing his chair back, he comes out and leans against the door, arms folded. There's a long silence.

Taking a tissue out of my pocket, I wipe the smudge off his window.

'What are you sorry about, Olivia?' Rosco's voice is neutral.

This could be a trick question. I'd better be careful I don't confess to all sorts of things. Like stealing his lightsaber ten years ago. I don't think he knows about that. It pays to remember Rosco is trained to get information out of guilty offenders.

'I'm sorry I didn't see anyone taking shots of Georgia Hansen.'

Rosco nods, but doesn't say anything.

'I'm also sorry I missed your calls on the weekend. My phone goes flat really quickly so I keep it in aeroplane mode most of the time to save the battery. Then by the time I got the calls I figured it was too late.' That silent treatment works.

I rack my brain. Is there anything else I should apologise for while I'm at it? 'I'm sorry we lost Ajay on Friday night, but it wasn't totally my fault and it *was* me who ate that Mars Bar you left in the fridge, but I thought you'd had enough.' It's good to come clean. Mostly clean. There's still the lightsaber.

Rosco runs his hands through his hair, making it stick up at odd angles. 'We've lost a lot of ground with Rochelle Randall because of those photos, but I've talked her into keeping us on. Bottom line is, I need you back there. Double objective now – find out if Ajay's cheating and who's got it in for him. So, what's your lead?'

I fill him in on the proposed McSushi franchise in Byron Bay. 'Luna, this yoga instructor, who may also be a local sushi-maker, is leading the opposition. She's also being sued by Ajay for teaching speed yoga. So she has plenty of motive.'

Rosco isn't as impressed as I thought he'd be. 'We need hard evidence.' He snaps his fingers and points a finger at me. 'Line yourself up a job at Lighthouse Bliss so you can get among it. Keep an eye on this Luna girl, but remember, it could be anyone. Work on the speed dating angle too; find out what's going on there.'

I don't like his bossy tone. 'And while I'm doing all that, you'll be ...?'

'Don't worry about me. I've got plenty on.'

This isn't how I thought it would be when I applied for this job. I'd imagined Rosco and I studying footprints. *He has a limp and a clubfoot,* I'd murmur, and he'd be impressed with my sagacity. 'I was hoping to move on to a different assignment,' I say.

Rosco cracks one of his knuckles. He always used to do that as a kid when we argued. It's quite irritating. 'Olivia, I could fill this position tomorrow if you don't want it. What's more, I could fill it with someone who doesn't eat my Mars Bars.'

That's a low blow. 'I want the job.' I turn to go.

'And Olivia.'

I swivel.

'Sort out your phone issues. If you turn it off on me again ...' he pauses.

I wait for the ultimatum.

'Just don't, that's all.'

I stare at him. Is he threatening me? I'd challenge him to a Jedi fight to the death, but clearly inappropriate that would be.

So Rosco, AKA Darth Vader, has made himself clear – I need to get myself a job at Lighthouse Bliss, pronto. It's a big ask, but I can only try. Maybe they need a cleaner or a shop assistant. I'm pretty sure I could make wheatgrass juice if I had to. It can't be that hard.

Sitting at my desk, I glare at Rosco while I dial the number on the brochure. Things were so much simpler back in the day. I imagine myself bursting into his office, lightsaber in hand. *Vader, I challenge you to a duel—*

'Lighthouse Bliss, this is Madeleine.' A breathy voice startles me. 'How can I assist you today?'

'Yes, hello.' I try for a mellow tone, but probably sound constipated. 'I was interested to know if you had any job openings?'

'Are you a yoga instructor?'

My mind goes blank. *Yes? No?* 'Yes. Definitely.'

'We're desperate for instructors. Can you start tomorrow?'

'Sure, tomorrow, yes,' I blurt. I can't believe this is happening. *Yoga instructor?*

'Okay. I'll put you down tentatively for the midday class. Can you come in tomorrow morning for an interview?'

'Ah, yes, no problem.'

'I didn't catch your name.'

'Olivia Gr—' *Damn.* I should have used an alias. I cough. 'Excuse me. Olivia Granolo,'

'Okay, we'll see you tomorrow, Olivia. Bring a copy of your qualifications please,' she adds.

I put down the phone and panic. How am I going to turn myself into a yoga instructor before tomorrow, let alone have the qualifications to prove it?

As always, when faced with a question I can't answer, I call on my good friend Google. I type in 'yoga instructor quick', press 'go' and hit the jackpot. The site isn't titled 'get your dodgy yoga certification here', but it might as well be. A picture of a most unlikely looking yoga guru fills the screen. With chubby cheeks, a collared polo shirt and a tuft of red hair, he looks more like a used-car salesman, but he's good enough for me. It costs a hundred dollars, but I figure I'll claim it on expenses. I just need to do a brief online exam. They don't make it too hard – all the answers are on the site.

I find out the word *yoga* means unity, *asanas* are the poses, *pranayama* is the practice of breath control and alignment is important. I also match a few Sanskrit words with their meanings. It's like primary school homework.

One hour later I proudly print out my 'School of Harmonic Bliss, Accredited Yoga Instructor' certificate, in the name of Olivia Granolo. I prop it on my snow-dome surfer. Yeah, I'm kicking goals. Elite dater and now yoga instructor.

Before I go home, I download *Yoga for Beginners* onto my laptop, ready for a hard night of study.

'I'll drop off your expenses later,' says Rosco as I leave. 'I've got to go to the bank first. See you soon.'

Not if I see you first, Vader. I shut the door with a bang.

Jacq's playing with her extensive Lego collection when I get back to Nan's, but she turns her face up for a kiss.

'What was Rosco doing in Byron Bay?' she asks.

'It wasn't Rosco.'

'Yes, it was.' Jacq turns back to her Lego. She appears to be building a gigantic blue wave with a surfer on it.

Nan sees the yoga lesson cued on my laptop while we're chopping vegetables for dinner. 'Are you planning on doing some yoga, Olivia? It *is* excellent for toning the derriere.' She eyes my baggy tracksuit pants.

I straighten my back. 'Yeah, I've got a job as a yoga instructor at Ajay's joint.'

Nan drops her knife. 'You what?'

I pull my instructor's certificate out from underneath the laptop and brandish it. 'See? I am an accomplished yoga instructor.' I whisk it away before she spots my unusual surname.

Nan snorts. 'If you're a yoga instructor, then I'm the cat's pyjamas,' she mutters as she dices her carrots.

I ignore her. Jealousy is a curse.

Being Monday, it is chicken curry night, which is appropriate. I put on some Bollywood music on Spotify to help the mood along. 'Tonight after dinner, I will lead you in a yoga class,' I say.

'Knock knock,' says Jacq in reply.

'Who's there?'

'Yoga.'

'Yoga who?'

'Yoga to try this, it feels gooood.'

'Who told you that one?' I ask.

'Kid at soccer.' Jacq chases her curry around the plate. 'His mother's a yoga teacher.'

'Like your sister.' Nan smiles brightly. 'You know there are lots of different types of yoga, don't you, Olivia? Which type do *you* teach?'

She's trying to catch me out. 'Hatha yoga.' *Ha.* I had that one in the test.

'Well, of course Hatha yoga.' She clears the dishes. 'But is it Iyengar, Ashtanga, Bikram, Kundalini, Jivamukti? There are so many types.'

She must be making it up, there can't be that many types, can there? I glance at my laptop. Underneath *Yoga for beginners*, it says *Iyengar style*. 'Iyengar.'

'Iyengar?'

I don't like her tone. 'Yeah, Iyengar.'

'There are easier types to master, darling. There are lots of props and so on with Iyengar.'

'I – am – an – Iyengar – instructor.'

Nan turns the kettle on. 'You always overreach. Do you want a hot chocolate, Jacq, before Livvy gives you your *Iyengar* yoga lesson?'

Jacq is already on the floor in perfect lotus pose. Leaning forward, she walks on her knees towards me. 'Yes please, Nan. Livvy, how many yogis does it take to change a light bulb?'

'I don't know. How many yogis does it take to change a light bulb?'

'Into what?'

'What?'

'That's the answer,' says Jacq. 'Into what?'

I laugh. 'I get it.' I push her off her knees onto her bottom. 'Look at you – you don't need to do yoga, you're already as bendy as a banana.'

I turn down the Bollywood music and press play on the yoga class. My pupils, Nan, Jacq and Kevin, line up obediently in front of me. We stretch and bend together. Except for Kevin, who rolls over and goes to sleep.

Nan has lots of helpful tips. As we lie and lift our legs into shoulder stand she calls out, 'Don't stick your bottom out so much.' In tree pose it's, 'suck in your stomach.'

'*I'm* the instructor,' I say after one tip too many. I try to think of a cutting remark that will demonstrate my superior knowledge. 'Your alignment's all wrong.' Half my class turns surly at that point, but Jacq's impressed.

It's Jacq's bedtime after the first half of the video. Nan takes her off for tooth brushing and doesn't come back. *The West Wing* blares from under her door soon after – Nan has the entire series on DVD – so I'm left to study on my own.

I leave the video on pause while I do some extra headstand practice. I can take my legs off the wall for a few moments at a time now without falling over. The smell of success is in my nostrils as I press 'play'.

The video is an old one – the instructor's hair is set in immovable blonde waves around her pretty face – but she knows her stuff. In the second half she brings out the props – belts, blocks, balls, blankets and bolsters. I'll never admit it to Nan, but this Iyengar yoga is tricky stuff.

I'm getting tired by this stage, but I follow her moves, using stuff from around the house in place of the proper equipment.

At ten o'clock I move onto *Intermediate Yoga* and things get hardcore.

Half an hour later, I'm on my back, knees pressed either side of my ears, looking at a hole in the crutch of my tracksuit pants. I have a dressing gown cord tied around my ankles, Jacq's soccer ball between my thighs, multiple copies of Nan's Nancy Drew books tucked under my bum, a pillow off the lounge under my shoulder blades and my head is resting on a picnic blanket.

'Breathe deeply and enjoy the deep serenity these poses bring,' says my instructor.

I moan. I don't feel serene – I feel trapped. I should have released the dressing gown cord before wedging my head between my knees.

'Let your legs separate from your body,' croons the video.

I must have misheard – my knees are blocking my ears. I start to panic. What if I can't get out of the pose? I'll be stuck here until morning.

'Relax. Extend your spine. With each breath allow yourself to sink a little deeper.'

I can't see the video, but an evil note seems to have entered her voice. I try to block the idea that she's metamorphosing into a vile creature with manky black hair – if only I'd never watched *The Grudge.* I just want her to leave me alone.

'Lift your bellybutton away from your navel,' she says in a sinister tone.

No, no, no, I shriek mentally. *Anything but that.* It doesn't even make sense. As I ponder the meaning of her instruction, there's a knock at the door.

Who on earth knocks on doors at this time of night? I struggle, swaying from side to side, but it's no good. I can't escape – the evil yoga teacher has me trapped. I moan louder – I can't talk, a soccer ball is pressing into my nose.

The knocking gets louder, then stops. Next thing there's a bang, followed by a crashing sound. I scream, swivel my eyes, see two legs coming towards me and scream again, though not very loudly as I'm still muffled by the soccer ball.

Kevin leaps up from where he's sleeping. His legs blur as he runs past me – not towards the intruder, but away.

The door to Nan's room opens and her bare legs run out. Kevin follows – bolder now. There's a confusion of sounds – growling (Kevin), squealing (Nan) and grunting (me, as I try to free myself).

'No,' says a familiar man's voice.

'You bastard,' says Nan. The sound of something hard hitting bone follows.

The man moans.

I give a gigantic heave and roll over onto my side, the soccer ball coming free as I do so.

Nan, in a short lacy negligee, is standing over a man who lies on the ground, his hands over his head. Kevin, in a delirium of excitement, has his teeth locked on his T-shirt. He growls, snarls and slobbers, the hero of the day in his little canine mind.

I focus on the figure on the ground.

'Are you all right, Olivia? I'll take care of him.' Nan raises her baseball bat, panting. She too is starring in an action-packed drama. My family is crazed with blood-lust – only Jacq, bless her, sleeps on.

'No, Nan,' I yell. 'It's Rosco.'

Nan glances over at me, not releasing the bat, then back at Rosco. She squints at him. She's clearly taken her contacts out. 'So it is. Well, why are you tied up like that?'

Rosco moans. 'Don't hit me again.' He sits up, rubbing his head.

Kevin backs off, barking – he's only brave when his prey is on the ground.

'I just wanted to give Olivia her expenses for Byron Bay. I was going to tuck them under the door, but I saw the light was on. When no one answered I looked through the keyhole. It looked like she was in trouble.'

Nan turns to watch me disentangling myself from my pose. 'Did *you* get yourself into this state, Olivia?' She lowers the bat reluctantly, shaking her head. 'I did warn you about Iyengar yoga.' A snort of laughter escapes her lips. 'You look like a trussed-up chicken.'

On my laptop, my yoga instructor is now coming to the end of her routine. Her face has gone back to serenity – but a hint of evil lingers in her doll-like eyes. 'Relax, rid yourself of negative thoughts. Breathe in the silver, blow out the black.'

Rosco's hair is tousled and falling over his eyes. He doesn't look much like Prince Phillip right now. He looks more like Han Solo after he fought the giant otter.

I have an urge to smooth his hair out, but instead I breathe deeply. 'Thanks for dropping off my expenses. I need to finish up my yoga practice now.'

'*Touch marine life wonders and experience a world of exciting rides and attractions including the amazing Shark Bay. Visit our special polar bears ...*'

My radio alarm goes off early and I jump out of bed, ready for a big day. *Not.* Thanks to Ms Iyengar – AKA *The Grudge* – I have a cricked neck, an aching back and I fervently wish my legs *would* separate from my body and quit giving me hell.

My stomach squirms as I see the broken door, which Rosco has jammed shut. But there's no point in dwelling on last night. As Ms Iyengar says, breathe in the silver, blow out the black. Today stay positive I must. Not only am I making my debut as a yoga instructor, but I have a hot date with Mr Bouncy back on the Gold Coast in the evening. It's a high-achieving day. I take a photo of my yoga instructor certificate, making sure 'Granolo' is out of frame, and post it – *Inhale the future, exhale the past #namaste #yogaislife #yogini.*

After a quick trip into Active Sports for some chic yoga wear – psychedelic tights and a black lycra singlet with a picture of a whale on it – I'm on my way to Lighthouse Bliss.

Forty-five minutes later, the familiar streets surround me. The pavement is teeming with the usual frenzied mix: hippies down from the hills, European backpackers, spiky-haired Japanese surfers and gold-sandalled blondes in white linen beach wear.

As I drive through the main street, a familiar face goes past my window. *Brooklyn from Brooklyn. What's she doing in Byron Bay?* Her long hair is pulled into a sleek bun and her black business suit would be more at home in Melbourne or New York. She's holding a mobile phone the size of a book to her mouth and talking animatedly. She looks like she's in one of those Netflix shows about glamorous lawyers. I follow her with my eyes for a moment, then drive on – my new job beckons.

Lighthouse Bliss is only a couple of minutes out of town. I park among the bangalow palms and make my way past the flowering lily pond to reception.

The usual South American panpipes are playing and lavender wafts from an aromatherapy burner. A pair of pale, slender feet appear to be staffing the reception desk. Peering over, I see a girl in a headstand. Her back is as straight as a ruler. Jealousy stabs me. Will I ever be able to do that?

She isn't even using her arms to support herself. She is holding a book, which she appears to be reading. Tilting my head, I read the upside-down title – *How to Be a Yoga Rock Star.* 'Hello,' I say.

She brings her legs down slowly, pausing halfway before dropping them to the ground. Getting to her feet, she smiles. 'Hello, I'm Madeleine. How can I help you?' It's the breathy voice I heard on the phone. She's about my age and striking, with red hair, slanted green eyes and tiny freckles that dot her creamy skin. She's carefully made-up, with glossy red lipstick, eyeliner and even fake eyelashes. I hope that's not a pre-requisite for yoga instructors as my own face is au naturel.

'Hi, I'm here about the yoga teacher position. Olivia Granolo.'

Madeleine nods. 'Come this way.' She sets off down the corridor, treading with the precise step of a ballet dancer.

'Nice headstand.' I hope I sound like a true connoisseur.

'Thanks. I try to do an hour a day. How about you?'

'Same.' *In my dreams.*

'The pose begins when you want to get out of it, right?'

'Absolutely.' I have no idea what she's talking about and I'm worried I'm sounding too sycophantic, but she seems to buy it.

Above her tight iridescent-blue stretch pants Madeleine is wearing a singlet with a cartoon of people eating sushi. As she moves ahead of me I read the caption on the back – *Scientific whaling in progress.*

'It totally sucks doesn't it – eating whale meat?' I'm mainly trying to bond, but who doesn't love whales?

Madeleine shakes her head, her silky hair falling around her face. 'I can't believe it. It's like eating people. Worse. Whales are so pure. Their spirits are so innocent.'

Madeleine and I sit down on white armchairs in an all-white room. She crosses her legs and I notice a tattoo of a shark on her ankle. She barely glances at my qualification. 'So, Olivia, how long have you been practising yoga?' she asks.

A few days would probably not go down well. 'Ah, I started when I was thirteen. Five years.'

She nods slowly. 'I started at eight. It would have been good to start earlier.'

Damn. 'I mean, obviously I started before thirteen, but that was when I got serious.'

'Right.' She looks sceptical. 'And how long have you been teaching?'

'Two years.' Clearly she didn't notice that my certificate was dated yesterday, or she wouldn't have asked. 'How about you?'

'I left school when I was fifteen to train as an instructor, four years ago. So, in the time you've been teaching, what are some of the challenges you've faced?'

I don't think *getting trapped in my yoga equipment* is a job-winning answer. 'Ah, I love yoga so much, my main challenge is having enough hours in the day to do all the yoga I want to do.'

Madeleine nods, she isn't giving much away. 'Who was your teacher?'

I rack my brain for a place she won't know. 'Oh, I trained in Iceland when I was there on a student exchange, under Lars Vindendigger.'

Now, her face lights up. 'Wow.' Her whale earrings dance with excitement. 'Iceland; I'd love to go there. You'll have to tell me all about it. Hey,' she eyes the whale on my lycra singlet, 'you weren't involved in demonstrations against whaling in Iceland, were you?'

I nod modestly.

'That is *so* cool.' My whale activism has tipped the balance in my favour as she hands me the key to the studio. 'Your first class is at twelve. The studio space is free now if you want to warm up.'

'Oh, great. I'll do that. Is Ajay around today?' I ask.

'Why, do you want an autograph?' Madeleine's voice has a cool undertone.

'No, just wondering. I guess you get a lot of that. You know, groupies.'

'You have no idea.' Madeleine rolls her eyes. 'He's got over a million followers on Instagram, so ...'

'I don't know how his wife puts up with it.'

Madeleine looks at me intently. 'You know Rochelle?'

I shake my head quickly. 'No. She was in *Woman's Weekly*. I read it at the doctor's.'

Madeleine grimaces. 'I don't think Rochelle cares too much. She's got her life on the Gold Coast, he's got his here. As long as the money rolls in.' She stands up and points out through the door. 'That's your studio over there. It's got everything you need.' She glides down the corridor away from me.

There's half an hour until my lesson and my stomach is rumbling so I head over to the health food bar. Eying the selection, I grab the most edible looking thing in sight: a bran, oatmeal, craisin and chia muffin. I gobble it down and it sinks like a rock to the bottom of my stomach.

My yoga class starts filing in at about five to twelve. Most of them look alarmingly fit. *Breathe in the silver, blow out the black. I am cool, calm, relaxed*, I tell myself. *I am a yoga guru*.

'What sort of class is this?' asks one of the women.

I'm ready for that. 'Iyengar.'

'Oh good; I like Iyengar, it's more painful,' she murmurs to her companion.

It doesn't go too badly at first. I repeat lots of salutes to the sun. That fills in some time. Then I make an on-the-spot decision to get stuck into all the props that line the walls. Soon I have them all on their backs, balls squeezed between their legs doing backbends. This is much easier to say, than to do, so it's lucky I'm saying not doing.

The main difficulty is, my body appears to be rejecting the

bran muffin. Loud gurgles and rumblings emanate from beneath my psychedelic tights. I'd have been all right, though, if not for the woman with the sinewy arms and legs in the front row.

'Can you demonstrate a handstand?' she asks.

A handstand? I've never done one of those in my life. But maybe they're easier than they look. The class waits expectantly. There doesn't seem to be any alternative, so I put my hands on the ground, fling my legs up and ... topple over sideways, emitting a loud muffin-fuelled burp as I do so. As I land on the mat, I hear screams. Rolling over, I see my students stampeding for the door. *Wow.* I know it wasn't a great handstand, and the burp was kind of gross, but—

A small black shape runs after them. I blink. Another one runs past. And another. I sit up and focus. *Rats!* They're everywhere – nestled among the fluffy blankets, chewing at the imported Indian belts, climbing the Ajay brand blocks. It's like Nancy Drew's *Mystery of the Brass-bound Trunk*.

Two of the biggest rats I've ever seen run towards me, their front teeth bared. I jump to my feet. *Code red, code red. Espionage.* It must be. There's no way all these rats could just appear in a posh place like Lighthouse Bliss. I run to the corner of the studio, pull my phone out of my gym bag and snap off some shots of the furry invaders. Where did they come from? One minute I've got a pile of top quality props, the next they're swarming with rodents.

Alarmed by the squeals and commotion, the rats have now dived for cover. I tiptoe towards the part of the studio where they first appeared. Glass louvres across one wall open onto a palm forest. One of the louvres at the front, near the prop boxes, is open. It would have been easy to feed a few rats through while the class was distracted with my ludicrous handstand. I peer out at the palm forest, but there's nothing there except a brilliant blue and green bird, hopping among the leaf litter.

A rat scurries over my foot. I squeal and run from the studio. Outside, yoga students clump in quacking huddles like well-toned geese. One girl giggles nervously as I appear. I toss my studio keys on the deserted front desk. Guess I'm not going to be a rock star yoga guru anytime soon.

I stop at a coffee shop to lick my wounds and pick up a copy of the *Lighthouse News*. Plan A hasn't gone too well; it's time to move on to plan B – checking out my main suspect.

First the candid yoga shock pics and now rats in the studio. Someone sure has it in for Ajay. If they're trying to ruin his business they're doing a good job of it. Rats scuttling across your feet do nothing for a place's tranquil oasis feel.

The café is packed with hipsters having intense discussions. I order a double strength latte and a chocolate muffin.

Turning to the back of the paper, I check the yoga schedule at the Pink House. Luna Nakamura is leading an advanced power yoga class at three pm.

Great. Just great. Can't wait.

14

Whale songs greet me in reception at the Pink House and the ubiquitous oil burner releases a spicy aroma, but there's no one around. I glance at my watch. It's five past three; the class has already started. I can't say I'm in a big hurry to join in.

Brochures line the walls. I run my fingers over the rack. If I want to try ten types of massage, four types of past-life therapy, have my colon irrigated, oil dripped on my head or my aura read, this is the place to be. Every brochure offers the promise of a new, improved me. I take one of each and pop them in my shoulder bag. As I slip into the back of the packed-out yoga class, I feel more spiritual already.

'Now, keeping your legs together, push up into a handstand.' Luna places her hands on the ground and effortlessly lifts her legs.

Not handstands again. I would have liked to hold off for the easy class at six o'clock, but that would have cut into my big date. Considering I've been doing yoga all night and all day, my date had better be something sedentary. Dinner and a movie would be okay.

Luna is suntanned and muscular. Her sun-streaked brown hair falls over her face as she hovers upside-down, before slowly lowering her legs to the ground. Unlike Madeleine at Lighthouse

Bliss, she is not dressed in skin-tight lycra, but in loose off-white pants and a white singlet. Her gold-skinned face is make-up free. Madeleine and Luna are the Yin and Yang of yoga instructors.

'Coming down, jump back into crocodile,' she says in her high-pitched voice.

I didn't bother attempting the handstand, but now I jump back into crocodile, which is basically a push-up. My arms protest and I collapse – a crocodile door mat.

Why is yoga so hardcore now? Where is the 'yoga for slackers' class? Luna might not be as fast as Ajay, but they're neck and neck for difficulty. It's a credit to my professionalism that I not only make it through the class, but also summon the strength to ask her a few questions at the end.

Tottering to the front as the room empties, I cough and raise my voice by two octaves. 'Excuse me?' Rosco says that copying someone's speech patterns helps to build trust.

'Yes?' Luna turns, looking unnaturally cool for someone who's led two hours of torture.

'Hey, I'm Olivia. I just wanted to say, I enjoyed your class.' *Not.*

'Oh, cheers,' she drawls. 'You know, it's hard at first, but it gets easier. Yoga is a joy and a blessing, isn't it?'

'Yeah, totally. I heard you on the radio the other day. And I was, like, interested to hear you used to work with Ajay.'

'Yes, I used to be one of his instructors. Do you know Ajay?'

Using my keen intuition, I take a chance. 'Enough to know he's a slimy weasel.'

'Sounds like you know Ajay.' Luna is too spiritual to come straight out and say she wouldn't spit on him if his hotpants were on fire, but I can read between the lines.

'I wondered what your experience with him was.'

'I don't talk about it. Negative vibes.'

For someone who's moved on, she still sounds angry.

'Nice top.' She eyes my whale singlet.

'Thanks. I like your outfit too. It's very ... flowy.'

Luna smiles. 'I'm not into lycra.' She eyes my tights. 'No offence. Natural fibres boost your nervous system and white magnifies your aura. Hemp is best. It's more sustainable than cotton. You should try it.'

'Right. I didn't realise that. I will. Anyway, I've done yoga with Ajay and now yoga with you and I can tell you one thing. You beat him hands down. The way you demonstrated that half lord of the chickens posture? I've never seen it done so well.'

Luna's eyebrows crinkle.

Perhaps I've got that wrong; time to extricate myself. 'Well, namaste and goodbye.' I turn to go.

'Hey,' she says.

I turn back.

'I'm getting a group together. You might be interested?'

I try not to look too eager. Joining the Women Against McSushi group would be a major coup. I could find out if they're the ones who have it in for Ajay. 'Yeah, maybe. What sort of group?'

Luna picks up a few mats and packs them into her bag. I get the impression she's thinking over her answer. 'We do this and that. Take action when needed. If you give me your number I'll give you a call when something's on.' She pulls out her phone.

I recite my mobile number. 'Okay, thanks. See you next time.' I'm going to be late for my date if I don't get going.

She stares into my eyes. Hers are so dark, they're almost black. 'You're either on the bus, or off the bus, Olivia.'

I nod like I know where she's coming from. 'Totally.' Leaving Luna to pack up, I head for the car park.

There are only two cars left outside the building, mine and an old model Ford with a *Magic Happens* sticker on the back and a dreamcatcher hanging from the rear-view mirror. I peer in through the windows, but see nothing unusual. I glance behind me. No sign of Luna. It's time to try something that isn't in Rosco's instruction manual. *Nothing illegal, Olivia,* he has drilled me. But what he doesn't know won't hurt him. Nancy Drew and Veronica Mars never take too much notice of rules and regulations.

As I regularly lock myself out of my car, I find it handy to carry a strip of plastic packaging tape which slips inside windows. Luna's car is an old model like mine, so it should work. My heart pounds as I slide the tape down, flick the lock and open the door. Under the seats I find only a damp towel and a bikini. But when I open the boot a distinctive smell hits me – rats. The animals themselves aren't here, but a few dark hairs have caught on the carpet. *Bingo.*

On the way out of town I'm past the McSushi billboard before it registers. Something's changed. I do a U-turn and pull over in front of it. Someone's gone crazy with a spray can. Red letters like knife wounds plaster Ajay's rippling muscles – *Stop the Whale Killers.* I reach up and touch them. The paint's still wet.

Whale killers? I take a photo. Things are sure hotting up around here.

15

'Home to more attractions than any other destination in the Southern Hemisphere, the Gold Coast has the fastest, the longest, the highest and the most exciting thrill rides in the country ...'

I moan at my radio alarm, roll out of bed and stagger into the kitchen. Heaping two teaspoons of instant coffee into my cup, I add hot water and drain it in one shot.

Nan pauses, her mug half-rinsed. 'Are you alright? You look like you've been run over by a truck.' She, herself, looks amazing. The more haggard I get, the more Nan blooms. It's like that movie, *Dorian Gray*, with me playing the role of the hidden painting. Today Nan looks like she's going to play tennis. It's probably a tennis-themed shopping outfit though.

'Not truck.' I press my hand to my temple. My head is thumping. 'Half man, half dog.'

The corners of Nan's mouth twitch. 'Tell me more.'

I sigh; the evening is a blur of fluffy blond hair. Gareth, the graphic design student, had arrived dressed in tight red-striped pants, a flowered Hawaiian shirt and a baseball cap worn backwards. He'd dragged me from dance floor to dance floor, barely pausing to drink guarana- and caffeine-laden soft drinks. I'd finally escaped at two am, only for him to ring at three am to tell me what a great time he'd had. It's obvious why he's into speed dating – he wouldn't have the attention span for a normal date.

I don't have the stamina for that kind of relationship. Particularly after overdosing on yoga. And I've still got a date coming up with the American Bloke on Friday. Only inertia stops me cancelling – it's easier to let it stand.

'Why don't you find a nice boy and settle down?' asks Nan. 'All this gadding about like Britney Spears.' She peers closely at me. 'I hate to say it, darling, but it's not agreeing with you. Your complexion ...'

I'm too weak to retaliate. Besides, she's right.

Jacq's computer game beeps and shrieks in the lounge room. She glances at me as I come in. 'Got him.' The computer gives a loud wail. 'He was stupid, that guy last night. Only idiots wear their caps backwards.'

'You're right. He was stupid.'

'He smelt, too.'

'Yes, he did. He smelt like rotten eggs.' I know this game.

'He smelt like poop,' Jacq pauses, 'with tinned fish on top.'

'And sprinkles of rotten cheese.'

'And vomit sauce.'

My head's going to explode. I can't face any more yoga today. I pick up the landline; maybe Rosco will let me off going back to Byron today when I tell him about the rats. A pretty impressive result, finding the hairs in Luna's car.

I'm pressing his number when I remember the defaced McSushi poster. It had slipped my mind in the morning blur. *What was that about? Ajay is a whale killer? Or McSushi?* I put the phone down again. I should look into that before I talk to Rosco.

My computer boots up slowly. I find the McSushi website, but Jacq's computer game is overloading the wifi and it takes an age to load. I lie on my bed to wait.

I float in blue. Pushing with my tail, I propel myself through the water. A song comes to me – it echoes and vibrates through my flesh. Oooo, eeeee, aaa. Ooo, eee aaa. Olivia. That's my name. Olivia, Olivia. With a power thrust I burst from the water, falling back onto—

My bed.

'Olivia.'

I rub my eyes. *Rosco.* What's he doing here so early in the morning? My eyes go to my clock as it ticks over to eleven o'clock. *Oh no.* It all comes back to me. It's eleven o'clock and I'm still in bed. How am I going to explain this?

'Olivia.' Rosco knocks loudly. It's polite of him not to push the door down – the repair man is coming today for the other door, after all. 'Are you in there?'

I snatch my mobile from the bedside table. It's flat. *Double oh no. Must be a problem with the reception,* I rehearse. *I've been ...* What the hell *have* I been doing, apart from dreaming I'm a whale? That's right, computer research.

'Coming,' I call, scanning the McSushi site for a titbit to justify being in bed at eleven o'clock in the morning. *Hmm, corporate information – nothing, global markets – nothing, menu –* I try to ignore Rosco's knocking. *Special feature in our Tokyo and Iceland branches ...* I stare at the menu, hardly able to believe it.

Whale meat.

Ajay is endorsing a company that sells whale-meat sushi.

It's amazing what celebrities will do when they think no one they know is watching. The links fall into place as I rush to the door. 'Rosco, what are you doing here?'

'I could ask you the same question.' Rosco's eyes linger on the side of my head. 'I've been trying to call you.'

I pat my hair, fluffing up the flat bed head. 'Really? There must be a problem with reception.'

Rosco glances at my phone, which is still in my hand.

I slide it casually into my pocket, in case he is tempted to check if it's on. It's time for my big Nancy Drew moment. 'You wouldn't believe what I've found out. I know who's got it in for Ajay and why.'

I pull Rosco into my bedroom and point at the screen. 'McSushi sells whale meat in their restaurants in Tokyo and Reykjavik.'

Rosco looks underwhelmed.

'That's dynamite in a place like Byron Bay.'

'Yes, it would be.' Rosco pauses. 'Good work.'

Good work? Is that all he has to say to my amazing breakthrough?

'So that's the why. What about the who?' Rosco sounds like a teacher coaching a slow pupil.

'Luna Nakamura. I think she released rats at his yoga studio yesterday.' I fill Rosco in on the rats in the studio and rat hair in the car story, skipping over some minor details, like my car break in. 'She asked me to join her group.'

'So there's a group? And you've been invited to join?' Rosco is more interested now.

I nod.

He smiles. 'Excellent work. Better than I expected. I want you to play along, find out who their members are, what they're up to.'

'You want me to dob them in?' Now I know Ajay's on the side

of the whale killers, I don't know if I want to be on his team any more. Or his wife's team anyway.

'He who pays the PI ...' Rosco says.

Calls the tune. 'Yeah, I know, I know.' It's one of his favourite sayings. 'Anyway, it's not like I can do anything right now. She said she'd call me when there's an action on.' *And my phone could well be flat that day ...*

It's like he knows what I'm thinking. 'You're going to have to toughen up, Olivia. I'd never make a buck if I only took on clients I like.'

'No. I know that.' I force a smile. 'It's okay. I'm tough.'

'Right, come back into the office. I've got a new client coming in at twelve you might be able to handle. But as soon as Luna rings, I want you on it.'

I nod. 'Are you going to pass on my results about the rats?'

'Yeah, I'll let Rochelle know – suggest she gets the police to search Luna's car. Your evidence won't be admissible, of course – being obtained illegally.'

Clearly he has deduced how I discovered the rat hairs.

He walks towards the door. 'See you there in a few minutes.'

'Where do you draw the line?'

I'd spoken quietly and hadn't expected an answer, but Rosco freezes, halfway out the door. He turns. 'The line? You're talking about ethics?'

I nod.

'You draw it at a point that lets you make a profit, but doesn't stop you sleeping. I'm sleeping well, how about you?'

'I'm sleeping okay so far.'

'When you're not, let me know.' He pulls the broken door shut behind him.

My stomach churns uneasily as I get ready for work. I don't feel good about the idea of identifying the members of Luna's group. Why didn't I tell Rosco this? *Because I want the job.* I hope Luna gives her car a clean before the police get there. She's a hippie nut in hemp clothing, but I like her. Her heart's in the right place, which is more than I can say for Ajay.

I pull out a clean white, immune-system-boosting cotton T-shirt, team it with my blue cargo pants and pick up my shoulder bag. Hopefully my new client will be more to my taste.

In Rosco's office, a man leans back on his chair, his arms dangling beside him.

'Olivia, this is Brad Cahill,' says Rosco as I take a seat.

He looks familiar, but it's not until he pushes his daughter's photo across the table that it falls into place. He's the man-fish. His daughter is Maya, heiress to the world longboarding title, or so he'd have us believe.

'She's got the title right here,' he smacks his palm, 'if she'd get her act together, but she keeps buggering off when she should be training.' Brad's blue eyes drill Rosco. He's a handsome man – broad shouldered, strong-jawed – but his suntanned hands are clenched. He looks like he wants to hit someone and he wants us to make sure he's got the right person. *Great.*

I look sideways to Rosco, hoping for a flicker of eye contact to tell me we're on the same wavelength. But Rosco is sitting forward on his chair focused on Brad. As the interview winds up, he does something bizarre.

'Hey.' Rosco pushes a pad across the table. 'D'you reckon I could get an autograph?'

Brad grins, obviously delighted. He scrawls his name on the paper. After a vigorous handshake – Rosco's – and a brief nod – mine – he strides out the door.

After he's gone, I turn to Rosco. 'What was that all about?'

He glances at the signature, tears it off the pad and places it carefully in his desk drawer. 'Brad Cahill – you haven't heard of him?'

'Nuh.'

'You're joking.'

'No.'

'Well you've got some catching up to do. Where to start? Five times world champion. Started professional surfing as we know it – big sponsorship, cosmetics contracts, movie deals, you name it – all his idea. They used to call him the Ultimate Wave Machine.' He sounds like he's talking about Nelson Mandela.

The Ultimate Wave Machine? I don't get it, but it's obvious Rosco does.

'Some people reckon it was the end of surfing in its pure form, what he did. Budgie Goldsworth – you must have heard of him?'

I shake my head.

Rosco's eyes widen. 'Last of the old-style surfers, the soul surfers – you know, in it for the love. Brad pushed him off his perch in 1992. They haven't spoken since – never appear at an event together.'

'A philosophical difference of opinion?'

'I suppose you could say that – hate each other's guts is how I'd put it. Mate of mine met Brad at a party – got mixed up and called him Budgie by mistake. He won't make that mistake again.' Rosco smacks his fist into his palm. 'Can't believe you've never heard that story.'

'I don't follow competitive surfing.' I gaze at the photo of Maya. Her hair is wet, she has a surfboard under her arm and a medal around her neck. 'I've met her, in the surf. Looked like she had some issues with her dad.'

'Will she recognise you?'

'Nah, it was brief. She's nice though – let me share her wave.' I take Maya's file, realising as I do that I'm on the wrong side of the fence again. *Damn.*

'She let you share her wave? Sounds like she lacks the killer instinct all right. Okay, it's up to you, Olivia. Save her from herself. Find out what she's up to – drugs, boys, punk music. Whatever she's doing, it can't be as important as winning that title. Looks like Byron Bay is calling your name again.'

'Doesn't Byron have its own PI?'

'Not that I've heard of. Maybe I should open a branch there.' Rosco wanders out to the kitchen for a coffee. While he's there the phone rings. I pick it up. 'Gold Star Investigations.'

'Yeah, it's Kenny here.' The voice on the end of the line is terse. He sounds like I ought to know who he is.

'Do you want to speak to Ross?'

The man snorts. 'Nah, tell him Kenny called. He'll know what it means.' He hangs up.

'Kenny called,' I say to Rosco as he comes out of the kitchen.

'Urgh.' Rosco slops coffee over his shirt. He puts his cup down and tries to mop at it with a piece of paper.

'Is there a problem?'

'No, I'll be right.'

I think he's talking about the coffee rather than Kenny, but I let it pass. I turn to go.

'You're doing okay, Olivia.'

I turn back to Rosco. 'I am?' Relief washes over me.

He gives a crooked smile, like Han Solo after he escapes the aggressive space slug. 'May the horse be with you.'

My stomach skips. And here was me thinking he'd forgotten.

After Rosco gave me the flick as his playmate, we didn't talk to each other for a long time. We moved in different orbits. Then, a couple of years ago, we ran into each other by chance, right outside my house.

It was late. I'd been at a party and Frannie's mum had just dropped me off when Rosco came up the street with his surfboard under his arm.

I paused at the gate when I saw him. 'Hey, Rosco.'

'Hey, Olivia. How have you been? Is the horse still with you?'

I laughed. 'Of course. And with you?'

'Absolutely.'

I noticed he was dripping wet. 'You been surfing?'

'Yeah.'

'In the dark?'

'It's not so dark.' He looked up at the sky. 'Moon's almost full. You should try it some time, night surfing. It's amazing.'

'Maybe I will.' There had always been something different about Rosco, I realised. He never followed the herd.

We perched on my garden wall and chatted for a while, under the streetlight. He didn't seem in any hurry to move on. It slowly occurred to me that *something* was happening. We were holding each other's gazes, our hands resting closer and closer on the wall. The air around us was still with expectation.

Mum opened the front door eventually. 'You coming in, Olivia?'

I gave her a wave. 'Won't be a minute.'

She closed the door again.

'Guess I'd better be getting on.' I wondered if it was inappropriate to want to kiss someone you used to play *Star Wars* with.

'Why don't we go night surfing together some time?' said Rosco.

A thrill ran through me. 'I'd love to. I'm going to Byron tomorrow with Abbey for a couple of weeks. After that?'

'Sure. It's nice to see you again.' And then, the moment that I call the Notable Exception happened. He leaned over and kissed my cheek.

A firecracker exploded inside me. My whole body went warm and tingly. What would have happened if he'd kissed my lips?

I never found out, though, because after what happened in Byron the last thing I wanted was to go night surfing with Rosco or anyone else. I gave him the cold shoulder when he called around to make a date. And that was that.

I still think about that night sometimes, though, because I've never had that firecracker feeling again. Never come close.

17

Back in Byron the next day, I hit the streets looking for Maya. If she isn't doing her duty in the waves maybe she's in one of the coffee shops that line the main street.

After doing the rounds of a few cafés, I'm ready for a break. I order a latte and slump into a chair. I glance at the girl sitting at the table next to me. She has shiny red hair and is wearing a tightly fitted singlet and flower-patterned lycra tights. It's Madeleine from Lighthouse Bliss – she of the perfect headstand, perfect make-up and synthetic clothing. The Yang yoga instructor to Luna's Yin.

She has her back half-turned and is writing in a leather-bound notebook. A glass of green tea stands beside her. I can't help but see the words on the page. Okay, I could have helped it, but I'm paid to be nosy.

How will I become a rock star yoga teacher? she's written at the top in neat handwriting. Underneath it she prints the word *headstand.*

Interesting. Maybe I'm not so far wrong in my quest. Here's someone else who feels the answer to getting ahead is a headstand.

Madeleine underlines *headstand* three times, then gets a

pink highlighter out of her bag and highlights it. Next to it she prints *Sydney*. She contemplates her words, draws a pink arrow between them, drains her tea and closes the notebook. At this stage I become very interested in a painting on the opposite wall. When I turn around, she has gone. I finish my coffee and go up to pay the bill.

The café is styled as a funky sixties surf joint. An old wooden Malibu board hangs behind the bar. Signatures of surfers I assume are of some note are scrawled across it. I see Maya's there and use it as an opening.

'Does Maya come in here much?' I say to the girl behind the cash register, gesturing at the surfboard. 'I thought I'd catch her in the surf, but she hasn't been out at all.'

'Naomi,' she calls. A teenager with wild springy hair in low-slung jeans and a midriff-baring top looks up from her milkshake. 'Where's Maya at these days?'

The girl shrugs. 'Dunno.'

Even Nancy Drew has her dud moments.

I finally track down Maya at the Byron Bay RSL on Thursday evening. Sipping a beer, I perch at a table down the back where I can take photos without being noticed. It's open mike comedy night and she's just taken the stage. The crowd is a mixture – young hip surfies mingled with your typical middle-aged RSL drinkers.

Maya is wearing a fifties-style dress that hangs loosely off her athletic frame. Yellow ballet shoes complete an outfit that makes her look like a cross between Gidget and a child gymnast. I'd have picked her as a Roxy and Billabong girl myself.

'I got a new longboard for my boyfriend. Good trade huh?

No, seriously though, when you're a girl in the surf you need to have some comebacks ready for those boys who've overdosed on testosterone and adrenaline. There's a lot of them out there – here's a few suggestions.'

She's a natural. The contrast between her cute gap-toothed smile and the stuff she's saying gives her an extra edge. I snap off a couple of photos.

'You know, Byron Bay gets pretty crowded. I often get confused when I'm sitting in the line-up and think I'm at Blues Fest. I keep thinking I should have worn my gumboots. I've found out you can scare off the non-locals with a bit of hocus pocus though. "Watch out; you're crushing my aura" works well.'

The crowd laughs all the way through her routine, and when she finishes she gets a huge round of applause. She jumps off the stage and runs to kiss a guy who's sitting in the front row. I click and catch his image. He's in his early twenties – a few years older than Maya. Shoulder length brown hair, a few tatts – cute, in an edgy, self-confident way.

I put my phone down as a guy in a trilby hat with a cockatoo feather comes to pick up glasses. He's fighting a losing war with a lock of greasy black hair that keeps falling over his eyes. 'She was good,' I say.

'Who, Maya? Yeah, she's a funny chick.' He flicks back his fringe with a practised twitch as he stacks the empties.

'Some people have it all, don't they?' I prompt.

'How'd you mean?'

'Well, surfing, comedy ...'

The glass guy glances towards the front of the room where Maya and her boyfriend are hugging each other. 'Unlucky in love though.'

'Why, what's wrong with him?' He looks alright to me.

The glass guy balances his tower of glasses and lets his hair fall over his eyes. 'Oh, there's nothing wrong with *him*.' He obviously regrets saying anything. Without another word he moves on to the next table.

The announcer picks up the microphone. 'Our next act is James Goldsworth.'

Goldsworth. The name sounds familiar.

Maya's young man bounds up on stage and it clicks. *Budgie Goldsworth, Brad pushed him off his perch in 1992. They haven't spoken since.* Could James be the son of Maya's father's nemesis? That would explain the glass guy's comments.

I look from Maya to James and back again and only one thing comes to mind – Montagues and Capulets. The man-fish is not going to be happy. And I'm the one who gets to break it to him. I flick through the photos on my phone. Should I delete them?

I think of Rosco. *You stop at a point that lets you sleep at night.* For the first time, I wonder if I'm in the wrong game.

I plonk the report on Rosco's desk on Friday morning.

He flicks through it. 'Good work. Pretty straightforward case for a change.'

I glance at the photos of Maya in front of the microphone. I feel like a hunter who's brought down a deer. An uneasy mixture of guilt and pride churns in my stomach. 'What do you think will happen now?'

'We'll invoice Brad, he'll pay.'

'No, I ...'

'I know what you mean. Not your problem.' He looks at me. 'Here's something you'll be interested to know. The police checked Luna's car, found ...' He sorts through the papers on his desk and reads from his notes. 'Twenty yoga mats, one swimsuit (two-piece, made of hemp), one book (on aura analysis), a pair of chopsticks (used) and ... some rat hair. They questioned her, but don't have enough evidence to lay any charges yet. They'll be keeping an eye on her.'

'So what's the next step?'

Rosco grimaces. 'We're off the case. Rochelle isn't happy with our progress.'

'What? But I'm the one who put her onto Luna. Why'd she dump us?'

Rosco spreads his hands out on the table. There's something guarded about his face.

'Was it something I did?'

'She thought it was strange we were there when the photos were taken and the rats released, but we still don't have any definite ID.'

We? He means me. 'Oh.' The breath puffs out of me. 'Sorry, I tried.'

His face isn't giving much away. 'Yeah, I know. Don't sweat it.' Rosco glances at the clock and pushes his hair off his forehead. It's ten thirty. 'Want to have lunch with me today?' His voice is casual.

This hasn't happened before. 'What are you after?'

'Nothing. Just lunch.' Rosco looks at me innocently.

I still think he's after something, but I shrug. 'Okay, sure. Why not?'

Going back to my computer, I hum as I type out a report. I might have lost us a client, but at least Rosco and I are friends again. And maybe this lunch signals the start of something new. Maybe he's going to bring me in on the American operation. I can't say I'm sorry to have seen the last of Ajay, anyway.

Something is niggling at the back of my mind. Luna is an animal lover and a hippie. Wouldn't she find the idea of releasing rats into a yoga studio unethical from a rat welfare point of view? Well, I suppose people are unpredictable.

My watch alarm goes off spontaneously at twelve o'clock. I really need to get myself a new watch. This one lulls me into thinking it's got over its incontinence problem and then *beep, beep, beep, beep.*

My stomach rumbles. Catching Rosco's eye, I rub my stomach. He holds up a finger – one minute.

I go to the bathroom, comb my hair and go back out. As the door squeaks shut behind me, I stop dead in my tracks. A girl is standing in the office doorway, her hand on the doorknob. It takes me a moment to realise who it is – Brooklyn from Brooklyn. She looks completely different and not at all like a Netflix lawyer. She's ditched the business suit and boutique clothing and is wearing a full-length flowing dress in some sort of tribal pattern. She is make-up free, her nose sunburnt, and she has a hibiscus behind her ear. In her hand is a brightly painted didgeridoo.

Rosco bounds out of his office. 'Brooklyn. Been shopping?'

'Yes.' Brooklyn holds up her purchase. 'I've bought an authentic dodgeridoo,' she drawls. 'Isn't it cool?'

'Didgeridoo,' says Rosco.

Brooklyn laughs her honking laugh and flicks her glossy hair. 'Didgeridoo.'

But it looks more like a dodgeridoo to me. I'm pretty sure you'd find *made in China* on there somewhere.

'I have something I need to discuss with you, Ross.' She ignores me. 'Can we have lunch?'

'Yes, of course,' says Rosco. 'I'll grab my wallet.'

I flop onto my chair.

As Rosco comes out of his office he does a double take. 'Oh, sorry, Olivia. You don't mind, do you? It's business.'

Yeah, right. I stick a pen in my mouth and grind it with my teeth as they leave, Brooklyn's shoes clacking down the stairs. The American operation, whatever it is, clearly does not require my input.

I don't feel like going to lunch on my own now, so I go out to the kitchen and look in the fridge. Inside are four of Rosco's Mars Bars. I pick them all up, go back to my desk and rip the wrapper off the first one. What's Rosco up to with Brooklyn? Work or play?

My eyes linger on his office as I chew. He'll have the file in there somewhere. I can find out what's going on with this American operation. Maybe I can figure out a way to get involved. It's what Nancy Drew would do. Rosco's been holding me back; I need to show him what I can do.

Stuffing the second Mars Bar in my mouth, I go into his office and pull open his filing cabinet. The files are in alphabetical order. I flick to B, but there's nothing. What's Brooklyn's second name? I have no idea. Okay, I'll have to look at each file. It takes a long time. After half an hour, I'm up to H and halfway through the third Mars Bar. I glance at my watch. He'll be at least another half-hour.

I find her under the M's. As soon as I pick up the file I see it all. Why didn't Rosco tell me Brooklyn works for McSushi?

Sitting at Rosco's desk, I read through the file, my pulse rate rising. No wonder he wasn't surprised when I told him McSushi sold whale meat, or that they were trying to open a shop in Byron Bay. He's let me run around chasing up stuff he already knows. He pretended he wasn't involved with McSushi. Why? I grind my teeth.

I pull out a company report, flick through it and find a picture of Brooklyn in full corporate clobber – fitted grey suit, pulled-back hair, broad smile, red lipstick. *Public Relations Officer,* she's called. I note she has the same surname as the CEO, who is the guy she came in with the first time. She's probably his daughter.

I read on. It doesn't get any better. McSushi has hired Rosco to find out the members of the activist group who are opposing their new franchise in Byron Bay and, if possible, to infiltrate and bring them down, in order to smooth the way for their north coast expansion. And now, he's out to lunch with Brooklyn. To be honest, I'm not sure which of these things makes me angrier. He was supposed to be having lunch with me. I hadn't admitted it to myself, but maybe I'd been hoping for something more than just work talk.

My cheeks burn as I think back over the past couple of weeks. I've been so pleased with my progress, but the whole time Rosco was keeping this from me. I thought we had an understanding. I thought we were friends. Not only did he hide the McSushi contract from me, he was getting me to do his dirty work with Luna's group.

It *was* him in Byron Bay on the weekend – doing his own snooping. He lied to me. I've eaten another Mars Bar while I've been looking through the file and now I bite on the last one like it's Rosco himself between my teeth. Taking out my phone, I photograph the pages in the file, in case I want to refer to them later.

With four Mars Bars worth of sugar racing through my blood, I rip a sheet from his pad, put it on top of the file and, in a furious rush before I change my mind, write, *Do your own dirty work. I quit!* For good measure, I stuff the Mars Bar wrappers inside the file. My heart is pounding with sugar and anger. Picking up my bag, I fling my souvenirs inside and let myself out the door, banging it behind me.

I've only stomped halfway down the stairwell when the outside door opens and Rosco comes in.

'Olivia? Are you going out for lunch?'

I gaze at him without speaking for a moment. 'I left you a note.' I take a deep breath. 'You ...' I inhale again. 'You ...'

He climbs the stairs towards me. 'Are you all right? You're not having an asthma attack, are you?'

'You've gone to the dark side.' I push past him.

He touches my arm. 'What's this about? Come upstairs and talk about it.' He pauses. 'I haven't gone to the dark side. You're the one who's acting like they've gone to the dark side.'

'Me? I could never go to the dark side.' Raising my leg, Ninja style, I kick him in the shins. 'Ha.' Too much sugar always makes me emotional.

'Ow,' Rosco hops, clutching his leg.

I have a flashback to the last time I kicked him. It was ten years ago, when he told me he didn't want to play *Star Wars* with me anymore. 'The horse was never with you,' I yell, as I did back then.

Jumping the last few stairs, I burst onto the street like a Jedi starfighter escaping a death star. It's only when I get to the car and look in my rear-view mirror that I see the chocolate smeared all around my mouth. My hand shakes as I wipe it off.

I start the car. This appalling day isn't over yet – date with the American Bloke to contend with, I still have.

Back home, I tell Jacq and Nan I'm going out for work again, as I did for my previous date. It's easier than explaining why I'll be wearing a blonde wig and a push-up bra and they have to call me Anna.

Obviously, I don't tell them I've quit my job. Still, every time I think about Rosco, fury rises like a tsunami fuelled by a Mars Bar sugar explosion. It's probably a good thing I'm going out on a date. I won't have any tooth enamel left if I don't keep my mind on other things.

My phone rings as I'm getting ready. I don't recognise the number, so I let it go to message bank – I'm too angry for conversation. If it's Rosco, calling to apologise, I'd possibly be open to that I suppose. If it's a good apology.

But it's Luna. I recognise her high-pitched voice straight away. 'Hey, we're having an action tonight for whales. If you want to come along and help, give me a call?'

Whales? Is that the same as Women Against McSushi? In either case, pass.

I parade the second outfit from my 'femme fatale' bag – black fake-leather pants and a spaghetti-strapped lycra top with 'sexy' written on it in some sparkly stuff. It's not unlike the outfit Olivia Newton John wore when she shed her goody goody image in *Grease* back in 1978. In fact, judging by the little moth holes on the top, which you can hardly notice, it may even be the same outfit. I saw the stage production of *Grease* in Brisbane a couple of years ago and it was so much fun I downloaded the music on Spotify afterwards.

'You look like Barbie,' says Jacq, looking up from her dinner. Knowing her feelings about Barbie, it's not a compliment.

'You look very nice, Olivia,' says Nan. Considering Nan's taste in clothes, this is also not a compliment.

There's a knock on the door and Nan opens it. She eyes the American Bloke and looks back at me in a way that says she's onto me. 'Your date's here ... Anna.'

Jacq spikes her fish finger hard enough to bend the fork prongs and mutters, 'He looks stupid.'

In a strange serendipity, the American Bloke, who is called Brandon, looks like John Travolta in *Grease* – tight jeans, white T-shirt, slicked-back hair. He seems okay.

On the street, Brandon opens the door of his spotlessly clean old Holden for me.

I flutter my eyelashes at him. I never know what's going to happen when I put on my disguises, it's almost like they're enchanted. Off come the daggy clothes and, voila, I'm someone else. Considering my current circumstances, it makes a nice change.

Brandon's booked a table at a Mexican restaurant. Usually I hate Mexican, but tonight, it turns out, I don't. Hot Tamales specialises in funky 'New Mexican'. The food isn't bad – not as heavy on the cheese and beans as usual. It's a nice contrast to the Mars Bars.

'It's hard to find places in Australia that do good Mexican.' Brandon sips his margarita.

I stick with water. I don't want to add alcohol to the volatile mix already in my system. 'We're spoiled rotten in America.'

It turns out he's an actor and a dancer – I might have seen him on *Dancing with the Stars*? I haven't, but am impressed nonetheless. 'I love *Dancing with the Stars*,' I say.

He goes a bit vague when I ask him what he's working on at the moment and mumbles something about 'resting'.

I tell him I'm a law student. Come to think of it, that might be the truth. As of today, I need to reconsider my options. I don't want to think about that now. 'Why'd you go to speed dating?' I ask.

'I'm into speed. My take is, something good can only be improved by doing it faster. To be honest though, it was awful. Can you believe those laminated questions? I did meet you, though, so it wasn't all bad.'

After dinner, he asks me back to his place for a coffee.

I hesitate. Going back to guys' places is not my thing. In fact, I've never done it before. I'm about to say no when he speaks again.

'Just for dancing.' Brandon smiles.

Dancing sounds harmless. I could do with some fun after the wreckage of today. I have pepper spray, a phone with triple zero on quick dial and a super-loud emergency whistle in my handbag if required. 'Okay. Why not?'

Brandon lives on the twentieth floor of a Surfers Paradise apartment – Casa Del Rio. There's a lot of that Mediterranean thing about. As we whiz up in the lift I catch a glimpse of myself in the mirror. My blonde hair is tousled and my lipstick smudged. I take my high heels off at the door.

'Take a seat.' Brandon gestures at the couch and vanishes into the kitchen, returning with two cups of coffee. His eyes twinkle as he hands me a coffee.

It's lucky I'm in an adventurous mood as things quickly turn a little strange.

'I've got a treat for you.' He slips a record on an old-style vinyl record player and leaves the room.

The music's familiar. *Grease*. What a coincidence.

As 'Greased Lightning' starts Brandon reappears. He is now dressed in black leather pants and a black singlet. Striking a pose, he tosses his head back, John Travolta-style, moving into a hip-thrusting dance number.

I bite my lip to stop myself giggling. But it's kind of cool. He's a great dancer. After a few moments, he puts out his hand and I stand to join him. He twirls me and dips me so effortlessly, it makes me feel like I can dance.

As the music fades Brandon dashes from the room. A 1950s-style bikie, complete with bikie cap, dances in for 'Summer Lovin''. My participation doesn't seem to be required for this one so I watch from the couch and sip my coffee. Brandon winks as he struts from the room at the end of the song. The grand finale is *Saturday Night Fever* and I'm not surprised to see him emerge in a white suit.

Brandon smiles as the song ends, his legs spread wide and finger pointing to the ceiling. 'You like?'

I giggle. I do like. 'You're a John Travolta impersonator.'

Brandon nods. 'Among other things.' He struts towards me, peeling off his white jacket. He has no shirt underneath. 'You're the one that I want,' he sings. 'Oo, oo, oo.'

My pulse goes faster. 'It might be time for me to—'

But he reaches down, slips his fingers under the front of my wig, and rips it off.

'Ow.' I rub my forehead.

'Much better. You have beautiful hair. You shouldn't hide it.'

I'm disconcerted, but he's smiling. 'How'd you know I was wearing a wig?'

'I'm in the biz, babe. I know a wig when I see it.'

The biz? He's a PI too? 'What biz?' I try to sound unconcerned.

'Showbiz. What biz did you think I meant?'

'Oh, nothing.'

'So why were you wearing a wig?'

'I ... I wanted to make an impression at speed dating. Then I was stuck with it.'

Brandon looks into my eyes. 'You would make an impression dressed in a sack.'

My face burns. 'I think I should—'

'No, don't go yet. I'll get us something to eat.' He nods towards the balcony. 'Why don't you check out the view?' He heads to the kitchen.

I debate whether to leave, but he seems harmless and I wouldn't mind a snack so I go out onto the balcony. The twinkling lights and dark sea give the Gold Coast a beauty it doesn't have at ground level. It's calming looking out at gleaming blackness all the way to the horizon.

Brandon comes out with a plate of cheese and biscuits. He's put the white suit coat on again, which is good.

'You're an amazing dancer,' I say through a mouthful of cheese and cracker, wiping the crumbs from my mouth.

Brandon shrugs. 'Dime a dozen.'

'Do you live here by yourself?' It's a nice apartment for such a young guy. Especially one who is 'resting'.

'Yeah.' He leans on the balcony beside me. 'I get a pretty sweet deal.' At that moment, his phone rings and he pulls it out of his pants. 'Yeah, yeah. Okay,' he drawls into the receiver. 'You what?' There's a pause before he abruptly turns the phone off. When he turns to me the mood has broken.

'Something come up?'

Brandon gives a forced smile. 'Yeah, it's my agent. Turns out I've got an early start in the morning – an acting gig.'

I take the hint. 'Right, I'd better head off; I've got an early start too. I'm taking my sister to Ocean World for her seventh birthday.'

Brandon blinks. 'Ocean World? You know there's a roller-coaster there that's the fastest in the Southern Hemisphere?'

'Thanks for that. I know to avoid it now.'

'I wouldn't worry about the waterski show; I hear it's pretty bad,' he says.

'Right. Hot tip.' My wig lies on the coffee table like a dead silky terrier. I pick it up and stuff it in my handbag.

Brandon calls me a taxi. 'We'll get back together soon?' He kisses my cheek, but his heart doesn't seem to be in it.

I nod vaguely. It's not a definite commitment.

I check my phone on the way home in the taxi, but there's still no message from Rosco.

It looks like we're having a Mexican stand-off. I replay our stair-corridor showdown. It's possible that I may have over-reacted, but I'm not going to be the one to apologise first. That would be setting a bad precedent.

20

'Witness the dolphins' amazing agility and grace as they interact with their trainers at Dolphin Cove ...'

Ocean World is a lot of fun at first. It's good therapy. I'm too busy to check my phone every few minutes to see if I've missed a call from Rosco. He is, however, still on my mind.

There's no way I'm going to apologise. He's the one who acted like a jerk, concealing the McSushi case from me. *Not to mention having lunch with Brooklyn, when he was supposed to be having lunch with me.* But I don't know what I'm going to do with my life if I can't be a PI. And maybe I wouldn't have kicked him in the shin if I hadn't eaten all those Mars Bars. Too much sugar does terrible things to my judgement. I heard someone pleaded diminished responsibility in a murder case once, due to eating too much chocolate. I can understand that. Anyway, all things considered, I'm open to the idea of a grovelling apology. From Rosco, that is. Not from me.

In the meantime, there are the dolphins. The way they burst from the water, spin and leap, it makes my blood sing.

'Dolphins have always been a source of wonder for humans,' says the announcer, a girl with long burnished hair, as one of the dolphins does an effortless backflip. 'There are many stories of them rescuing people from shipwrecks or driving away sharks.'

I've always been a sucker for dolphins – me and everyone else, I guess. As I watch the dolphins race around the pool, I wonder what's in it for them. The crowd loves it, the dolphin trainers are ready to explode with excitement, the dolphins – well, they seem to be having fun, but how would you know? The trouble with a permanently smiling face is that nobody knows when you're sad.

Jacq is hooked from the first second. 'How do you get to be a dolphin trainer?' she asks me, adding it to her career dreams. I imagine most of the kids in the crowd are asking the exact same question. From the look of the trainers, being young and good-looking are pre-requisites. Maybe a PhD in animal psychology ranks a close third.

It begins to rain as we move on to the waterski show but it doesn't dampen our spirits. Brandon was right, though; it's a pretty weak act – lots of girls dressed as meter maids and boys dressed as bikies. I wander off for a cup of coffee while Jacq watches the show, riveted.

The trouble with theme parks is, they don't know when to stop. It's not enough having dolphins, polar bears, dugongs, seals, waterskiers, penguins and pelicans; they have to have rides, 4D movies, junk food, rides and more rides. I defy anyone over ten to face a day of this without becoming crabby. It can't be just me. By mid-afternoon I'm ready to karate chop any penguin who gets between me and a lie down.

My watch crawls gradually towards five o'clock. Closing time can't come soon enough. The constant drizzle has turned to rain. People in plastic ponchos mill around like cut-price *Lord of the Rings* extras. Nearby, a family in sodden Gold Coast T-shirts pose in front of a dispirited polar bear.

We've done the Waterski Wipe-out, the Quest for the Golden Seal and the Dolphin Show. We rode the Pirate Ship until I was green and staggered from fairy floss to hot dogs to ice-cream. This has been the longest birthday celebration of my life.

'Thank you for visiting us at Ocean World. The attractions are now closed. Please make your way to the exits. Gates close at five-thirty,' coos a woman's voice over the loud speaker.

Oh hallelujah, praise the Lord. 'Time to go, chook.' I pull up the hood on Jacq's poncho. Jacq has the deranged look of an overstimulated child. Her cheeks are flushed and there's a stubborn set to her chin. Tears may come at any time. As I steer her over the bridge spanning the shark pool she digs in her heels and grasps the handrail. 'Look. Look there. The shark's swimming funny.'

I look down, sighing. I've already seen sharks swimming funny. Oh yes, and seals jumping funny, dugongs looking funny and kids throwing up funny. I'm pretty much over funny. Plus, I can barely see through the raindrops plastering my glasses. *Lighten up, Scrooge,* I tell myself. *It's your sister's birthday. Go the distance.*

I take my glasses off, wipe them on my damp T-shirt and replace them, focusing on the pool.

In the unnaturally blue water below us, a large shark seems to be doing the cha cha to an unheard rhythm, its body wiggling from side to side. We aren't the only ones to notice. Others pause, keen for one last smidgen of excitement.

'Maybe it's going to have a baby,' says Jacq.

It does appear to have a bulge around its midriff. With one last frantic wiggle it opens its mouth. The crowd hushes as a whitish object floats from between its jaws.

'It's a baby shark,' Jacq squeals.

I shake my head. 'Might be a fish.' I didn't do high school biology for nothing.

The woman beside me screams through a mouthful of ice-cream. 'It's an arm.'

My stomach contracts as I peer more closely. Floating on the water's surface is a hand and part of an arm. It rolls palm up with the current, revealing a tattoo on the wrist. I pull Jacq away as a gentle wave of water washes over the black outline of a man cross-legged in lotus pose.

21

'Stand clear of the shark pool. Please stand clear of the shark pool.'

News spreads quickly across the theme park. It's like someone has yelled 'free beer'. The exiting crowd rushes back to the shark pool, pushing at the fence like a wave against a breakwall. Mayhem ensues.

After a few minutes of mob rule, the Ocean World staff take control of the situation, moving the shell-shocked crowd away. A girl in a blue T-shirt and shorts touches my arm.

'Miss? We're trying to clear the area.'

'I'd better stay,' I say. 'I know that arm.'

It doesn't take long for the R to arrive. They tape off the shark pool while Jacq and I watch, huddled under a cafeteria umbrella. The rain is falling heavily now, cascading off the points of the umbrella and splashing onto our feet. The Ocean World girl points at me and one of the cops swaggers over.

I know as soon as I see him we're not going to get on. He's about fifty, ruddy faced, his stomach straining at the buttons of his blue shirt. His mouth is set into a suspicious scowl. I bet he's one of those men who get off on power.

'Why don't you check out the underwater tunnel, Jacq, while I talk to the policeman?' I point at the viewing area opposite and

Jacq trudges off. In retrospect, it's not the most sensitive place to send her. Still, she can't afford to develop a morbid fear of aquaria if she's going to be a dolphin trainer when she grows up.

The cop slides a notebook out of his tight back pocket. He takes my details and narrows his eyes when I tell him how I know Ajay.

'Bit of a coincidence, wouldn't you say? We'll have to talk to your boss.' He consults his notebook. 'Mr Ledger at Gold Star Investigations?'

'I don't work there anymore.'

'Since when?'

'Since yesterday – I resigned.'

He fixes his washed out eyes on me and I feel as guilty as hell. 'Hm.' He makes a note. Hopefully Rosco will vouch for my innocence. 'Do you have any thoughts about who might have done this?'

Where to start? I tell him almost everything – McSushi, the whale meat, Luna and her group, the rats, the Georgia Hansen photograph. There's only one thing I leave out: Luna's call to me last night.

I'm not sure why I don't tell him – an instinct to protect her, or at least give her a chance? It's too damning. *We're having an action for whales tonight* – and next day the arm of Ajay, who promotes McSushi with whale meat in it, turns up in the shark pool. Sending this guy after Luna feels wrong. It would be like sending a pit bull terrier after a tiny fluffy dog in a hemp jacket. Or something like that.

The cop pulls a card out of his back pocket and gives it to me. 'We might need to talk to you again. Give me a call if there's anything else you want to tell us.' Again his eyes drill me. Either he knows I'm keeping something back or that's his standard technique.

I take the card and glance at his name. Dan Ferris. 'I'll do that, Dan.' I sound guilty, even to myself.

At that moment, one of the policemen up at the pool calls down. 'False alarm. It's a fake.'

Dan looks up. 'A fake arm?'

'Yep. It's plastic.'

Dan looks back at me. 'Anything to add?'

I shake my head. Why would you throw a fake arm with Ajay's tattoo on it into the shark pool? It makes no sense at all.

Dan hitches his pants and saunters back to the shark pool, his bottom pressing at the seams of his navy-blue pants.

Fingering his card, I glance over at Jacq. Her nose is pressed against the glass, watching the sharks' never-resting circle of the tank.

I'd like to talk to Rosco about this. But going to be the first to call, I am not.

'Faster, faster,' yells Ajay. The sweat streams off me. He bellows commands – ardha chandrasana, garudasana, tadasana, utkatasana, uttanasana. Straighten your front leg, round your back, lift your pelvis, pull your stomach in. My body is clumsy and disobedient. His hand comes towards me, the tattoo of a man in lotus pose flashes before my eyes. He hits me and his arm detaches ...

I wake with a start. Opening the windows, I peer out, my sweaty body drying in the light westerly wind. The rain has stopped. In the gaps between apartment buildings the sky has a washed clean look. My dream lingers like a bitter aftertaste.

Jacq is up, building a huge rocket out of the Lego I got her for her birthday. Nan's present, a hair accessory set, full of hair bands, bows, feathers and jewels, was not as much of a success.

'Look, you can make hair bands to match your clothes,' Nan had said, but Jacq was yet to open the box. Personal grooming is not one of her priorities.

'Can I have pancakes for breakfast?' Jacq asks when she sees me. She seems to have recovered from the shock of seeing the shark spit out the arm.

'Okay, but we'll need to go down the shop for some eggs.'

I pick up my purse and Kevin jumps up, wagging his tail – ready for action.

He's a funny dog, Kevin. Scarred for life by living with Nan, of course, he has gas problems, hypochondria, and a delusion he's a chick magnet. Nan always says he has a lot in common with her ex-husband. I haven't seen a lot of my grandfather since he ran off with his secretary when I was ten, so I wouldn't know.

'Heel, Kevin. Sit.' I say as we wait to cross the road. Kevin is well trained. Nan got great pleasure out of taking him to obedience classes. It's not a coincidence that Kevin is also my grandfather's name.

I grab the *Gold Coast Times* from the newsagent as we go past and scan the front page.

Fake Arm Creates Mayhem, but Where is Guru?

I scan the story.

Mayhem reigned ... bull shark disgorged ... celebrity yoga guru, Ajay.

Bystander Kylie Jackson of Brisbane ... 'We were just about to go home,' Ms Jackson said, 'when some kid yelled out the shark was swimming funny ... I saw the fingers. I screamed. It was total chaos ... My son Derek threw up his ice-cream all over his ... It's supposed to be a family attraction. I won't be coming back.'

The striking tattoo ... Ajay, owner of the Bikini Beach Body Boot Camp Speed Yoga empire.

Last night, the police reported the arm was a fake. There are still concerns for Ajay, however, who cannot be located. His wife Rochelle has asked for help to find her husband.

I look away from the paper. Ajay is missing.

The newspaper rustles in my hands as the breeze freshens. Below the headline, the classic hotpants photo of Ajay overlaps that of a shark.

While clearly disappointed that the arm is a fake, the newspaper still can't get enough of the story. It continues with a two-page spread in the middle. I learn Ajay started Beach Bikini Body Speed Yoga Boot Camp five years ago and the brand is now estimated to be worth $40 million – American.

There's a small picture of Rochelle, a still from some forgotten horror movie. She's wearing a strategically torn T-shirt and not much else.

They've even found a couple of minor celebrities to give gushing quotes.

Channel Nine weather girl Sally Sergeant says:

Ajay is a spiritual leader who re-drew the map of yoga. I myself was privileged to be among the huge crowd who saw him in action last week at the Sydney International Yoga Meet. Here at Channel Nine we will be holding our breaths and hoping he's all right.

ABC financial analyst Darryl Polglase is:

... shocked to hear of this incident. Ajay's yoga empire is worth millions. He is an astute businessman who hooked into the health obsession of the new millennium.

I scan the page. A small line at the bottom reads, *Police are still seeking a Byron Bay yoga instructor, Luna Nakamura, who is believed to have relevant information.* Luna. She's disappeared.

I bite my lip. Disappearing is bad. It makes you look guilty. The question no one seems to be asking though is, what's with the fake arm? Why would you throw an arm with Ajay's tattoo on it into the shark pool? *Why?*

Jacq tugs on my sleeve. 'Are we getting the eggs, Livvy?'

I fold the newspaper and we continue to the corner store. Taking advantage of my distracted state, Jacq runs around tossing junk food into the trolley. Pushing past the big cold cabinets at the end, I head back up the aisle towards the cash register.

Jacq grabs my arm. 'There's someone waving at us in the ice-cream.' She waves at the ice-cream.

'Nice try. I'm not buying ice-cream. You've already got,' I glance at the trolley, 'Tim Tams, chips and Coco Pops. Since when do we eat Coco Pops?'

'No, really, Livvy. There's someone in there.' Jacq grabs the front of my trolley and pulls it around. 'There, see, behind the ice-cream.'

I peer into the freezer cabinet. Behind the tubs of ice-cream a figure in a blue singlet and floaty pants is jumping up and down. It's never occurred to me you can get in behind the ice-cream, but I suppose that's how they restock it. Are they stuck in there?

I look around, but there's no staff nearby. Striding to the cabinet, I open the door. An icy mist floats over me. Through the fog, a familiar face appears. I feel a strange sense of dislocation. Like I'm in Nancy Drew *Murder on Ice*. Or maybe *Wuthering Heights*. I can practically hear the dogs howling on the moors. 'Luna?'

Luna's long hair is covered in frost. She puts her finger to her lips and glances from side to side. 'Here, take this.' She pushes a tub of Extra Deluxe Rich Chocolate Ice-cream towards me.

Jacq's eyes light up and she snatches it.

I take it from her. 'We've got ice-cream at home.' I try to put it back in the freezer.

Luna blocks me. 'Take it,' she hisses. She rubs her arms. Frost is forming on her eyebrows now. Without another word, she turns and vanishes through a door out the back of the freezer.

There is so much that is weird about this exchange, I don't know which bit to tackle first. I push my trolley towards the door, my mind spinning. Was she waiting in the ice-cream for me? Is she stalking me? Or was she planning to give the ice-cream to the first person who came along? Had it really happened? I glance back at the cabinet – there's no sign of anything untoward. The frozen food is as neat and tranquil as always.

'*She* was nice.' Jacq gazes at the ice-cream as we stand in the checkout.

I nod, bemused. She must have been there if Jacq saw her too. So Luna is on the run. But why hide out in an ice-cream cabinet? And why give me the ice-cream? Is there a message inside?

Pulling the lid off, I peer inside as we walk back home, expecting to find, 'Help me – I didn't do it' scratched into it, but there is nothing.

'Don't be greedy. Wait 'til you get home,' says Jacq.

Back home, I rip the article on Ajay out of the paper and stick it in the kitchen drawer before making Jacq a pancake with a scoop of ice-cream on top. Maybe the ice-cream isn't the point. *What is the point then?* I rub my temples, my brain hurting.

The afternoon moves slower than a theme park queue. Jacq goes to play with a new friend from holiday program, Nan goes out with Reggie and I am left alone. This gives me time to reflect on my situation, which isn't a good thing. I could have been swanning around in South-East Asia with my friends, but instead I am unemployed on the Gold Coast. There must be something wrong with my decision-making process.

To distract myself, I put on my Spotify mix and, turning it up loud, dance around the room. 'Greased Lightning' comes on, which reminds me of my date with Brandon. It was weird, but kind of fun. Maybe I wouldn't mind seeing him again.

The dancing makes me feel better. Outside, the sun is sinking towards the horizon. There are a few clouds around, but it looks like it could be a good sunset. I decide to go out for a walk.

I stride along the esplanade beside the beach, weaving my way between bus-loads of tourists with cameras ready for the sunset. When I reach Cavill Avenue, I turn around. The weather to the south looks ominous now. Dark clouds are building and a gust of wind whips up whitecaps in the sea.

Sure enough, not five minutes down the road it starts to rain. *That'd be right.* I could be snorkelling on a reef in Thailand, but no, I have chosen to be walking in Surfers Paradise in the rain. What is wrong with me?

I trudge on, the rain growing heavier, soaking my T-shirt and running down my face. The streets are suddenly empty; the tourists have retreated. A rumble of thunder fills the air. A car pulls up beside me and beeps. I ignore it, walking faster.

'Olivia.'

I turn. Rosco waves at me out of the window. The sight of him produces a confusing mixture of emotions. I walk towards him and stand with my arms crossed next to the car, rain drumming on my head. 'What do *you* want?'

His mouth twitches into a half-smile. 'Want a lift?'

I hesitate, then lightning flashes over the sea and the rain intensifies. I abandon the moral high ground and climb in, slamming the door behind me.

The radio plays softly as we drive along. Rain beats against the windscreen, drowning out the music. We don't talk. I'm happy with that. There are things we need to discuss, but they can wait.

Rosco glances over once, before looking back at the road. It seems the Mexican stand-off is still in force. Rosco and I used to fight a lot as kids. Afterwards, he was always the one to crack first, coming over to my place to see if I wanted to play again. I'm not about to start changing the rules now.

Eventually he pulls over outside Nan's flat, turns off the car and swivels in his seat to face me. He pushes his hair out of his eyes. 'I'm sorry I didn't fill you in on the McSushi case, Olivia. I didn't think you'd like it. I was right, wasn't I?'

I nod. 'It's still not a good reason not to tell me.'

'No, I'm sorry. It – it seemed easier. You know how you were asking me where I draw the line?'

'Yeah?'

'Well, I draw it somewhere different to you. It doesn't mean I've gone to the dark side. I'm just trying to make a buck.'

The wipers flick back and forth across the windscreen. 'How does identifying a group of activists to a company selling whale meat fit in?'

'I've dropped the McSushi contract. They'll go somewhere else, but our hands will be clean.'

I blink. 'You've dropped the contract? Did you do that for me?'

'I did it for me, alright? Now do you want to come back to work?'

I meet his gaze. 'Maybe.'

'Will you kick me in the shins again?'

'Possibly. If I think it's called for.'

'You always did have a good kick on you.'

'You're the only person I've ever kicked.'

'Should I be flattered?'

'Probably not.'

'Are we cool?' he asks. His eyes meet mine and …

Whoa. Was that a spark? Heat spreads over my face. 'We're cool.'

Rosco's cheeks are flushed too. He taps his fingers on the steering wheel. 'Abbey and Frannie went off to South-East Asia, huh?'

'Yeah.'

'You didn't want to go?'

I bite my lip. 'I wanted the job.'

He gives me a long look. 'Why?' he says at last.

My tongue seems to be tying itself in knots. 'I've … I've always wanted to be a PI.'

'Is it what you expected?'

'No. I guess I thought I'd be like Nancy Drew, pursuing justice and all that. Sleuthing around, solving mysteries, making the bad guys pay. Stupid, right? How about you?'

'I suppose I thought that too. Hardy Boys though, not Nancy Drew.' Rosco looks out the window, then back at me. 'You're different to how you used to be.'

My heart thumps in my chest. 'Different how?'

'You're still … exuberant. But … your fuse is shorter. You get angry more quickly.'

I look out the window. I don't want to have this conversation.

'Did something happen in Byron?' Rosco's voice is quiet. 'When you went there with Abbey?'

I feel like the car is swaying. That's the last thing I expected him to say. We stare at each other. My mouth is dry.

I close my eyes, listening to the thump of the rain.

'I'm sorry. I shouldn't have said anything.'

I shake my head. 'No, that's okay.' I look out at the rain. 'Yes. Something happened.'

'You want to talk about it?'

I watch the rain pound on the footpath. I've never told anyone except Abbey, not even my parents – especially not my parents – but now ... it seems that I want to tell Rosco. 'I was ...' I pause. 'I was ...'

Rosco touches my hand.

'I went out night surfing. I got the idea from you. Abbey wouldn't come, she was afraid of sharks and ... this guy ...' I gnaw my lip. 'He attacked me. It wasn't as bad as it could have been. Some people came up the beach and he took off. But still ...' I think of that night. The darkness. The fear. His weight on top of me. 'When something like that happens, you realise ... The world isn't the way you thought it was. Something shifts.'

Rosco is holding my hand now. 'I'm sorry that happened to you, Olivia. If I ever find that ...' his voice trails off. After a few moments, he lets go of my hand. It feels cold after the warmth of his touch. 'You didn't tell the police?'

I shake my head. 'Abbey didn't want her parents to know. They would have cracked down on her. On us. And there was no point. I never saw him.'

'He shouldn't have got away with that,' says Rosco.

'No. But I couldn't ...'

'I know. I understand.'

I clench my fists. 'The thing that makes me most angry is,

it's not like it's even that uncommon. It happens all the time.'

'Some people don't deserve to exist.'

'I suppose that's part of the reason I wanted to do this.'

'Be a PI?'

'Yeah. I thought maybe, it's stupid, but I thought maybe I could help.'

Rosco nods.

We're silent for a while, looking out at the teeming rain.

'That's not stupid,' he says at last.

'It is. It's stupid.'

'No it's not.'

'Yes it is.'

'No it's not.'

We smile at each other weakly. Whenever one of us used to say, *that's stupid*, the other always had to deny it.

'Is that why you gave up surfing?'

'Yeah. When I pulled my surfboard out it made me feel ... It reminded me.' My skin feels too thin, like my emotions are seeping out. I look down. 'I've made a puddle on your seat.'

'It doesn't matter.'

'Were you following me tonight?'

He looks embarrassed. 'I'm not stalking you. I just thought it would be easier if we talked face to face. I'm used to you now. I don't want to have to break in another assistant.'

It's warm in the car and, now the engine's off, the windows have fogged up. As the rain drums on the roof, it's like we're in a private cocoon.

'What about you?' I ask. 'Why'd you want to be a PI? Apart from the Hardy Boys, I mean.'

'To make money?'

I laugh. 'How's that working out for you?'

'Not so well. I do have another reason, but it's stupid.'

'It's not stupid.'

'Yes it is.' He smiles. 'My dad was a PI.'

'Your dad?' I've never heard Rosco mention his dad. Rosco's mum was a single parent as far as I knew.

'Yeah. It's pretty mixed up. He was the PI Mum used for her divorce. She only told me when I turned sixteen. I thought the guy who ran out on Mum was my father.'

'Wow. Have you met him?'

'No. Maybe I will one day. I know who he is. He works in Sydney. So, when I learnt that, I felt like it was in the blood. I decided I had to give it a go.'

'Do you still go night surfing?'

'Yeah. I do. Every full moon. You should come with me some time.'

I feel like I've been here before, like we're back sitting on the wall outside my house the week before I went to Byron.

Rosco's eyes meet mine and there's something different in them. It's not the flash I felt before; it's steadier than that.

I know what's going to happen next and can't deal with that. I need to get out of here. 'I should go now. I'll see you back in the office.' I jump out of the car and run through the rain to Nan's unit. From the doorway, I look back.

Rosco raises a hand before driving off.

The unit is quiet when I come in. Lightning flashes outside followed by the low rumble of thunder. My mind is turning over and over. I feel raw, exposed.

My stomach growls and I open the freezer. Pulling out the

chocolate ice-cream Luna gave me, I dig in, spoon moving from ice-cream to lips in a feeding frenzy. Eating always helps. It doesn't stop the memory coming back though.

I was on my way back, head in the clouds, when it happened ... My spoon catches on something.

I scoop some more and a triangle of plastic comes into view. Further scraping produces a plastic sleeve. *A message from Luna.* Heart thumping, I pull it out and wipe off the ice-cream to reveal an envelope inside. I slide it out.

Scrawled across the front of the envelope in felt pen it says, *found this in the boot of my car.* I open the envelope. Inside is a McSushi wrapper. I turn the McSushi wrapper over and examine the back, but there's nothing there. I sniff it. It smells of wasabi.

It's a message – apparently an important one – but what does it mean? My head hurts. Why did Luna brave the freezer to give it to me? What was she trying to tell me? Maybe it will make more sense in the morning ...

I shower and climb between my sheets.

It was beautiful in the surf that night. There was no one else out. I tried not to think of what might be underneath me. But then a wave came and I was gliding over the moon-shiny darkness. It was just as amazing as Rosco had said.

I breathe deeply, trying to control it, but the fury rises so fast I can hardly breathe.

In the morning, I slip on shorts and a T-shirt, let myself out of the flat and pad down the street, my feet bare on the cold pavement. The skyscrapers are dull today – clouds drift in their mirrored windows. On a fine day they'll burn your retinas if you're not careful. Kevin trots behind me in his jacket, his nails clicking on the cement.

The sound of the surf is almost deafening as I step onto the sand. Massive walls of grey water roll in, crash onto the beach and suck back out. I jog along to the headland, the southerly wind whipping at my hair. A few drops of rain splatter my glasses. Summer is gone – today we are back to winter.

Reaching my favourite viewing position, I squat, hugging my knees. The car park is full already – there are as many spectators as surfers. Guys in hoodies with zoom lenses perch on the rocks ready for the money shot. 'Corduroy lines ... hollow ... walls ...' Their voices drift over to me. I pull out my phone and add more words to my list.

Surfers run past me at full pelt, eager to fling themselves into the ocean. Their zinc-cream-plastered faces are fixed on the sea. If you get in the way of these guys, they'll run you down. There's a fever in the air; you can see it latch on to them as they get out of their cars. The ones on their way out of the surf are different. Their eyes are bloodshot, their movements loose and unhurried, their zinc cream faded. They've had their fix.

An extra-large set of waves roars towards one guy caught inside the break. Seeing what's in front of him, he paddles faster and faster. I urge him on, but it's too late. The wave smashes on top of him. I hold my breath in sympathy – he's under for a long time – and gasp as he pops up the other side. But there's no rest, another wave is coming. Again, he paddles – my breath steadies as he makes it over.

I think of Rosco in the car last night. Of the way he held my hand. How I felt that one time he kissed me. Then I remember what Maya said – *you need to commit more. Ask yourself: what's the worst that can happen?*

I watch a few surfers take off on vertical faces, get smashed beneath the whitewash and limp from the water, worse for wear. Broken pieces of surfboards drift in on the foam, their owners left to catch a wave on the part still attached to their leg.

You take risks, you get smashed, but ... you survive.

Rosco is poring over the *Gold Coast Times* in the office kitchen when I get in. My heart does a rapid tap dance at the sight of him. *Commit more. Don't run away.*

He looks up and our eyes lock. 'Welcome back.'

I adjust my glasses.

Rosco turns the page.

It seems that if there's an elephant lurking in the room we are both going to ignore it. *Oh, that elephant over there. Nope, can't see it.* Here I am ready to take a risk and Rosco is calmly reading the paper. I'm not sure what I was expecting after the way I jumped out of the car last night. And perhaps I was wrong, perhaps nothing was going to happen. I swallow the lump in my throat and adopt a brisk, businesslike air, but the open paper catches my eye.

The Ajay arm case has been relegated to page three. He is still missing. There are no new leads, but a lot of speculation. No one has any idea what the fake arm means.

Next to a picture of Rochelle lunching with an unidentified man at a Surfers Paradise café, the headline reads, **Police Still Searching for Ajay: Guru's wife set to inherit multi-million-dollar business.** The picture shows only the back of the man's head. He has dark hair and broad shoulders. Rochelle is leaning over the table exposing her sensational bosom. Apparently she is coping well.

Police are still 'following a number of leads'. That means they haven't found Luna. A sub-story queries, *Who Will Be the Next Face of McSushi?* It appears Ajay's contract has concluded. A few predictable faces accompany the story – Chris Hemsworth, Guy Sebastian, Margot Robbie …

'What do you reckon?' Rosco doesn't look up from the paper. 'Do you think this Luna's knocked him off?'

'No.' My hand goes to my shoulder bag – her envelope is inside. 'She's a hippie love child, not a killer.'

'Uh huh.' He looks up and assumes his usual instructor's tone. 'Let's say he was knocked off. What type of person do you think would have done it?'

I know what he's getting at – murderers won't always be sharpening their daggers, wearing eye-patches and casting shifty looks the way they do in Nancy Drew. But Luna …

'Any thoughts?' says Rosco.

I look at the newspaper. 'He's the kind of guy who makes enemies.'

'Jealous husband?'

I gaze at the picture of Rochelle. 'Or jealous wife?'

Rosco grunts. 'It's possible. Still, not our problem now, I suppose. I'll let the police worry about that one.' He folds the paper.

'Can I keep it?'

Rosco hands me the paper. His eyes question me, but then his phone rings.

Back at my desk I pull out the envelope I found in the ice-cream, open it and look at the McSushi wrapper. I'm hoping I missed something last night, but it's still just a McSushi wrapper. I know what Rosco will say if I show it to him. *Not our problem. Give it to the police.*

I remember the cop at Ocean World. He's already suspicious of me – if I give it to him questions will be asked. Questions I don't want to answer, like, why did she give it to you? *Because I'm a member of her activist group?* It's the only reason that makes sense. But that will bring me closer to having to tell a direct lie about Luna's call the night before the arm incident. My mind turns to the fake arm again. *What's with that?*

I google 'fake arms' and get a list of websites offering information about prostheses. I type *fake arm* into Instagram. This is slightly more promising. A hashtag *#fakearm* has some funny photos – people hiding their phone on a school desk with a fake arm, and arms hanging out of car boots. I scroll down further and find a picture of a fake arm lying on some grass. As well as *#fakearm*, it's also hashtagged *#fakearmsagainstharassment*. The poster is called sharkgirl and their profile picture is a shark. There's no other information. I search #fakearmsagainstharassment but nothing else comes up. *Dead end.*

I slip the envelope back in my bag with the newspaper article. What does Luna expect me to do about it? She's the main suspect in what could be a murder investigation. Maybe she thought killing Ajay would save whales. It's certainly stopped him endorsing McSushi.

I think back to how she looked in the ice-cream cabinet – nervous and cold. But who wouldn't be nervous if they were being hunted by the police – by grouchy-faced Dan Ferris? I file the envelope in the too-hard basket. For now, I need to concentrate on keeping my job. I glance over at Rosco and our eyes meet. He looks away first.

I also need to figure out what, if anything, is going down with me and Rosco. *Ask yourself: what's the worst that can happen ...*

The day goes by without incident; as does the next. Rosco is briskly professional. I'm beginning to think I imagined the Spark between us in the car. Maybe I did. In one way this is a relief, but in another way I wish I hadn't jumped out of the car quite so quickly. It would be good to know if Rosco is still a Notable Exception.

On Tuesday afternoon, Rosco goes out for a meeting. I yawn. It's been such a slow day I'm half-asleep. Maybe a quick headstand will wake me up. I've been practising every day – taking my feet off the wall for short periods, wobbling, putting them back. It's become a superstition: *the day I can do a headstand without the wall my life will be perfect.*

Putting my head on the carpeted floor next to my desk, I lift my legs, slowly taking them off the wall. I'm almost balanced when the door bangs. I squeak and fall over.

'Forgot my car keys.' Rosco looks at my empty chair then at the floor. 'Is this what you usually get up to when I'm out of the office?'

I climb to my feet, adjusting my glasses. 'No, hardly ever. You caught me at a bad time.' More explanation seems to be called for. 'I was doing a headstand – it helps me concentrate.'

'Uh huh.' He swings his car keys on his finger. 'Don't get yourself into any position you can't get out of. I'll be gone for a few hours. I wouldn't like to think of you here with no one to untangle you.'

I flush. 'That only happened once.'

'Give me a call if it happens again. I could do with a laugh.' He winks and shuts the door behind him.

I stare after him. Is he flirting with me? I decide not.

On Wednesday I go out for lunch and find the local McSushi pulling down its Ajay posters. By Thursday, new ones are up. Stopping in the street, I stare at them in shock. It isn't Chris, Guy or Margot.

It's Maya.

She is wearing a green bikini, carrying a surfboard and smiling her gap-toothed smile. *Australian longboard champion Maya Cahill* is plastered across the top. *McSushi gives me the energy I need when I'm on a wave*, reads the endorsement. *Oh Maya, bad idea.* I bet her father's behind this.

I come back in to find Rosco on the phone. He's doing some fast talking, pulling at his hair, like he always does when he's tense. I pause for a second as I go past his door and catch a fragment of conversation. 'Not too much longer, Kenny.'

Who is this Kenny? It's the third time I've heard his name and each time Rosco's got all worked up. When he puts the phone down I walk over to his door. 'Who's Kenny?'

Rosco looks up. 'Kenny the King.'

I look at him blankly.

'You haven't heard of him?'

I shake my head.

'Huh. Thought everyone knew Kenny. The landlord. He owns half of Surfers. You really haven't heard of him?'

I shake my head. *If Kenny's the landlord ...* 'Are you having financial problems?'

Rosco looks tired. 'Nothing I can't handle.'

I feel bad. I'd no idea things were difficult. 'I'm sorry I made you drop the McSushi case. And lost us Rochelle. I didn't know.'

'Olivia, I told you, dropping McSushi had nothing to do with you, alright? It wasn't working out. And you did your best with the Ajay thing. You did well, in fact. Don't worry about it. That's my job.'

'I had wondered.'

'What?'

'What your job was.'

Rosco's phone rings. 'Well, now you know.'

For the rest of the week, I continue to be a model employee. I stop in at the supermarket every day, pausing in front of the ice-cream section, but the frosty figure of Luna never reappears. I feel uneasy, like invisible events are happening around me. Luna's envelope is always on my mind, but remains in the too-hard basket.

I almost show it to Rosco several times, but the idea of having to go to the police puts me off. Whichever way I look at it, it's still just a McSushi wrapper.

Brandon doesn't call. I hadn't planned on seeing him again, but it would have been nice to be asked. My Instagram feed shows Frannie and Abbey riding elephants and swimming in waterfalls. I have nothing to post – *#dullweekend*.

On Monday, I come into work to find Brad Cahill sitting across the desk from Rosco. Rosco glances up, but doesn't smile. Something serious is going on. Brad half swivels in his chair, sees me and turns back to Rosco.

'Sit down, Olivia,' says Rosco. 'Brad's here about Maya.'

My stomach turns cold, like it already knows what he's going to say.

'She's gone missing.'

I slide into a chair, my mouth dry. Scenarios flash through my head, none of them good.

Brad's face is drawn and his eyes are red. 'She was getting it back together. She's been training four, five hours every day. And getting the McSushi endorsement – it was the biggest deal she's ever had. They're going to sponsor her whole world tour; all she needs to do is have their logo on her wetsuit ...' His voice trails off.

'Have the police been told?' I ask.

Brad darts me a contemptuous look. 'Girls that age – they wander off all the time. "We'll make a few inquiries",' he mimics. 'They're useless.'

'No letter?'

Brad rolls his eyes.

Just asking. 'What about her boyfriend?'

'He's out of the picture,' Brad snaps.

'Does he know anything, though?' I press.

Brad's face goes red. 'I told you – he's out of the picture. The police have spoken to him; he hasn't seen her for a week. If I get you on this job I don't want you wasting my time sniffing around the Goldsworths. Maya knew they were out of bounds.' Brad clenches his hands, the muscles standing up on his forearms.

I have a feeling Maya mightn't have been as compliant boyfriend-wise as he thinks. I saw them together at the RSL; they were pretty keen on each other. 'You're the boss,' I say.

Rosco shakes hands with Brad at the door and grasps his shoulder. 'We'll get onto to it straight away. If she can be found, we'll find her.'

Brad glances back at me. 'Find my girl.'

'I'll do everything I can, Mr Cahill. She's a great girl.'

He half-smiles. 'Yes, she makes me proud.'

Something about the way he says it gets my back up. *What if she didn't make you proud? Would you still want to find her?*

Rosco comes back in and sits opposite me. 'What do you think?'

I chew the inside of my lip. 'She might have run away. I would, if I had a father like him. On the other hand ...' I don't like to voice what's on my mind, but Rosco knows. We're both thinking about what happened to the last face of McSushi. It could be a coincidence, but then again ... 'I'll get down to Byron Bay.'

'Talk to everyone who knows her.'

'The boyfriend?'

'He's first.'

It takes me all day to track James Goldsworth down. I finally score with one of the surfers towelling off in the Wategos Beach car park. 'That's Goldie out there.' He points towards the horizon – there's only one person left in the water. He's lying face-down on his surfboard right out the back, letting wave after wave go by. The sun is setting and the waves are turning from gold to black.

Sunset is shark feeding time so I'm not too keen, but it doesn't look like James is getting out any time soon. I struggle into my too-tight wetsuit – I really should buy a new one – and paddle out.

'Hey,' I call as I get closer. I don't want to startle him. It looks like he might be asleep, although that seems unlikely. 'James?'

He lifts his head from the board, his face in shadow. 'Yeah?' His tone isn't welcoming.

As I get closer I see the dark bruise around his eye. His eyelid is swollen and purple and a yellowish tinge spreads all the way down to his cheekbone. Someone's given him a good whack. 'I wanted to talk to you about Maya.'

His face twitches. He puts his forehead back on the board. 'I've already talked to the police.'

'I'm not the police. I'm a private investigator. You might be able to help.'

'I don't know where Maya is.' His voice is muffled by the board. 'I wish I did. I haven't seen her since ...' He sits up. 'I haven't seen her since someone took photos of us together at the RSL.' His voice is sharper now. He focuses on me. 'That would be you, I take it?'

I change the subject. 'Who gave you the black eye?'

'Who do you reckon? Same guy who's paying your bills.' He spits the words out.

This isn't going as well as I'd hoped. 'Don't you want to help Maya?'

'Look – the only thing that would help Maya would be getting a divorce from her father. I can't help. I don't know where she is.'

The light is fading, turning the water dark beneath us. I pull my legs up onto my board. 'I'm sorry, James, about the photos. It's my job.'

'What kind of a job is that?'

'A dirty job some of the time, I guess. But I took it because I wanted to do something good. Finding Maya would be good. I like her.'

There's a long pause before he speaks. 'Everyone likes Maya.'

We sit there in silence for a while. I sense a slight thawing in our relationship. 'It must be tough – your families ...'

'Hating each other? Yeah. Jesus, it's total crap. I'm sick of being a Goldsworth. It's like there's this stupid legacy I need to carry around. I'm supposed to surf in a certain way, think in a certain way, go out with certain people. My dad's as bad as Maya's and he sees himself as the white hat in this feud. He's the hippie soul surfer while Brad's the big, bad capitalist. As far as I'm concerned they both suck.'

'A plague on both your houses.' I don't expect him to catch the reference.

'They have made worm's meat of me.' James fingers his black eye, his face bitter.

I shouldn't be surprised that he knows his Shakespeare – he's studying acting at TAFE after all. I looked into his background for my report.

'Where would Maya go if she ran away?'

'Apart from away from her dad?' James's eyes linger on the shore where lights are coming on in the houses. 'I don't know. All I can think of is she loves comedy. I mean, she loves surfing too, but she's kind of over it. She's been pushed too hard for too long. First the Australian titles, now he wants her to take the world titles. He's reliving his glory days through her. But comedy, that's something all her own – hers and mine.'

Comedy. It's not much of a lead, but it's better than nothing. 'Anything big happening comedy-wise?'

'There's the Brisbane Comedy Festival next week.' James's voice is brighter now. 'They have, like, heats you can go in and if you're a finalist you get to go to the Melbourne Comedy Festival. We were talking about it, Maya and I, before ...' He touches his eye. 'We've heard Melbourne's pretty cool.'

The Brisbane Comedy Festival. It's not much of a lead. 'I'll keep it in mind.' It's almost dark now. I shiver. 'D'you reckon we could catch a wave in?' It's a long paddle to shore and I don't want to do it on my own.

'Sure.' James glances over his shoulder, gives two strokes and is on a wave and out of sight before I can say, 'Wait for me.'

'We,' I mutter. 'I said *we*.' I breathe deeply to ease the rising panic. It's getting dark. I need to get into shore before James leaves me on the beach alone. I paddle for a wave and miss it; paddle for another one and miss that too. I'm so busy not thinking about what's lurking in the dark sea beneath me, I have no room in my head for wave selection. I see another wave coming and paddle. It's only when I'm at the point of no return, staring down the face, that I realise it's a set wave – the one in a series that is extra large.

It's bigger than anything I've ever ridden before but it's too late to pull out now. *You need to commit more.* I give two strong strokes and leap to my feet. My board shoots vertically down the face. I know I have to turn before the bottom or I'll nose-dive and crash. *Into the sharky water.* Taking a step backwards, I drive the right-hand edge in hard. Miraculously, the board turns before the bottom and I skim along the face – riding it for what seems like hours, all the way into the beach. James stands on the sand, his board under his arm, watching. My heart racing from the adrenaline, I step off my board.

'Nice wave,' he says, as if it's an everyday event rather than a record-breaking personal best.

I feel like punching the air, but that would be uncool. 'Do you reckon,' I pant, 'that I will ever in my life be able to do that again?'

All week I search for Maya. I talk to her friends and check her Facebook page. It's full of inspirational surfing quotes – 'The best day working is not as good as the worst day surfing' – and photos from her life – Maya on waves in Fiji, Indonesia, Samoa. But there is no indication of a darker side, and no clues.

I hang out at the surf breaks from sunup to sundown – long hours, but light work – striking up conversations with all the surfers. There's a general consensus that Maya's father was driving her crazy, but not much else to go on.

They're all full of talk on the Ajay disappearance, though. I keep my ears pricked for news of Luna. The McSushi wrapper plays on my mind but no course of action presents itself.

Everyone has a rumour to pass on.

'I heard his body washed in at Coffs Harbour, but they're keeping it secret.'

'Luna? Yeah, she did it. Good on her.'

'I reckon Georgia Hansen hired a hitman after that photo. I would've if I was her.'

'He was a sex addict; there wasn't a single woman in his classes he hadn't hit on.'

'They say he's the father of Georgia Hansen's baby.'

'I reckon that Himalayan guru came after him 'cos he was, like, cheapening yoga.'

'How were those rats in the studio, hey? Dude had some enemies all right.'

'The fake arm? Reckon he might have slapped one too many people.'

The *Lighthouse News* weighs in with a two-page investigation into the yoga scene.

Speed Yoga or Fast Prophets?

After 5000 years on the outer, yoga is now mainstream. Target sells yoga videos; K-mart sells yoga wear. In the Bay, every second person is a yoga teacher. One of the figures at the heart of this boom is Ajay, who made Bikini Beach Body Boot Camp Speed Yoga into a multi-million-dollar franchise. Ajay never pulled any punches when asked about his business empire. 'I know my techniques might offend some people, but if more people are getting into yoga because of me that's a good thing, right?' Ajay said in an interview with the Lighthouse News *a month ago.*

As the investigation into his disappearance drags on speculation is rife. Could a yoga purist be the culprit?

'Yoga is a spiritual practice,' said a source who wishes to remain anonymous. 'Many people in the yoga movement are angry about the way Ajay bent it to his own ends. I'm not saying it's right, but some of that anger might have gone too far.'

I keep the article to add to my collection. I don't envy the police the job of untangling all these stories. For that matter, I don't envy my own job – finding Maya. Even after a week I have nothing to go on.

I've come to a dead end.

On Thursday afternoon I get in my car to head back to the Gold Coast no wiser than when I left. All my hopes now rest on the Brisbane Comedy Festival. James is convinced she's run off to escape her father. I like this theory. It's better than the alternative.

I call James before I leave the Bay. 'So, this comedy festival – can you get us tickets? I figure we should go up there, hang out, talk to some people at least.'

'I'm working on it.'

'What, is there a problem?'

'Turns out tickets sold out weeks ago. Don't worry; I'll fix it. We've got to be there. I've got a feeling about it.'

'Okay. I'll see you then.' I'm sure he'll sort something out.

On my way home I stop off at Big W and pick up the prints from Jacq's birthday at Ocean World. Jacq's old fashioned when it comes to photography. She doesn't believe it's a real photo unless it's in print. I know how she feels. I like the anticipation of waiting for prints, too.

I flick through the photos, close-ups of stranger's knees feature prominently. Jacq's excited to see them though. She pores over them while I get dinner ready. Nan's out at the movies with Reggie.

'Hey look, Livvy. It's that guy who came around here the other night – the stupid American one, not the stupid one with the cap on backwards.'

'Huh?' I glance up from the saucepan.

Jacq brings the photo over to me. 'Here, see? See how dumb he looks?'

It's one of the photos Jacq took of the waterski show, while I was off having a coffee break. It seems to have a *Grease* theme. In the foreground, an out-of-focus female waterskier in a tight black singlet and black stretch pants flies over a ski jump.

The background is in focus. There's a line of female dancers in flared skirts and headbands and behind them a line of men with swept-back hair in white T-shirts. Any one of them could be Brandon.

'Yeah, they look like him, don't they?' I turn back to my stirring.

'No.' Jacq is insistent. She pulls at my arm. 'There.' Her finger points to one of the faces.

I pull the pot off the hotplate and peer closer. 'How can you tell it's him? They all look the same.'

Jacq gives me the 'you are so dumb' look she's been perfecting lately. 'Get yourself some better glasses.' She picks up Nan's glasses and hands them to me.

Maybe I do need to update my glasses. I hold Nan's glasses in front of the photo. It *does* look like Brandon, but surely he'd have said something. I told him I was going to Ocean World. We even talked about the roller-coaster. 'I don't think it's him.'

'I was right about Rosco, wasn't I?' says Jacq. 'At Byron Bay. It was him wasn't it?'

'Yes, but ...'

Jacq stabs her finger at the photo. She isn't taking any more lip from me. 'It's him. You can tell by that dumb dimple in the middle of his chin.'

I keep thinking about it during dinner. After Jacq's gone to bed I pick up the photo and study it again. Nan comes home and I hand the photo to her. 'See anyone you recognise in that photo?'

She peers at it closely. 'That isn't you going over the jump, is it?'

'No, that isn't me going over the jump. Anyone else?'

Nan purses her lips. 'Those men in the background ...'

'Yes?'

'They all look like that fellow who came around here the other night – the American one. How did things go with him?'

'Fine. I can't tell you much – confidentiality clause.'

Nan sniffs. 'I always know when you're lying, Olivia.' She puts on the kettle. 'What's happening with you and Rosco?'

'What? What do you mean what's happening? He's my boss.'

'Do most bosses break down their employee's doors late at night?'

'That was a misunderstanding. He thought I'd been tied up.'

'Maybe.' Nan is inscrutable.

'What do you mean, maybe? He did.'

'I think if a man breaks down your door it shows he has feelings for you.'

I shake my head. 'It's strictly an employer–employee relationship.'

Nan raises one eyebrow.

I wait for one of her pronouncements.

'You could do worse. It's impressive how he's started his

own business so young. Maybe if you put more effort into your appearance ...'

I grit my teeth. This is Nan's hobbyhorse. I'm used to it, but it still gets my back up.

Nan picks up her magazine and flicks through it. 'I saw something here. Yes, why don't you get your hair done like Taylor Swift? A nice fringe. You haven't changed your hairstyle since you were fifteen.' She holds up a picture of Taylor Swift looking sultry in a clinging silver dress.

'I don't want a new haircut.' I finger the strands of my straight shoulder-length hair. 'I wouldn't look like Taylor Swift, anyway. I'd look like, I don't know.' I take the mag off her and flick through it, coming to the makeover page. 'I'd look like one of these women in the "after" shots – too try-hard. It's stupid how in the "before" photographs they always look like they just got out of bed. It's not exactly hard to improve on that.'

Nan snorts. 'You take after your mother. She never made the best of herself either.'

Mum lectures in outdoor pursuits at TAFE and her idea of dressing up is a clean T-shirt and quick-dry pants. I'm a big disappointment to Nan, I know, but if I give in on the haircut it'll be open slather. Before I know it, she'll have me wearing pink lipstick and red nail polish and flower-patterned dresses. Despite my dating success with my femme fatale outfit, it's not a look I can carry off on a regular basis. It's too much effort. Besides, I don't like drawing attention to myself.

Nan goes to bed and I pick up the Ocean World photo again. There's no way of telling if it's Brandon or not. But if it is, he has a connection with Ocean World he hasn't told me about.

A memory comes back to me. At his apartment, he took a

phone call that disrupted our evening. That had been the night before the fake arm appeared in the shark pool. And he *had* been at speed dating. Could he have a connection with Ajay? If it wasn't for the McSushi wrapper I'd say it's none of my business, but I feel like I owe it to Luna to find out more.

It's not much to go on, but it's worth following up. *Besides.* My mind drifts back to *Saturday Night Fever.* I don't think he's my type, but we did have fun. I switch on my computer.

My fingers move over the keyboard. 'Hi there. Feel like getting back together for a bit more *Saturday Night Fever*?'

'You won't be a bystander on the Gold Coast; this city will inspire you to get involved and discover fun again ...'

On Friday night I park my car on the corner opposite Brandon's apartment and peer up at his window. I slip my hand into my handbag to check the contents – pepper spray, whistle, phone, purse. It's best to be prepared. I'm not sure what I'm getting into. *Dirty dancing or a date with death?* Turning the radio off, I climb out of the car.

Basically I want to suss him out, have a snoop around, put my misgivings to rest. And maybe do some more dancing.

Getting dressed for this occasion was a major dilemma. I'd done the slinky dress and the Olivia Newton John number. I was out of options. There was nothing in my wardrobe that fitted the Anna Smith personality – even without the wig. In the end, I threw myself on Nan's mercy. She was delighted.

'I have some clothes I bought before my last diet,' she said. 'They should fit.' Out of her closet came aquamarine pedal pushers, a yellow halter-neck top and sparkly high-heeled sandals. She even opened her jewel box for me and hung some droopy peacock feathers in my ears.

'You should dress like this more often,' she said as I tottered out of her bedroom.

I would have had a smart answer, but her pants were cutting off the blood supply to my brain. I smacked her hand away as she came at me with the hair-spray – enough was enough.

Brandon buzzes me in and I squint at myself in the lift mirror on the way up to his flat. I look like one of those people in the Sunday paper style section. *Captured on the streets of Surfers – Anna wears pants by Paris Hilton, top by Wonderbra and earrings by Andrew Peacock.*

Brandon answers the door as soon as I knock. His chest is bare and a pair of loose pants hang off his hips. 'Hey there.' He flashes his eyebrows at me. 'You look nice. I was just getting dressed. Come in.' He heads straight for the record player. 'You ready to boogie?'

'Sure am.'

'Any requests?' He flicks through his vinyl collection. 'I've got lots of musicals.'

Something complicated requiring numerous costume changes would be good. It might get him out of the room long enough for me to have a look around. *Jesus Christ Superstar?* Too religious. *Oklahoma?* Too farmy. *Mary Poppins?* Not enough costume changes. 'Can you do *Rocky Horror Picture Show?*'

'You're kidding. It's my all-time fave.' Brandon pulls out a record, lifts the lid of the turntable and slips it on. 'This is going to be good.' He bounds from the room.

The first song is a slow number, 'Science Fiction, Double Feature'. I'm pretty sure he won't make an appearance for this, so I go for it, phone ready to photograph any evidence. His apartment is strangely uncluttered, more like a holiday house than a home.

I don't like my chances of finding anything interesting. The only decorations in the lounge room are photographs of whales and dolphins. There are whales breaching, dolphins back-lit by rainbows, dolphins riding waves. *I guess he likes dolphins.*

I slip into the kitchen. Unlike at home, there's nothing stuck to the fridge, no useless junk in the cutlery drawer and no stash of loose change, business cards and unwanted safety pins in a bowl. Opening the pantry door, I inspect the rows of perfectly aligned vitamins, spices and sauces.

As the song winds up, I walk back to the couch, take a sip of mineral water and wait for Brandon to appear.

Brandon's bedroom door opens to the opening bars of 'Time Warp'. *Rocky Horror* was a good choice. He's worked hard on his outfit – black tail-coat, tight black pants, black shoes and white socks pulled over the pants. The stage make-up has come out. His face is white, eyes outlined in black and red lipstick glistens on his lips. 'Ta da. I've been waiting my whole life for this.' He spreads his arms.

'It's astounding,' I say.

'Time is fleeting.' Brandon takes my hand and pulls me up to dance.

It's fun. It reminds me of my Year Ten school disco. A whole bunch of us had lined up – *it's just a jump to the left ...*

At the end of the song Brandon bends me over backwards in a dip. 'You're a sucker for this stuff, aren't you?' he says.

I nod. 'Do another outfit. I love it.'

He smiles. 'Okay, just for you. It'll be a good one.' He disappears into the bedroom.

I walk down the corridor. If Brandon appears I can always say I'm going to the loo.

The door next to the bathroom is closed. I open it carefully, glancing back at Brandon's bedroom. The record is playing 'Sweet Transvestite'. Checking that his door remains shut, I step inside.

The room is set up as an office – a tidy one. A laptop sits on the desk near the window. I'd like to check it out, but I don't have time. A compact filing cabinet stands next to the desk. I pull it open. *Bank statements, Contracts, Expenses, Holidays, Income, Media, Tax ...* For a young guy, he's very organised. His whole life is in alphabetical order. It would take too long to go through it all. I go straight to the drop file marked bank statements.

My throat tightens as I see the line item. *Ocean World, salary.* So he does work at Ocean World. I take a photo and I'm about to thrust it back when I notice an envelope sitting at the bottom of the file. I pull it out and open it. It's stuffed with fifty-dollar notes. There must be thousands of dollars in there. I don't have time to think about what that might mean now. Placing the envelope back and sliding the cabinet door shut, I come out into the corridor – and almost collide with Brandon.

'Hi there,' he drawls. 'Looking for the bathroom?'

I lick my lips and nod. Brandon is wearing skin-tight gold hot pants and nothing else except a short blonde wig. 'Rocky?' I croak.

The record is now playing 'Toucha Toucha Touch Me'. Brandon has clearly timed his entrance for this.

'You wanna get dirty?' he sings, flashing his eyebrows at me.

I don't. I so don't. Maybe he'd just forgotten to mention he worked at Ocean World, but on the other hand ... My heart thumps loudly. What were those payments? *And how does a guy his age afford an apartment like this?*

Brandon dances towards me in his gold hotpants.

'I'm not feeling well,' I squeak.

He dances closer, singing along to the song.

'No, really. Can we call it a day?'

In answer, Brandon dances even closer. We are practically chest to chest.

He's not listening. My fists clench and something snaps inside me. I kick his shin as hard as I can, shove him backwards and run for the door.

'Ow, what was that for?' he says, but I don't stop. All I can think about is getting out of there.

It's not until I'm looking at my car in the street that I remember I've left my handbag with my pepper spray, whistle, purse and car keys in his flat.

There's no way I'm going back up there and I don't want to hang around here either – what if he comes looking for me? It's too late to call Nan; she'd have to wake up Jacq to come out. And I don't have any money for a taxi or bus. There's only one thing for it.

I put in a call to Rosco.

'The sun doesn't set on Australia's Gold Coast. The end of the day just means the start of a new ...'

Rosco plonks two cups of coffee on the table and slides one across to me.

'Thanks.' I place my hands around the cup to warm them. It's not a cold night, but a sea breeze blows into the café, making me shiver.

I see Rosco take in my outfit – the tight pants and halter top. 'Here.' He unzips his sweatshirt and passes it across the table. 'Femme fatale?'

'Yes.' His body warmth still hugs the fleece as I slide my arms in. 'They're not my clothes. They're Nan's.'

Rosco whistles. 'Your nan's a foxy dresser.'

'I know. It's like we've traded places, right?' It's close to midnight and the streets are busy with clubbers, drunk teenagers and beefy-looking men. I feel vulnerable.

Rosco hadn't said much when I'd asked him to come and pick me up. He must be biding his time.

I sip on my coffee. 'What have you been up to tonight?'

Rosco drains his coffee before replying. 'Just catching up with a mate for a drink.'

'Sorry to interrupt.'

'No, no problem. And you?'

'Not such a quiet one.'

'I figured that. Going to tell me about it?'

I shiver again. I'd wanted excitement in my life but wrestling with a guy in gold hotpants didn't fit the bill.

'You okay?' Rosco asks.

'Yeah.' I suppose I'm going to have to tell him. 'I've been investigating.'

'Right. Any leads on Maya?'

'Um, it's actually something else.'

'I haven't asked you to do anything else.'

'No, well …' I take a deep breath and it all comes out – *Rocky Horror*, the cash-filled envelope, the bit at the end which, now that I'm out of there, doesn't seem quite so scary anymore. It's possible I overreacted. I try to make it sound like a purely professional occasion, but I'm not sure if Rosco buys it.

He looks over my shoulder, not meeting my eyes. 'You met this guy at speed dating?'

I nod. 'I left my handbag there. It had my purse in it, and my car keys.'

'So, he works at Ocean World but he didn't mention it when you said you were going there, and he was at speed dating the same night as Ajay.' Rosco taps the side of his cup with a teaspoon.

'And someone's been paying him large amounts of cash. You should see his apartment.'

Rosco brings his eyes back to mine. 'You shouldn't have been there tonight. It's not safe.'

I don't like his bossy tone. 'I thought it was important.'

'I wouldn't have got you to do that. Besides, we're not being paid to investigate this case. Talk to the police. Maybe they'll want to follow it up if there's a link to Ajay. They're still looking for Luna as far as I know.'

Luna. She must be scared – out there on the run. I've let her down. It's on the tip of my tongue to tell Rosco about the McSushi wrapper, but he's already standing to pay the bill and he'd just say to tell the police.

What was Luna trying to tell me? She hates McSushi, so it couldn't have been her wrapper. Someone else must have put it there. Did someone else leave the rat hairs in her car too?

The waitress smiles as she hands over Rosco's change at the counter. A couple of long, dark tendrils have escaped from her bun and she pushes them back behind her ears. She reminds me of Brooklyn.

Brooklyn. I remember her on the street of Byron Bay in her power suit. She'd been there right before my ill-fated yoga class. What if she released the rats? But why would she do that? Ajay was the face of McSushi. They're supposed to be on the same team. But on the other hand, getting Luna out of the way is in her interests. McSushi stands a better chance of opening in Byron Bay without her around running the protest campaign. Could the McSushi wrapper point to Brooklyn? Was Luna saying she'd been framed?

By the time Rosco comes back to the table I have a plan.

Rosco drives me to my door. 'You'll be all right getting your car?'

'Yeah, I'll get it in the morning.' I slide off his jacket and hand it to him.

He looks into my eyes. 'So, I'll see you Monday?' There's

something about his voice that makes me think there's more he wants to say.

'Yeah, I'm in Brisbane on Sunday; following up on this comedy lead for Maya.'

'That's right. Hope it goes well.'

There is an awkward silence. Will the Spark strike again? I both want it and dread it.

'Take care, Olivia,' says Rosco. 'Do things by the book, okay? And talk to the police about Brandon.'

It seems the Spark is missing in action. I give him a guilty thumbs up and open the door. Doing things by the book, no intention I have.

29

The question I ponder as I catch the bus back to Brandon's apartment early the next morning, is where to find Brooklyn. Was there an address on her file? I pull out my phone and flick through the photos. Yes, here it is. The Blue Dolphin Motel.

My car's right where I left it and I let myself in with my spare key. I slide into the seat and feel something under my feet. It's my handbag. I check inside; everything's there. Brandon must have let himself in and left it for me. That was helpful of him. But I still think he's up to no good.

Back home, I consider what gear I need for a hard day of tailing Brooklyn. My wardrobe offers little inspiration. 'Do you mind if I borrow some of your clothes again, Nan? I've got a big job on today,' I call down the corridor.

Nan stalks out from the laundry holding her yellow halter-neck top. 'How on earth did you manage to get lipstick all over this Oliva?'

I gaze at the top. There is no part of last night that would make an acceptable excuse. 'Sorry Nan.' High-level negotiations ensue. In the end I promise to do the vacuuming this week in exchange for access to Nan's treasure trove.

I dive into Nan's walk-in wardrobe and flick the hangers.

There's the violet pant suit she wore to pick up Jacq from holiday program. The khaki safari suit she put on to get milk from the store. And for special occasions, there's the ... gold bikini. *Gold bikini?*

'What's this for?' I wander into the lounge room holding the bikini out like a dead rat.

Nan lifts her head from her *Vogue* magazine. 'Gorgeous, isn't it? It was on special at that little boutique on the corner.'

'Have you worn it yet?'

'No, but Reggie's taking me to Noosa in November. It'll be perfect for that.'

I think Nan's been on the Gold Coast too long. 'Right.' I wander back to her bedroom.

Fifteen minutes later I strut out wearing a thigh-length red dress with a peter pan collar, red platforms, enormous red sunglasses and, of course, my blonde wig. I've stashed a few extra outfits in my sports bag.

Nan looks up, puts down her magazine, and sighs. 'If only you'd dress like that more often, Olivia. You look just like Nancy Drew.' She leans over to her bookshelf, pulls out a tattered paperback copy of *The Secret in the Old Attic,* and holds it out to me.

Nancy Drew is holding a candle in a shadowy room. Her dress looks more demure than mine, but there is certainly a resemblance. Hopefully this is a good omen for the day ahead.

I haven't forgotten Rosco's instruction to pass on my information about Brandon to the police. I can't put it off any longer. I find the cop's card and call the station. I'm not looking forward to it. I know he doesn't like me. Whatever. I don't like him either. A female cop answers the phone.

'I'd like to speak to Dan Ferris.'

'He's out right now. Can I take a message, or do you want to talk to someone else?'

Yes! 'Just tell him Olivia Grace called.' I leave my number. Duty discharged, I'm ready to hit the road.

I park my car opposite Brooklyn's motel at nine am and wait. PI work is a lot like fishing – long periods of boredom interspersed with short bursts of excitement. And there's no guarantee she's in there, of course. But at ten am Brooklyn comes out. She is wearing a tie-dyed dress in psychedelic colours and her long hair is divided into multiple plaits decorated with beads. What is going on? She's nothing like the corporate powerbroker who first rocked into our office. It looks like she's gone feral. She turns left, heading towards Broadbeach.

I let her get ahead, before driving after her, pausing if I get too close. After about ten minutes she turns down a side-street. My pulse beats faster. I think I know where she's going.

Rosco's units are more down-market than Nan's – fibro instead of red brick. Very 1950s. I pull over to the side of the road and watch her walk up the stairs to Rosco's unit block, knock, and go in.

All is quiet for some time. What's she doing in there? Rosco said he'd dropped the McSushi contract, so it's not business, which only leaves … *None of my business*, I tell myself. But a hot-wasabi-green aura of jealousy seeps out of my skin. I think of the Spark. Have I been imagining it? After all, why would he be interested in me after the way I blew him off two years ago?

At eleven o'clock I get out of the car, stretch my legs and get back in again. By twelve o'clock they're still inside and I'm desperate for a pee. Rosco's mantra – *a good PI does not desert her target* – repeats in my head. He hadn't had to be too specific. I'd worked out the pee thing by myself – it required a wide-mouthed bottle and was only slightly messy.

Today, however, I've forgotten the wide-mouthed bottle.

At twelve thirty a woman with leathery skin wearing a tight yellow tracksuit knocks on the window. I wind it down. 'You've been sitting here for two hours. Why?'

I peer over the top of my sunglasses. 'Can't say too much – security reasons.'

The woman puts a hand to her mouth. 'Is it the man on the second floor?'

'Like I say – can't say too much.' I don't want to get some innocent bystander into trouble.

'I've seen him reading foreign newspapers.' She's keen to do her bit for national security.

I nod sharply, trying to imply I am well on top of the game and she'd better leave me to it.

'Have you got a number I can call in case I see something suspicious?'

'Just the usual hotline – you've got the fridge magnet, haven't you?'

She nods, her henna-orange curls bobbing. 'You're very brave, dear.'

'Just doing my job, ma'am.' This line should by rights be delivered in an American accent, but I resist the temptation.

The woman walks off with an extra spring in her stride.

By one thirty I'm in danger of leaving a puddle on the car seat.

Just as I'm thinking I'll have to desert my target, the door to Rosco's unit opens and he and Brooklyn come out. I slump in my seat as they walk past. I should tail them but all I can think about is my bladder.

I look over at the unit. I know where Rosco keeps his key – we'd called in there once to pick up some documents. I get out of the car and waddle across the road trying to keep my legs pressed together. The key is tucked in on top of the garage door. I run upstairs to the toilet and sigh with relief as I deflate. Flushing, I wander out.

Rosco's tiny lounge room is lined with old sixties surfing photos, taken on the Gold Coast. A surfboard with a big ding in it leans against the wall on the miniature veranda – it looks like he's doing some repair work. A wetsuit hangs over the railing.

What's he been up to with Brooklyn? The obvious, I suppose. Don't they say the simplest solution is usually right? I grind my teeth. An empty beer bottle sits on a low table near the TV. I nudge it onto the floor with my foot. *Take that, Rosco.* Dusty vertical blinds complete the bachelor pad decor. It's interesting, but I can't afford to linger.

I hear footsteps on the stairs. *Oh no.* This is bad. Very bad.

Turning around, I scan my options. Rosco's lounge room doesn't offer much in the way of shelter. I consider the verandah, but I don't think the surfboard will cover me. *The bedroom.* I run into his bedroom and dive into the cupboard.

The door opens and shuts. Rosco puts on some music.

I try to compose myself. Hopefully he'll leave soon, and I can escape.

But after about ten minutes Rosco comes into the bedroom. He sits at the desk in the corner of his room. I hear the distinctive bing, bong of the computer coming on.

Great.

I might have stood in the cupboard all afternoon listening to him type if it hadn't been for my watch. I thought I'd fixed it, but at three o'clock it goes off with a loud *beep, beep, beep*. I try to bring my arm up to turn it off, but there's no room to manoeuvre in the cupboard. *Beep, beep, beep* it trills, on and on and on.

Rosco walks towards the cupboard and I close my eyes like an ostrich putting its head in the sand. This isn't going to be pretty.

Light floods the cupboard. I keep my eyes tightly shut, trying to pretend this isn't happening.

'Olivia? What the hell?'

I wince. My eyes open and I blink in the glare from the window. He looks angry. I've never seen him look so angry. I wriggle out from among his clothes, trying to think of an excuse for being in his cupboard. One that doesn't make me sound like a crazy, obsessed lunatic. A crazy, obsessed lunatic with an imaginary Spark.

Rosco takes in my red mini-dress, platforms and the huge sunglasses on top of my wig. 'You're following me.' It's not a question.

I shake my head, my blonde hair flying in front of my face. 'No, not you.'

'You're following Brooklyn?'

I nod.

He folds his arms. 'Did I ask you to follow Brooklyn?'

I shake my head. 'You said you'd dropped the McSushi contract.'

'I *have* dropped the McSushi contract,' he says.

'So why was Brooklyn here?'

'That's not your problem.'

It feels like he's slapped me. Clearly she was here for the obvious reason. 'What *is* my problem, then?'

'Your problem is that you are hiding in my cupboard. It's unprofessional.'

'Unprofessional? I'm not the one who's ... who's ...' *Who's got something going on with Brooklyn, when I thought he had a Spark with me.* My eyes prickle. I think I'm going to cry. I don't want Rosco to see this, so I run for the door, my red platforms clopping on the floorboards.

'Olivia,' Rosco calls after me. 'Come back. Come back here right now.'

'No. I won't,' I yell. 'You can't make me.' I slam his front door behind me and race down the stairs. I know I'm overreacting again, but I have to get out of there before I do something worse. A shin kick isn't out of the question.

The door opens again and I hear Rosco's feet run down the stairs after me.

I speed up, almost bumping into the woman in the yellow tracksuit as she comes out of the downstairs unit. 'Excuse me,' I say.

She looks from me to Rosco, eyes wide. With an intake of breath, she retreats into her unit, not taking her eyes off Rosco.

I jump into the car and slam the door, taking off up the street. Rosco runs across the road, his hand reaching out as if to stop the car. I accelerate. He slaps his hand on the boot as I drive off.

Glancing in the rear-view mirror I see him standing in the middle of the street, his hands on his hips staring after me. A curtain twitches in the downstairs unit.

I wipe my nose with the back of my hand and sniff. Successful operation that was not.

I drive around aimlessly for some time, trying to calm down. I drive past the bungee jump tower, swanky six-star hotels, games parlours, clubbies in their clubhouse, nightclubs, meter maids, seagulls, and a mahogany-coloured man in tiny red Speedos.

I hate Surfers Paradise with a vengeance but I hate Rosco even more. The worst part is, I have no reason to feel like this. If Rosco has something going on with Brooklyn it's none of my business. I suppose, deep down, as strange as it is, I must have felt like we had something.

Finally, I turn into Cavill Avenue singing along to 'You're Not Sorry' by Taylor Swift on the radio. I need chocolate and I need it now. Pulling over, I get out of the car and walk down the mall. Seiji is out the front of his souvenir shop and outback bar. We nod as usual.

'Are you okay?' he asks. His accent is pure Australian.

I stop in my tracks. 'You speak English?'

He smiles. 'I was born on the Gold Coast.'

Seiji has spoken English all along. What kind of a PI am I, if I didn't even know that? 'But you've never spoken English to me before.'

'I save it for special occasions. I need to practise my Japanese, so I pretend I can't speak English. Here,' he reaches behind him, picks up a koala keyring and hands it to me. 'Present. You look like you need cheering up.'

'Thanks.' I smile. 'I do.' A flash of colour in the distance catches my eye. It's Brooklyn. A surge of adrenaline races through me. 'Got to go. Thanks for the koala.'

'No worries.'

I clop towards Brooklyn and see her seat herself at a table outside a café. She glances at her phone, and gestures the waiter away. She's waiting for someone.

I step into the nearest shop door, where I can watch her. It's a souvenir shop, but it's not like Seiji's. These are souvenirs for Aussies, not for overseas visitors. And what sort of souvenirs do Aussies buy on the Gold Coast? Belts that can hold six stubbies at a time, drinking mugs in the shape of a naked woman's torso ... *Ew.*

I look up and by accident catch the eye of the pimply-faced guy serving in the shop. He smirks. I look away, but find my eyes on the mug again. I scurry out, feeling dirty.

Brooklyn is typing on her enormous phone. I notice several string bracelets on her wrist, which complement her hippie dress. She's definitely been shopping in Byron Bay. Something major must have happened to transform her from corporate executive to north coast hippie in such a short space of time. After a few minutes a girl strolls up and takes a seat opposite her. Her straight red hair brushes toned white shoulders, exposed in a cutaway singlet. Below that is a pair of psychedelic lycra tights. I catch my breath as she turns her head. It's Madeleine from Lighthouse Bliss, the wannabe rock-star yoga teacher, she of the perfect headstand and perfect make-up. What on earth is she doing here?

I hover in the doorway. This is too intriguing. I have to get closer, but they both know me – can I rely on my disguise? Probably not. Maybe I've got something better in my bag.

I run back to the car and open my bag of tricks. *Nan's gym outfit? Nah. Her lacy 'lunch with the queen' frock? Nah.* The last item to come out of the bag is something I'd stuffed in on a whim – the gold bikini. My stomach churns. It's perfect, but I don't want to do it.

The whole street is lined with metered parking. What better excuse for wandering up and down? *A good PI does whatever it takes.* I slip the bikini on under my dress, find a pair of high-heeled shoes and, at the last moment, whip off my dress and step from the car.

I feel naked.

A cool wind blows across my exposed stomach. I suck it in, lock the car behind me, adjust my wig and sunglasses and mince up the street.

There's a pay-and-display machine right in front of where Brooklyn and Madeleine are sitting. I stop there, my back to them, and strain to hear their conversation.

'So, any luck?' Madeleine says.

'Not yet,' says Brooklyn. 'He covers his—'

'Are you going to feed the meter or what?' A red-faced man in a Fourex T-shirt appears beside me. 'That's my car there.'

I glare at him. He's made me miss the rest of the conversation. I open my purse, pull out two dollars, hold it up to him and put it in the pay-and-display machine.

'Is that all?' His eyes flick up and down. 'You don't look much like a meter maid.'

I'm in no mood to be messed with. 'If you don't mind, I'm busy here. I've fed your meter, now can you move along?'

The man's face goes redder. 'What do you mean you're busy? You're a meter maid.'

He's speaking loudly and Brooklyn and Madeleine look up.

It's time to beat a retreat. I turn on my heel and sashay off down the street.

The man's voice follows me. He sounds plaintive – like someone who's just found out there's no Santa. 'Meter maids aren't supposed to talk like that. It's not right.' His voice fades as I get further down the street. 'I'm going to ring the council.'

I round the corner and lean against the wall to collect my thoughts. I think I've got away with it. Brooklyn and Madeleine didn't see my face. *What was going on there?* Madeleine's a whale lover. Given the McSushi situation, she and Brooklyn should be in opposite camps, not conspiring in cafés.

Across the road, a girl with a blue beanie pulled down to her eyebrows and large sunglasses is sitting on a bench staring at me. I straighten my back. *What's wrong? Haven't you ever seen a well-rounded meter maid?* She isn't exactly a fashion plate herself. Her dull-coloured T-shirt and pants are dirty – like she's been sleeping rough.

The girl beckons for me to cross the road. I shake my head. I have enough to do. Although ... something about her is familiar. The neutral-coloured clothing ... Is that hemp? She beckons again and it suddenly hits me: it's Luna.

I break into a smile. I'm so happy to see her.

31

Dodging the slow-moving cars, I run across the road to Luna. A passing suit in a Commodore gives a piercing wolf-whistle that peters out as I glare at him.

Luna stands as I get near and, glancing over her shoulder, pushes through the door into Seiji's shop. I follow. Inside, it is shadowy and cavernous, fitted out with tables, chairs and an extensive souvenir display. Seiji is polishing glasses behind the bar, which is decorated with the bonnet of a battered four-wheel drive and a pair of what appear to be buffalo horns.

He raises his hand. 'Hi.'

'Hi.' I wave back.

'You know my brother?' asks Luna in her high-pitched voice.

'Your brother?'

'Yeah, Zander.'

'Zander?' I look over at him. 'I thought your name was Seiji.'

'Seiji's our dad,' he says. 'It's the family business.'

'Oh.' I glance from Luna to Zander/Seiji and back again. 'So, your parents were into interesting names, huh?' I say.

'Crazy hippies,' says Luna.

People in glass houses, I think, but don't say.

'They live on a collective up the back of the Gold Coast,' she adds.

'You want a drink?' asks Zander.

'Sure,' I say.

'A cocktail?'

I'm not really a drinker, but I could do with an anaesthetic to dull the strangeness of the day. 'Why not?'

'Give us two Nancy Drews would you, Zander?' Luna slumps at a table next to a life-size model of a camel.

Nancy Drews?

Zander drops two coasters on the table in front of us. He places a glass on each. 'Cheers.' He flicks his black hair off his face and ambles off to rearrange the souvenirs.

'I thought you'd be more of a wheatgrass juice girl,' I say to Luna. I've been reading people wrong all over the place. *Seiji speaks English. And his name's Zander.* Maybe I'm not a very good PI.

'I am usually. It's the stress,' says Luna.

'I know what you mean.' I sip my drink. 'This is good. What's in it?'

'Rum, ginger ale, lime.' Luna pulls off her beanie and her hair falls around her face. 'Can't stand that thing. Synthetic fibre.' She's lost the nose ring – it probably makes her too distinctive. 'I worked here for a while, so I know my cocktails.' She seems in no hurry to explain why she's ushered me in here.

'I got your envelope,' I say.

'Froze my tits off waiting for you.'

'How'd you know I'd be there? Why me?' The cocktail is taking effect already – the events of the day are now less painful.

'I followed you to the supermarket, but I knew the cops were looking for me, so I slipped in the back door. I didn't expect to end up in the freezer. Once I was there, the ice-cream seemed like a good idea.'

'Hm.' Putting a McSushi wrapper in a tub of ice-cream doesn't scream 'good idea' to me. 'How'd you get it in there?'

'I tipped the ice-cream out. If you warm it up on the edges with your hands it slips out okay, then I put the envelope in and sat the ice-cream back on top.'

'Right.' She hasn't answered the second part of my question, so I repeat it. 'Why me?'

'You're in my gang. WAG.' Luna finishes her drink and holds up two fingers to Zander, signalling for more.

'Wag?'

'Whale Action Group.'

'Oh. I thought I was in Women Against McSushi.'

'You're in both. And you're a PI.' It's not a question.

'You know I'm a PI?'

'Well, duh. Everyone knows you're a PI.'

'Everyone who? Everyone where?' The alcohol is affecting my ability to create proper sentences.

Luna waves her hand around airily. 'Just everyone.'

And I thought I was being so secretive. I put down my drink, remembering I have something important to tell her. 'Madeleine and Brooklyn ... You know Brooklyn, American girl? Loud New York voice.'

Luna nods. 'I've run into her in the Bay.'

'She works for McSushi.'

Luna's eyes widen. 'Really?'

Seiji places another couple of drinks in front of us. *Zander*.

We clink our glasses together. 'Brooklyn and Madeleine, they're planning something. I saw them together,' I say.

Luna pokes her ice with her finger, pondering this information. 'I reckon she's got it in for me – Brooklyn, I mean. Because of WAM.

Or it might be because of WAG. You know what?' Luna points her finger at me. 'I reckon Brooklyn released those rats in the yoga studio. I'd never do that – I love rats, they're really intelligent and affectionate. She must have planted the rat hairs in my car, too.'

'The McSushi wrapper …' I say.

'Yep.' Luna nods. 'She's setting me up. With me out of the way it'll be open slather for McSushi in Byron Bay.'

'I can see why Brooklyn would do that, but what about Madeleine? Isn't she a member of WAM?'

'Nah, she's a member of WAG.'

'WAG, WAM, whatever.' I sip my drink, feeling like I've made an incisive point.

Luna shrugs. 'Why do people do anything? Money, sex, power?' She waves her drink to emphasise her point. 'Wearing a whale singlet doesn't necessarily make you a whale lover. Madeleine's pretty intense, don't you think? She's ambitious. She wants to be a yoga rock star.'

'Yeah. I saw her reading the book, *How to Be a Yoga Rock Star.*'

'Right. You wouldn't want to get in her way. She's Scorpio with Scorpio rising. Definitely.'

I nod. I'm not into astrology, but after two Nancy Drews I'll agree with anything.

'She's a natural redhead, you know.'

I stare at her, not sure of the significance.

'Fiery. And all that lycra and make-up she wears … It can't be doing her chakras any good.' Luna's eyes open wide. 'I just worked it out. You know who murdered Ajay?'

My mouth drops open. 'No, who?'

Luna drops her voice. 'Brooklyn.'

'Brooklyn?' I know I'm not at my most clear-headed, but I

can't figure it out. 'Why would Brooklyn murder Ajay? He was the face of McSushi.'

Luna seems to be wondering how I ever got to be a PI. 'To get rid of me,' she hisses. She raises her finger and pokes it at my chest. 'Who had the most motive? Me – everyone knows he was suing me. Who does all the evidence point to? Me. They needed a new face of McSushi anyway – someone fresh for Byron Bay. Maya's the girl they need to ease their entrance into the Bay. Ajay's yesterday's news.'

'But she's gone missing.'

'Maya?'

I nod.

'I didn't know that.'

'You don't think ... You don't think someone's killing off the faces of McSushi, do you?' I finally voice my worst fear.

'Nah, that'd be stupid.' Luna pauses. 'Although, on the other hand, it could save a few whales.'

I drain my drink. I wish she hadn't said that.

'Float away into the sensory labyrinth of the Infinity Funhouse ...'

I wake at home the next morning, my mouth dry and my head thumping. I'm still wearing Nan's gold bikini, but wrapped around it, toga style, is one of the kangaroo-patterned tablecloths from Seiji's Outback Bar. It's lucky Nan isn't home to see the damage to her bikini. She's gone off to spend a couple of days with Reggie, taking Jacq with her.

Pinned to my bikini top is a note. 'Don't forget – action at Ocean World Monday night.' I moan, closing my eyes again. I *had* forgotten. Luna made me promise to join her for a protest against dolphins in captivity. It's all coming back to me now, unfortunately.

Luna had pressed my arm. 'It'll be great, you have to come. It'll be a joint action with WAG and WAM.'

'What happened to your last protest – the one you called me about? I didn't get the message until the next day,' I lied.

'Oh, that never went ahead. We didn't have enough people, but this time we will. You'll be there, won't you?'

I'd agreed enthusiastically but, in retrospect, it had been the Nancy Drews talking. Things had got a little strange at that point.

'I've been learning dolphin for it.' Luna gestured at her phone on the table.

'You've been learning about dolphins?'

Luna shook her head. 'No, dolphin, as in the language. I already know whale. Dolphin is similar – it's like the difference between, say ...' she paused. 'Swedish and Norwegian.'

'Swedish and Norwegian? Do they even have dolphins in Sweden?'

'I don't know.' Luna waved her hand. 'Spanish and Portuguese then.'

'Right, so whales are Spanish and dolphins are Portuguese?'

'Forget the Spanish and the Portuguese. I'm learning dolphin, okay? Here.' She handed me one earbud and placed the other in her ear.

I leaned my head next to hers as she tapped her phone. A clicking sound filled my ear, followed by squeaks, then clicks again.

'What do you think it's saying?' Luna leaned her cheek against mine.

'Its name is Juan and it likes paella.'

Luna pressed the off button. She pulled out her earbud and glared at me. 'Olivia, why are you resisting this? Is there something you're trying to suppress?'

I giggled. 'Like what? Inappropriate crushes on suave Spanish dolphins?'

Luna crossed her arms. 'Have you been having dreams about dolphins or whales lately?'

'No, uh ...' I remembered the dream. I'd been a whale, bursting from the water.

'I'm right, aren't I? Dreams about whales or dolphins are a sure sign they have something to share with you. The fact I'm here now to teach you dolphin when you most need it confirms it.'

I sipped my drink and leaned back in my chair.

'I can tell you're threatened by this, Olivia. You don't have anything to fear by accepting their teachings.'

I put the headphone back in my ear. 'Let's hear it.'

I yawn and stretch in bed, reluctant to get up. My memory of the dolphins' message is blurry. Luna said they were talking about peace and fish, or something to that effect. It had all been clicks and whistles to me.

The nightclub had filled around us as the night went on.

'You got a boyfriend, Olivia?' asked Luna at one stage.

'No. I've never had a proper boyfriend.'

'Girlfriend?'

I shook my head. 'I'm not good with relationships.' I sipped my drink.

'Would you like one?'

'A girlfriend?'

'Is that an option?'

'No, I don't think so.'

'Too bad. Boyfriend, then. Whatever.'

'Yeah ... Yeah I would. He'd have to be the right one though.'

'Hey, Zander,' Luna had called out at that point. 'Do you fancy Olivia?'

Zander paused in his glass-polishing and flicked his hair out of his eyes. He smiled. 'Yeah.'

'I'll let you know if he breaks up with his girlfriend,' said Luna.

'Thanks.' I leant on my elbow. 'Have you ever had a really sizzling kiss? You know, one that makes you melt?'

'Like in the movies?'

I nodded.

'No. All my kisses have just been, like, average. How about you?'

I shook my head. 'Below average. Except for one Notable Exception. But it wasn't a proper kiss.' I pause. 'Do you think if a guy breaks down your door at midnight it means he has feelings for you?'

Luna considered this. 'Well, it depends on the context.'

I explained about the yoga video and the mess I'd got into. 'He thought someone had tied me up.'

Luna snorted. 'I've never heard of that happening before.' She straightened her face. 'You must have been trying really hard. But, yeah, breaking down a door, it's a positive sign I think. If that's what you want.' Luna shrugged. 'You know, guys are hard to figure out.'

For some reason, this made me think of the horrible souvenir shop. 'What sort of a person buys a naked woman's torso mug as a holiday souvenir?' I said.

'Say what?'

I explained the concept.

'Ew, gross,' said Luna. 'A man.'

'Yeah, but what kind of man?'

'A sleazy kind of man. Like the ones who buy those "boars and babes" calendars.'

'You don't think it could be postmodern? Like a commentary?'

Luna shook her head. 'The Gold Coast is not postmodern, it's pre-modern. There are no hidden depths.'

'There must be some. I mean, I haven't found them yet, but …'

'Uh uh. Think of the Gold Coast as icing without the cake. You dig and you don't get wholemeal carrot cake like Byron Bay, or sponge cake like Brisbane, you just get tacky all the way down. Tacky, tacky, tacky.'

I felt like her metaphor was falling apart but I let it go.

Luna walked me home. I was going to ask her to stay the night, but she faded away, muttering something about wheatgrass juice.

I open one eye again, and the other. Sliding my feet to the floor I walk with a slow shuffle to the kitchen.

There's a voice message on my phone. I press it and hear Rosco. 'Olivia?' He sighs, there's a pause, then the message stops. I replay it a couple of times, but it's hard to read much into it. If he thinks I'll respond like a trained poodle to that, he's mistaken.

Kevin, who has been snoozing on his rug, suddenly jumps to his feet, yapping. Someone has slipped something under the door. I shuffle closer. It's a McSushi poster – one of the old ones – Ajay not Maya.

Red words are scrawled across his body. Bile rises in my throat as I read them.

I pull open the door, but the stairwell is empty. When I turn around the words are still there.

YOU'RE NEXT.

I double-bolt the doors, close the windows and put Kevin on full alert.

'If anyone gets in that door you gnaw their ankles, Kevin, okay?' Kevin sticks out the tip of his tongue in a terrifying demonstration of fierceness.

I call the police again. This time Dan Ferris is in. He sounds bored, but says he'll come around to look at the poster. I tell him my suspicions about Brandon, but this fails to impress. I slam the phone down. My impulse to call Rosco is firmly quashed. No one's going to rescue me except myself.

I eye the poster on the mat. *YOU'RE NEXT.* There are several interpretations: I'm next after Ajay, or next after Maya, or next after both of them. I don't like any of these options. My stomach clenches. I hope Maya's alright.

For lack of anything else to do I pull all my newspaper articles out of the kitchen drawer where I'd stashed them and lay them out on the counter. There's Ajay slapping Georgia Hansen, the *Lighthouse News* yoga exposé, Rochelle in the café with an unknown man ... I put on my glasses and inspect the photo more closely. It looks like Brandon's shoulders. It looks like his hair. It looks like his white T-shirt. But why would Brandon be in a café with Rochelle?

I pace up and down, tread on Kevin's tail and, finally, turn on the computer to distract myself.

There's a message from James Goldsworth, sent yesterday. With everything else going on, I'd missed it. 'Better start working on an act for the comedy festival.'

I email him back. 'Ha, ha, funny one. See you at my place at three o'clock.'

There's a sharp knock at the door. I peer through the peephole. My friend the cop has arrived. Opening the door, I gesture at the doormat where the poster lies. As instructed, I haven't touched it.

He snorts, pulls some rubber gloves out of his black case and picks it up. His face sets in crinkled lines of suspicion; he turns his puffy-rimmed eyes on me. 'People do this kind of thing all the time when someone in the public eye goes missing.' His voice is flat, gravelly. 'You've been in Byron Bay asking questions, haven't you?'

I nod. He makes it sound like a criminal offence.

'That sort of thing attracts attention. There are a lot of nuts out there.'

He places the poster in a plastic bag. 'Keep the door locked.'

And that's it – he's gone. *Right, thanks for your support.*

My computer beeps – another message from James. 'I'm serious. You know how there weren't any tickets left? I've wangled you a wild-card entry into the semis. The only way to get into the finals is by getting through the semis. There's no other way!' There's an attachment. I open it. *Get your stomach muscles toned – these newcomers will have you laughing – either at them or with them – in the sacrificial blood sport segment of the festival.* I scan the list of names. *Hooley dooley,* he isn't joking. Directly underneath *James Goldsworth* is *Olivia Grace.* I scan the rest of the list. Maya's name isn't there, but I hadn't expected it to be.

What was he thinking? I can't do that – I'm not a comedian. I freeze in front of a crowd. I was scarred for life by an incident at the school concert in Year Five. Unknown to me, my *Star Wars* undies were on show for an entire rendition of 'Thriller' with dance moves. The words 'school' and 'concert', when put together, still make me feel sick.

James is one step ahead of me though. My computer tings with another incoming email. 'Don't try to get out of it. You need to get your act ready now or you won't get into the finals! We'll fit into the scene better as performers anyway.'

Oh, crap. I can't resist his appeal to my most sensitive area – my professional pride. Okay, I have to prepare a routine – just what I need on a day when I've received a death threat and my brain is like a limp dishrag.

I type 'learn comedy fast' into Google. One hour later I've learnt there are many types of comedians – so many I instantly forget them all. To be successful, you have to deliver four to six laughs per minute. Timing is essential, and you need to know how to deal with hecklers. It's too hard. Isn't there a ready-made routine I can download somewhere? *Apparently not.*

I turn off the computer and lie on the couch. I've never felt less funny.

I'm woken by the sound of knocking on my door.

'Olivia.'

Damn. It's James and I still don't have a routine ready. 'Won't be a sec,' I call out. 'I'll see you down the car.' I run into Nan's room and riffle through her wardrobe. *What do comedians wear?*

The only comedians I can think of are men and Nan's wardrobe is lacking in the men's suit department.

A horn beeps on the street. *Hold your horses.* Panicking, I go for the safest option, black, and hastily apply some make-up.

I look out the window. James is sitting behind the wheel of his VW bug with the music turned up so loud I can hear it from inside the apartment. It's not any band I'm familiar with. The words 'gangsta' and 'homeboy' feature prominently.

I go downstairs. 'Can you turn that down?' I yell, climbing in. As I get in his car, I have a flashback to parking my car in Cavill Avenue yesterday. It's still there. I hope the meter maids are feeding the meter.

James hits the power button and the music dies. His eyes flicker up and down, taking in my black stockings, black mini skirt and black polo-neck top. 'I'm guessing you've got a Liza Minelli routine happening. Am I right?'

I lift my sunglasses and give him a killer stare.

James shrugs. 'Nice eyeliner.' We drive the first half-hour in silence. I eye the tatts on his suntanned forearms as he taps the wheel. A dragon curls around one arm and some Celtic symbols around the other.

'This is a long shot, isn't it?' I say finally. 'Do you really think Maya's going to be up there doing stand-up if she's run away from home?'

James's hands clench the wheel. 'You got any better suggestions, private investigator?' I don't. I don't tell James about the poster. I don't want to worry him. This is our last shot and we both know it.

Half an hour out of Brisbane CBD James breaks the silence. 'I think it was my fault.'

My depleted brain has been absorbed in the passing scene of cut-price furniture shops, car yards and fast food joints so I don't catch his meaning at first. 'Huh?'

'Maya disappearing. I think it was my fault.'

He's got my attention now. 'What do you mean? How is it your fault?'

He stares straight ahead. 'You know how we were talking about Romeo and Juliet?'

'Yeah?'

'D'you reckon Romeo would have given up if Juliet's father punched him out and told him Juliet was too busy getting ready for the world titles to see him?'

'I guess not, but you know, it's just a story. I don't think Juliet surfed anyway.' I'm trying to lighten things up.

James bangs his hand on the steering wheel. 'I gave up too easily. I should have kicked their door down.'

I stare at him. *Kick the door down* ... 'Is that what you do when you care for someone? Kick their door down?'

He gives me a strange look. 'Maybe. If necessary. She must have thought I was piss-weak, disappearing because her daddy told me to.' He lowers his voice. 'I thought she'd still be there when I came back for her. I was so stupid.'

'That wouldn't be enough to make her run away, would it?'

'You don't know Maya. She can't stand half-measures. She's a bridge burner from way back.'

'I've seen that side of her in the surf.' *Ask yourself: what's the worst that can happen?*

'It would have seemed like a total betrayal to her, slinking off after he hit me.'

I put my hand on his arm. 'Hey, you can play it differently next time you see her.'

James accelerates through a gap in the traffic. 'I keep looking for her everywhere. Every time I see a girl surfing I think it's her. It's stupid – no one else surfs like her.' Five minutes pass before he speaks again. 'She's the One. And I've lost her.'

The Kangaroo Point cliffs go past and I clear my throat. 'Have you got any tips on how to develop a comedy routine in about fifteen minutes?'

James lifts his sunglasses and gives me a look that makes me sink in my seat. 'You haven't got your routine ready? I told you, you won't be able to get into the finals unless you qualify.'

I waggle my head to imply it had been top of my list but events had overtaken me.

'Right.' James changes lanes sharply, making me press my foot to the ground where my brake pedal should have been. 'We need to do some quick thinking.'

I think quickly but it's like wheels spinning in mud. 'Um ...'

'What's funny about you?'

'Nothing.'

'There must be something.'

'I have an unfunny life. I'm eighteen. I've just left school. I'm enrolled to study law, but I don't want to do it. I'm a private investigator. I live with my grandmother; these are her clothes. I have no boyfriend.'

James sniggers.

'What?'

'You're an eighteen-year-old private investigator who lives with her grandmother. And you're wearing her clothes on the job. How funny is that? It's comedy gold. I wish I was an eighteen-year-old private investigator who lived with my grandmother.' He's laughing uncontrollably now. 'It's like – God, I don't know. It's like Nancy Drew on steroids.'

I maintain an offended silence.

'Does she make you polish your gun before you go out on a job? Does she iron your disguises for you? Or knit you a camouflage suit? Does she invite the bad guys in for tea and cake when they come around to threaten you?' James is laughing so hard I'm worried he's going to drift into the next lane.

'We turn right here,' I say frostily. The heats of the festival are being held at the Paddo Tavern and the finals, if we make it that far, at the Queensland Cultural Centre in South Bank. The street lights are coming on as we find a park.

James is still laughing. 'Can you imagine James Bond living with his grandmother?'

'I'm a PI, not a spy. There's a difference.'

'Not enough to matter.'

We make our way through the gathering crowd, looking everywhere for Maya, and finally take a seat near the front. Loud groups gather around tables, drinks in their hands, ready to be entertained. 'I can't do this,' I hiss. My heart is already pounding. 'I'll sneak into the finals or something.'

James looks at me like I've destroyed his chances of ever seeing Maya again.

'Fine. I'll die of fright and humiliation, but I'll try.' I glance at the program. James is third and I'm fourth.

The MC takes to the stage and my mind goes blank. I remember nothing of the first and second performers. They are poodles in tutus for all I know.

My attention comes back onto low beam for James's performance. He is funny in a self-deprecating nerdy way that plays well with the audience. 'I'm from Byron Bay.' Pause for laughs. 'Those of you who think that's funny, karma will get you in the end.'

I tune out. I'm on next. I glance down the aisle. It's not too late to make a run for it. I'm half-way to my feet when James's act finishes. He leaps down and grasps my arm, pushing me towards the stage.

The MC, a raggedy-looking bloke with long curly hair, calls my name. 'Our next sacrificial lamb is Olivia Grace.'

34

Time stops, then starts again. The MC's voice echoes in my head. *Olivia Grace, Olivia Grace, Olivia Grace.* For a wonderful moment, it seems like a dream. But my armpits are wet and I smell cigarette smoke. It must be real.

'Olivia,' James hisses. He jerks his head towards the stage. I plead with my eyes, but there's no pity there. He pushes the small of my back.

Et tu, Brute?

I totter onto the stage in my high heels and clear my throat, shielding my eyes from the glare. 'Umm ...' My voice screeches in the microphone. I jump back. I should have hidden under my seat while I had the chance. My hands shaking, I search out James in the audience. I don't know what I'm hoping for – cue cards?

His arms are folded and he is frowning. There's no help in that quarter.

'Umm ... I'm a private investigator.' Someone in the crowd laughs.

I pull my skirt down to check my undies aren't showing. 'No, really. I'm a private investigator.' I clear my throat and the microphone blares again. I open my mouth, not sure what's going to come out next.

'Some people think it's a glamorous job. It's not. It's weirder than you'd expect. Right now I'm here in Brisbane trying to be funny and I'm not.' Another nervous laugh comes from the corner of the room. 'No, I'm not.' There are a few more titters. I check my skirt again. *No undies on display.* 'Uh, do you want to hear about what it's like to be a private investigator?' The crowd roars assent.

I blink. *They do?* I run my tongue around the inside of my mouth. It's as dry as a Gold Coast winter. In contrast, my hands are practically dripping onto the floorboards. I can't wait to find out what I'm going to say next.

'I've had a difficult few days. There aren't many jobs where you get to dress as a meter maid.' It's like a ventriloquist is using my mouth. It's an out-of-body experience. I almost forget the crowd in front of me until a loud guffaw startles me as I relate the ice-cream cabinet story.

'It puts a whole new spin on the story of the spy who came in from the cold,' says someone who sounds like me.

The events of the past few weeks pour out. I change names and places to protect the innocent. Eventually I register the MC signalling time. 'So, being a PI is a good job for people who like dress-ups and don't mind making a fool of themselves.'

The crowd applauds and the stairs come closer. I have no memory of climbing from the stage.

James gives me a friendly punch on the shoulder as I sit. 'You *did* work on your routine.'

I gaze at him. My brain has been replaced with fairy floss.

'That was great. How'd you think of that stuff about the meter maid?'

I open and shut my mouth like a goldfish. 'It's a long story.'

One hour later they announce the results – James and I have both progressed to the finals. We slap our hands together. 'Alright!' We've got one hour to get over to South Bank.

South Bank is Brisbane's answer to the Parisian Left Bank, only not as trendy and bohemian. Obviously.

We park in the underground car park, our tyres squealing on the shiny black surface, and catch the lift up. The South Bank theatre is less intimate than the Paddo. Row after row of seats stretch from the stage. James and I give the doorman our competitors' passes and do the rounds, looking for Maya. There's no sign of her. I'm beginning to feel this is a dead end.

'I can't go on again,' I say to James. 'Once was enough. I'll watch the crowd. I'm here – that's all I wanted.'

As the lights go down it's hard to see anything. James has gone quiet. Pulling his notes out of his pocket, he scans them, then crumples them up. They fall to the ground as he makes his way backstage.

'Our first finalist is James Goldsworth, from Byron Bay,' says the announcer and James walks on stage.

He stands silently for a few moments, spotlit, clenching and unclenching his hands. When he speaks, it's in a quiet voice. 'I know a girl who can surf better than me. Not only can she surf better than me, she's much funnier than me. I know that won't surprise you.'

One or two people cough.

James wraps his hands around the microphone. He doesn't seem perturbed by the lack of response. 'I'm here because I didn't fight hard enough to keep her and now she's gone. Maya,' he shades his eyes. 'Maya, if you're out there, can you come home?

I was stupid to let you go, forgive me.' He looks at the front of the stage. A few people murmur.

'Maya – you're the One. If you don't come home, I don't know what I'll do.' The crowd is silent now. James stares out into the darkness. 'Yeah, so, sorry to have cast a dampener on things.' He starts to walks off. One or two people clap half-heartedly.

'James.'

I crane my neck to see who's spoken. A long way behind me, near the back of the theatre, stands a girl with black hair, wearing black lipstick and a loose black dress. I can't distinguish her face in the darkness.

James turns.

'What do you mean when you say I'm the One?'

'Maya?' James squints into the light. 'Can you ask me something easier?'

The girl is silent.

'Okay.' James leans into the microphone. 'You make me laugh. You finish my sentences. You cut me back to size when I'm full of myself. You know me. You're the only one who knows me. Is that enough?'

'Will you make friends with my father?' the girl calls out.

'I'll make friends with your father if that's what you want. I'll do better than that – I'll tell my father to make friends with your father. I'll make them both take out a full-page ad in the paper telling everyone they've kissed and made up. I'll send them on a Men Who Run with Wolves course together so they'll bond for life.'

My eyes are getting used to the darkness now and I see Maya smile, revealing the gap between her teeth. 'Will you stand up to Brad if he tells you I'm too busy training to see you?'

'I'll be through the door so fast he won't know what's hit him.' James has found Maya in the crowd now. A slow smile spreads across his face.

'Do you think it'll work?'

I look from her back to James. It's like the balcony scene in Romeo and Juliet. *But soft, what light through yonder window breaks?*

'It'll work. I love you, Maya.' James jumps from the stage and wends his way through the seats to where Maya stands, unmoving. People curl their legs back to let him pass. One or two pat his back. Murmurs of encouragement rise here and there.

'Go get her, son,' calls a man near the front.

The MC wanders back on stage. 'Never a dull moment at the Brisbane Comedy Festival folks.' He signals to the lighting guy and a spotlight hits James as he reaches Maya and hugs her.

There's an audible sigh from the audience. The guy next to me checks his program. 'Did we come to the wrong theatre?' he asks his girlfriend. 'I think this might be performance art.'

'Shut up.' She sniffs and wipes her eyes. 'That's the most romantic thing I've ever seen.'

35

'*Be seduced by the huge range of shopping choices, styles and experiences at some of Australia's largest shopping complexes and duty-free stores ...*'

Monday morning. Turning the radio off, I yawn. Well, that's one job well done. I hope Maya and James will be able to sort things out with their families now.

It turned out Maya had been hanging out in Brisbane the whole time. She'd got through the heats under a stage name – Shallow Sheila. James and I watched her act in the finals. It was pretty hilarious. She just missed out on going through to the next round, but we reckon she was robbed.

So, that's one less thing on my plate, which is good because my plate is still pretty full. I haven't forgotten about the poster. I'd double-locked the front door when I'd got home and briefed Kevin again on his responsibilities. The other major thing on my plate, of course, is Rosco. I remember his face in my rear-view mirror as I drove away. My stomach knots. I can't face him.

Jacq opens the door and bounds in, landing on my bed like a miniature hippo. 'You'll never guess what I did with Nan and Reggie.'

'What? Ate a broccoli pie? Went for a ten-kilometre run? Discovered you like bananas?'

'No, silly. Went to Timezone.'

'No broccoli pie?'

'No, we had hot dogs and coke.'

I'm not sure if Reggie is a good influence. I glance at the clock. It's only eight am. If I ring Gold Star Investigations now I won't have to speak to Rosco. While Nan drives Jacq to her holiday activities, I dial and get the usual message – 'Welcome to Gold Star Investigations, the Gold Coast's leading investigation agency, infidelity and relationship issues a speciality. Our investigators are the best in their field at covert and undercover surveillance. Please leave a message.' I hang up, then dial again, listening to Rosco's voice. This time I leave a message.

'Yeah, it's Olivia. We found Maya, so you can bill Brad. I won't be in today. I'm not feeling the best, and, you know, I worked Sunday. And, um …' I decide I have nothing more to say and hang up.

Nan is back now. 'I'm not going to work today,' I say. 'I'm sick.' Nan is wearing her 'at home' outfit – a lilac velveteen track-suit – which is unfortunate. I would have liked to be able to mope in peace.

I slump onto the couch and turn on the TV but it's no good. Daytime TV isn't enough to keep my mind off everything – Rosco, Ajay, Brandon, Luna, Brooklyn, Rosco …

'Did you see today's paper?' Nan passes me a cup of tea and a plate of carrot sticks. She is apparently taking my sickness at face value.

'No, why?' I eye the carrot sticks, but they're all wrong. I need comfort food, not vegetables. 'Aren't you playing golf today or something?'

'No, Reggie did his back in laser shooting at Timezone.' She pauses. 'They found the originals of those Georgia Hansen yoga photos. You remember, the ones of her being slapped?'

My head swivels away from the TV, a carrot stick in my mouth. 'Really? Where?'

'At the house of that girl they've been looking for, the yoga teacher. On her computer. She's obviously murdered him. I mean, if she took those photos ...' Nan settles herself on the sofa next to me and selects a carrot stick.

'Luna Nakamura?'

'Yes. Funny name, Luna.'

Luna took the photos? Somehow this never came up in conversation at the nightclub.

'She must have had it in for him to try to destroy his business like that.'

'Yeah, but—'

'Such a shame. I remember his wedding; it was in all the magazines. They got married in Bali, I think, or was it Thailand? Anyway, it was exotic. She was never good enough for him, of course, that woman.'

'Rochelle?'

'Always seemed like a gold-digger to me.' Apparently Nan thinks she would have made a more suitable wife for Ajay. 'They had a pre-nup of course.'

'They what?'

'They had a pre-nuptial agreement. That's usually the case when someone successful, like Ajay, marries someone who's less successful. Don't you ever read *Who*?'

'Only in the checkout. So, if Ajay and Rochelle divorced, she wouldn't inherit?'

'No, but if he's dead I suppose ...'

'She gets the lot.' I bite hard into a carrot stick.

'Juicy, aren't they?' Nan leans back to enjoy the show.

I frown, chewing. Rochelle hired us to follow Ajay because she was worried he was cheating. And she had good reason to be worried. If he divorced her, she'd get nothing.

But what about Brandon? He has an Ocean World connection. Is there any link between him and Ajay? Or him and Rochelle? I don't care if I'm working on the case or not, someone has threatened me. I need answers. Getting up from the couch, I pull the newspaper articles out again and look at the shot of Rochelle in the café. I'm well acquainted with Brandon's shoulders and they're a close match with the ones in the photo. What do I know about him, after all? Only that he does a mean disco dance.

'"I trust that everything happens for a reason, even when we're not wise enough to see it,"' Nan murmurs. 'That is so true. You're missing out, Olivia.'

'Mm, just got to look something up on the computer.'

I do a quick google on the name Brandon Sims. A couple of references to minor roles in TV shows come up, and a movie from about five years ago, *The Mystic*, which was apparently a student production while he was at film school. So, that's consistent with what he told me. I take note of the name of the movie. If I'm going to sit around all day, I may as well watch it. I don't have anything better to do.

I download it. The cover doesn't look promising; an Indian guy dressed in white glares at a square-jawed young Harrison Ford look-alike. I scan the blurb, but Brandon's name doesn't appear. He must have had a minor role.

Nan is up and dusting now. She frowns at me as I press play

on the laptop. 'Haven't you got anything better to do? You don't look sick to me.'

'It's for work, Nan.' I search the kitchen for something yummy, but in the end grab myself a banana and settle in to watch.

The movie is an action adventure thing. I don't get the plot, but it involves this Indian guy, Rakesh, putting hexes on people and being foiled by the cut-price Harrison Ford and his curvaceous sidekick.

Rakesh is a yoga fiend with lightning fast moves. First, he drops into warrior pose to hex Harrison. Then, *pow*, he segues into a handstand before dropping into a back bend and taking Harrison out with his feet on the way down. I've never seen yoga like this before. It's awe-inspiring.

Nan ignores the movie at first, tidying around me in a pointed way, but eventually even she falls prey to the power of Rakesh's yoga moves.

'Goodness, I've never seen anyone kick like that from tree pose.' She pauses in her polishing. 'He's flexible, isn't he?'

The movie is half-over before Brandon makes his entrance. He saunters in, serves Rakesh a drink and departs. I wait for him to re-appear, but he never does.

Then something surprising happens. I would have missed it if it hadn't been for Nan. There's a big crowd scene. Rakesh is warrior posing his way through the market hexing left right and centre. Harrison has a gun, but every time he shoots at Rakesh he drops to the ground in crocodile pose. Rakesh magically produces a giant cobra that creates havoc through the crowd.

'Did you see that?' Nan squeals.

'Shush, I'm listening.' Harrison and his girl are having a romantic moment among the chaos.

'Rewind it.' Nan snatches the mouse off me and rewinds. 'There.' She points to the screen.

In the corner of the market crowd a familiar face appears, is struck by the cobra and falls dead. *Ajay?* I didn't know he was an actor. I replay the scene a couple more times, and it's definitely him. His hair is shorter, and he isn't as buffed as the Ajay I'm used to, but there's no mistaking that face.

'Well, isn't that interesting?' says Nan.

I watch the video through to the end but neither Brandon nor Ajay reappear. The credits roll and Brandon's name scrolls across the screen eventually, but not Ajay's. Maybe Ajay is a name he took on to go with his yoga guru status.

I look at the date on the movie – 2014. Wasn't Ajay supposed to be doing something else at that time? Going to my room, I pull my travel bag out of the bottom of the cupboard and feel around in its pockets. As I'd hoped, I'd left a Lighthouse Bliss brochure in there. I open it.

Ajay has studied yoga all his life. In 2005, as a teenager, he went to India. Lost in a blizzard on a pilgrimage to a Himalayan temple, he stumbled across a cave. Inside was the guru Rakesh – a holy man – doing a pure form of yoga unique to that area. Ajay studied under Rakesh for ten years. He found the Indo-Tibetan speed yoga led to enlightenment twice as fast as the slow yoga of the plains. Upon his death bed, Rakesh made Ajay promise to take his yoga to the world – a promise Ajay has since kept with the creation of Bikini Beach Body Boot Camp Speed Yoga.

It's a nice story. It has all the right elements to appeal to a world craving a quick dose of spirituality. The thing that gets me is he even used the name Rakesh. He must have been damn confident no one would ever make the connection.

I gaze at the picture of Ajay on the back of the brochure. *You big fraud.* I bet that movie was the closest you ever got to India. *And Brandon, he knew your secret.* The guru-cave thing was central to Ajay's sales pitch. Without that, what was he? Just another buffed yoga teacher. I remember the cash-stuffed envelope. *Maybe he's being paid hush money?*

My hand is halfway to the phone to tell Rosco what I've found out when I withdraw it again. I almost forgot we're not on good terms.

I glance at my watch. The second ski show at Ocean World is at three pm. If I hurry, I might be able to catch Brandon after his show.

36

'And now, our lovely Candy will execute an amazing twist turn ...'

I pay my money and slip through the gate into Ocean World. The waterski area is right in front of me and the show is in progress. A light wind ruffles the surface of the lake. Ignoring the girl going over the jump and the amplified squawk of the excited commentator, I focus on the dancers near the water.

Five John Travolta look-alikes are boogieing to 'Rock around the Clock'. The viewing area is packed. I can't get close enough to see if one of them is Brandon. I'll have to wait until the show finishes.

I take up position on the grass near the pathway to the dancers' change room. As the song ends I stand, peering intently at the John Travoltas heading my way.

'Hey,' I put my arm out and stop the first one. The guy lifts his sunglasses and gives me a look that says *Yeah, I know I'm gorgeous, but hands off.* 'Oh, sorry.' The next one isn't Brandon either, or the next. The last John Travolta is running past me when I stick out my foot. He stumbles, puts his hands out to save himself and falls heavily on top of me, his sunglasses flying from his face. I flop onto the ground, landing hard on my bum. We both lift our heads, our chests pressing together.

For a few seconds we stare at each other. Then Brandon grimaces. 'What is it with you? I thought we were having a good time, but you kick me and run away without saying goodbye. Now I'm minding my own business and you attack me. Have you got anger management problems?' He sounds perplexed, but I'm not falling for his Mr Innocent routine.

'Why didn't you tell me you worked at Ocean World? And can you get off me?'

'What, you got something against Ocean World? Is that what this is all about?' Brandon rolls off me and sits up on the grass. One of the John Travoltas has stopped and is looking back. Brandon waves his hand at him. 'I'm alright,' he calls. 'I'll catch up with you in a minute.'

'No, but I told you I was going to Ocean World and you didn't say, "I work at Ocean World." That would be the normal thing to do, you know, if someone told you they were going to Ocean World and you worked there.' This isn't going the way I planned. It sounds more like a lesson on etiquette than an incisive interrogation.

Brandon brushes at his white T-shirt. 'Damn, I've got grass stains now. Yeah, well, sorry I didn't tell you I work at Ocean World. I wanted you to think I was a serious actor, that's all. Was that why you ran away?'

'That was part of the reason.' I try to inject a sinister tone into my voice.

'You didn't like my outfit?'

I think back to the gold hotpants. 'No, I didn't like your outfit, but that wasn't it.'

'So, you gunna tell me, Anna? Or do I have to guess?' He leans a little closer. 'Or should I say, Olivia? Did you get your pepper spray and whistle back, private investigator?'

'Yeah, I did.' I push him away. 'You were blackmailing Ajay, weren't you?'

'Oh, you know about that do you?' He doesn't sound overly concerned. 'I was just getting some of what was mine.'

'What do you mean?'

'That whole speed yoga thing – whose idea do you reckon it was?'

I remember his obsession with speed. 'Yours?'

'Damn straight. We did this stupid movie together a few years ago. When we were in acting school.'

'*The Mystic.*'

'You've seen it? Wow, that makes at least two people. Yeah, well I got the idea from that. Ajay – he used to be called Darren, by the way – stole it. Next thing he's changed his name, invented this history of cave gurus and Himalayas, and he's coaching celebrities. I mean, what a winning idea, hey? If there's one thing we're lacking it's time, right?'

'You developed the routine?'

'All me. Who wants to hang around in downward-facing dog for a minute? Speed it up, speed it up.' He snaps his fingers. 'More exercise and enlightenment for your buck. It was one of the best ideas I've ever had. To give Ajay his due, he milked it. The beach body bikini boot camp part was his idea. That's his main skill – marketing. All I wanted was a cut, but he did a runner to Australia.'

'So you came here and blackmailed him.'

'I guess you could call it blackmail. I said I'd out him as a B-grade actor who'd never been anywhere near India unless he paid up.' Brandon pauses to put his sunglasses back on. 'He was pretty freaked out. No one likes a fraud.'

'And the speed dating?'

'My idea of a joke, you know, to rub it in. Speed dating, speed yoga. I wanted to make sure he didn't forget whose idea this speed thing was.' He laughs. 'I dreamed up all these crazy places for him to hand over the cash. I'd make him meet me at the speedway, the roller-coaster ... He hated it. The more he hated it, the more I loved it. I was always looking for new ideas; anything to do with speed.' Brandon chuckles. 'I was having so much fun – I hadn't nearly finished with him.'

I take a deep breath, ready for my big Nancy Drew moment. 'And then Rochelle got you to kill him, so she'd inherit. She knew their marriage was on the rocks and she couldn't risk a divorce.'

Usually when Nancy Drew confronts her villains they break down and confess everything, but Brandon straightens. 'What? Oh, no, you got that wrong. Rochelle saw me in the pictures you took at speed dating. We go way back; she was at acting school with me and Ajay. She got in touch because she'd worked out what I was up to. She knows his history, of course, and said she'd pay me off to leave him alone. Where'd you get the idea I killed him?'

'That first night I was at your place, the night before his fake arm showed up. You took a phone call – it seemed kind of suspicious.'

'No, that was something else.' Brandon sounds evasive. 'I mean, knowing Ajay he's off having a fling with some new flame and he'll turn up soon.'

'Hey, I didn't know you two knew each other.'

I turn my head. Standing on the grass beside us is Luna. She's wearing a khaki-coloured sweatshirt with the hood pulled up and *Hemp Hemp Hooray* written on it. She also has short shorts, big sunglasses and a bigger smile.

'What, you two know each other?' Brandon and I speak at the same time.

'How do you know Luna?' I ask.

'Brandon's a member of WAG. He's our man on the inside.' She shifts from one leg to the other, like she has energy to burn.

'On the inside?' *Oh no.* I'd forgotten today is Luna's dolphin action day.

'Brandon and I were in the same pod in our past lives,' Luna adds casually.

'Pod?' I repeat. I stop myself from adding 'past lives?' like a talking parrot.

Brandon lifts his shoulders as if to disclaim all knowledge of the pod.

Luna laughs. 'He's shy about it. We met at a past lives workshop in Byron Bay. That's when we found out we were both whales in our past lives.'

That explains the whale and dolphin photos at Brandon's apartment. They're the family ancestors.

'He wanted to mate with me, but he never did,' says Luna. 'He only ever got as far as secondary escort.'

Brandon flushes, apparently embarrassed at the sexual failings of his former cetacean self.

'You all ready?' Luna sounds excited.

'Shouldn't you be in hiding?' Brandon clears his throat. 'It said in the papers they'd found the photos at your place.'

Luna narrows her eyes. 'Yeah, well, it's hardly illegal, taking photos, is it? Paparazzi do it all the time. I was just getting a bit of my own back.'

'He's still missing, though,' says Brandon. 'It looks bad.'

Luna shrugs. 'Never mind Ajay. Check this out.' She opens the sports bag she's carrying.

Inside is a bundle of what look like singlets. I pick one up.

'Don't take it out,' Luna hisses.

I unfold the singlet inside the bag, noting its unusual design. Suddenly Luna's plan is clear. My stomach sinks.

'They're fantastic, aren't they?' Luna giggles. 'They're made of hemp, too. Okay, where are we hiding out, pod buddy?'

'Over in the staff rooms,' says Brandon.

I hesitate as Luna and Brandon head off. I'm here under false pretences. I'm not convinced dolphin action is my thing.

Luna glances back. 'What's up, Olivia? Don't you want to help the dolphins?'

What sort of a question's that? I may as well admit to being a granny-killing psychopath. Reluctantly, I slink after them.

37

Luna and I wait outside until the other John Travoltas leave then Brandon ushers us into their changing room and opens the cupboard door.

'We'll wait in here until it's all quiet,' he says.

We stand in the cupboard for a long time. Brandon breathes into my ear. I'm not sure if it's deliberate, but I jab him with my elbow anyway.

Luna is a bundle of nerves, dancing around on the spot and snorting impatiently. 'Can we go yet?' she whispers.

'Soon.' Brandon's breath tickles my ear again. I stamp on his foot. 'Anger management,' he murmurs.

'Manage your own anger,' I mutter back.

While we wait, I rehearse ways to tell Luna a dolphin protest isn't my thing. *It doesn't bother me that much if dolphins are held in captivity.* Or, *I know it's stressful for them to be kept here, but it's not my issue.* Or, *I'm with you in spirit, but I can't afford to get a criminal record.*

It's no good. There's no way I can get out of this without looking bad. In fact, the more I think about it the more I feel Luna is right. Sure, I'd enjoyed the dolphin show, but in hindsight hadn't it been a little degrading making them do those tricks? It's like that old argument about pornography: the women are doing it because they want to. Well, maybe, but it doesn't make it right. People will do all sorts of things for money – or, in this case, fish.

At last the noise dies down outside. We open the door and Luna springs out like a jack-in-the-box. I dislodge a broom from my back and follow her. The changing room is pitch black. We shuffle forwards with our hands held out in front.

'We'll need to watch out for security guards,' Brandon says, opening the door.

Ocean World is a different place without the crowds. It's kind of spooky. We follow a shadowy laneway. Luna takes the lead, followed by Brandon, then me.

'Hide,' Brandon hisses.

We duck into the aquarium doorway as a security guard's torchlight approaches, then recedes.

Before long we're at the dolphin pools.

'How's this going to work, Luna?' says Brandon.

'It'll be fine. I'm a dolphin whisperer.' Luna pulls a small esky from her bag. 'And I've got fish.' She begins to pull a long piece of material out. 'Olivia, string this up along the fence while Brandon and I work with the dolphins.'

Great. I get to put up a banner while Luna and Brandon cuddle the dolphins. *Just because I wasn't a whale in my past life.* I tie one corner of the banner and stretch it out. Its message appears to have been developed by a committee.

I glance over at Luna, who is in the water up to her waist, waving a fish. 'It's a bit wordy.'

'Yeah. It's hard when you're working with two groups. We had to get the WAG and the WAM messages on it. I think it worked in the end, though.'

Luna and Brandon fit a hemp singlet to the first dolphin. Luna begins to sing.

'Is that Spanish or Portuguese?' I call in a low voice.

Luna ignores this. 'Hey, Olivia. She wants to say hello to you.' She waves me towards the pool.

I step across the grass. 'What, it specifically asked for me?'

Luna nods. 'Yeah, *she* did. She says she's excited to see you and she asks for a meeting of heart, soul and mind.'

Yeah right. I do like Luna, but ... I look at the dolphin. She is lying in the shallows. Her dark eyes meet mine. My trouble, I suppose, is that I can be suggestible. I go with the flow, even if I feel weird about it. Besides, it's flattering, the dolphin wanting to meet me. I wade into the water.

'You know, Olivia, dolphins can see right inside your body with their sonar,' says Luna.

'Yeah, I studied biology at school.'

'I bet they didn't tell you they can see your emotions too. There's no lying to a dolphin.'

That's a scary thought if it's true. 'Should I touch her?'

'She'd like that I think.'

I bend over and lay my hand on the dolphin's head, in front of her blow hole. She is smooth and rubbery. A puff of air comes out of her hole.

'Brandon and I had better move on to the next dolphin,' says Luna.

I feel like I'm being deserted at a party by the only person I know. 'Aren't you going to stay and interpret for me?'

'Just feel it with your heart.' Luna and Brandon move down the pool towards the next dolphin.

I crouch. 'So, hi dolphin.' A kind of peace creeps over me as I squat in the water. I try to open my mind and commune with her on a deeper level. I can sense the intelligence behind her dark eyes. It's calming.

Brandon and Luna have just fitted the singlet to the next dolphin when we hear voices. They're at a distance, but coming closer. I stand.

'Quick, take the photo,' says Luna.

Brandon pulls a phone from his pocket. He snaps a photo of the banner, my dolphin lying in the shallows and ... the money shot. The second dolphin leaps from the water in front of the banner. The words on the singlet are the same as the banner – 'Would you eat us? No McSushi for Byron Bay. Let the dolphins swim free.'

I don't bother to point out that dolphins aren't on the menu at McSushi. It's the vibe that counts.

The footsteps come closer.

I wave at my dolphin. She flicks her tail and swims off into the deep.

'Split up,' whispers Luna. 'Make sure the photo gets to the media.'

Brandon nods and we all run in different directions.

It's lucky I'm familiar with Ocean World. Running away from the voices, I swing left and duck into the shark viewing tunnel. Outside, three policemen run past, Dan Ferris in the lead. He is puffing, but surprisingly fast for a guy carrying so much weight. I press myself against the tunnel wall. If they find me I'll never work as a PI again. Or a lawyer. Maybe I never will anyway, but it's best to keep my options open.

It's surprisingly noisy here in the tunnel tonight. Music is pumping out over the speakers. Salt-n-Pepa's 'Push it' is finishing and Joe Cocker kicks off with 'Leave Your Hat on'. Weird choice of music.

The dark silhouettes of the sharks appear out of the gloom, swim along the glass and disappear again. A groper big enough to swallow me whole idles past as Justin Timberlake sings 'Rock Your Body'. Who's programming this music? Someone with an eclectic taste, that's for sure. But why?

Bob Marley follows, then we're back to Salt-n-Pepa, Joe and Justin. There are only four songs on rotation. The stingrays press themselves against the glass, their mouths gaping. The sharks go past again, and the groper. The wildlife is on rotation too. It's mesmerising – boring after a while, but at the same time somehow enchanting. *Enchantingly boring.* As 'Push it' starts for the third time I decide it's safe to come out.

I follow the tunnel up to the platform that runs around the top of the shark pool. The music's even louder here. *Rock Your Body* reads the heading on a sign on the edge of the pool. At last, some explanation. The sign explains that research has proved these four songs are the most likely to put sharks in a sexy mood. In an effort to encourage mating, they're being played constantly.

Interesting. Clearly the sexy music compilation is a concept shared between species. I envisage the male shark leaning over in the car and selecting Salt-n-Pepa. *This'll get her going.*

What would do it for dolphins? Enya maybe? They'd have to be more spiritual than sharks.

I gaze into the pool. From here on the deck the water is inky. I know sharks are more active at night but only an occasional fin breaks the surface. There's no sign they're boogieing. My mind goes back to Ajay. Who threw that fake arm in? And why?

It would have to be someone who has access to Ocean World. That means a staff member like Brandon, or someone a staff member would let in. Like a member of WAG. That brings me back to Luna, or a member of her group.

Something rustles behind me. I spin around, hoping the cops haven't sprung me. 'Madeleine?'

Madeleine's pale skin glows in the dim lighting. She's only a few metres away. As she steps towards me her red hair lifts in the breeze. As always, she is immaculately made-up. Today her leggings are neon blue with a white shark pattern. Her feet are bare, which explains how she'd sneaked up on me.

'Enjoying the music?' she murmurs in her breathy voice.

'What are *you* doing here?' My mind's working overtime.

'I heard there was a WAG action on.' She's close enough now for a whiff of perfume to reach my nostrils.

'You're a bit late.'

'Oh, that's a shame. Was it successful?'

'It was until the police came. Didn't you see them?'

Madeleine twirls a strand of hair between her fingers. 'No. Did they catch anyone?'

I can't take any more of her Miss Innocent routine. 'I saw you in the café with Brooklyn. *You* sent the police, didn't you?'

Madeleine blinks. 'No. Why would I do that?'

'Why are you siding with Brooklyn, with McSushi? Didn't you say it's worse to eat whales than to eat people?'

'I'm not siding with McSushi. Brooklyn and I are ... well, never mind that.' She walks closer until her shoulder is brushing mine. 'You're a PI, aren't you?'

Talk about the worst-kept secret ever.

'You weren't a very good yoga instructor.'

I don't like her tone. 'Well, maybe you wouldn't make a very good PI.'

Her green eyes widen. 'Oh, I would.'

'You would?' She has something she wants to tell me. I just have to let it come out.

'Better than you.'

There's something I've missed, something big and she wants to rub it in. 'That wouldn't be hard. I'm not a PI anymore anyway. I've resigned.'

Madeleine tilts her head.

'Didn't get on with the boss.' Something tells me this is the right thing to say.

'Tell me about it.' Madeleine's eyes meet mine. 'I've worked for Ajay for almost two years.' A fin slides past us to the tune of 'No Woman No Cry'. 'And I'm still a junior instructor. It's not right. I'm an amazing yoga teacher. I know I am. I live for yoga.'

I remember the website – *I didn't like the way he humiliated his instructor.* 'Did he give you a hard time?'

Madeleine's hands grip the railing. 'I tried to make my headstands perfect.'

'They looked good to me.'

Madeleine's lip curls. 'They were perfect – perfect. But he always slapped me, always. I'd see that tattoo coming at me and it was like he hated me. That man in lotus position on his wrist,' she shudders. 'It haunted me.'

I think I've heard enough. I edge away.

'Where are you going?' Madeleine grasps my arm. 'He shouldn't have slapped me in front of all those people.' Her hands dig into my flesh. 'I tried so hard. I was up to two hours of headstands a day.'

'That's a lot.'

Madeleine's face contorts. 'But I still couldn't get ahead.'

'So what did you do? Where's Ajay now?'

'Wouldn't you like to know.'

I try to loosen my arm from her hold, but all those years of yoga have made her strong. *Where are the police?* I strain my eyes for torchlight, weighing up the pros and cons of trying to attract their attention. On one hand, it would confirm Dan Ferris's suspicions about me – *ugly.* On the other hand …

'I'm the senior instructor at Lighthouse Bliss now he's gone.' She smiles. 'I'm practically a yoga rock star. It's my job to keep speed yoga going. Rochelle hasn't got a clue. She'll take her share of the money, but she doesn't understand. It's not about money, it's about enlightenment. That guru passed his secret on to Ajay. It's my duty to carry that on.'

'It was a con, Madeleine. There was no guru, no India, no speed yoga. Brandon made it up.'

'Brandon?' For a moment she loosens her grip, but she tightens it again. 'I don't believe you.'

I don't like the look in her eyes. I yank my arm away but she won't let go. I kick out at her shin, but she's too quick.

Bending, she grasps my legs and tips me backwards over the fence.

I hang out over the inky water, struggling to get back up. 'Help, police,' I yell, the pros suddenly outweighing the cons.

A large fin slices the surface below as Salt-n-Pepa croon for me to 'Push it'. Twisting, I grab her hair trying to pull myself back over the fence. Madeleine prises my fingers free. Heaving my legs up she gives a push and I hit the water.

39

I come up spluttering. The water is cold and dark. Justin Timberlake is rocking his body, but mine is one big mass of terror. I try to suppress it – *the water, the darkness* – but the memory returns. *The moon-shiny darkness. The push from behind ...*

'I warned you with the poster, but you kept snooping around. Snooping, snooping, snooping.' Madeleine's face is pale behind the fence.

I snap back to the present, lunging for the edge, but the pool is landscaped with a steep, rocky ledge on this side. I can't get out. I tread water, willing myself to stay calm, to think my way out of this. *Don't panic.* Panic attracts sharks. *Will singing Taylor Swift songs repel them?* It's no good; I can't remember any. I'll have to hope Justin is making them so sexy they're more interested in mating than eating.

Madeleine peers over at me. 'Olivia, calm down. Just speak to the sharks. Pay your respects. If you respect them, they'll respect you. You're in their home, after all.'

Something brushes against my leg, scraping like coarse sandpaper. I scream. A fin as big as my head slices through the water towards me. I scream again. My breath comes in jagged gasps as a tide of panic rises again. *The darkness, the water.*

Something big bumps against me again, rasping my leg as it moves past. I'm pretty sure I'm bleeding. *Blood attracts sharks.* I have to get out of here.

'They're not going to eat you. Just tell them you don't mean them any harm,' Madeleine calls. 'You're probably frightening them.'

The fin disappears. I circle, looking for it. The ledge is lower on the other side of the pool. It's scary going further in instead of out, but I strike out for it.

It feels like the longest swim I've ever done. I keep swimming, as hard as I can, but the edge never comes any closer. Every second is a heart-thumping, fear-wracked eternity. I'm shaking by the time I reach the other side. Shadows move beneath me as I scrabble at the edge. I pull myself out, slumping onto the deck beside the pool, trembling. Behind me I imagine I hear the flick of a shark's tail.

Over the other side of the pool Madeleine has faded into the darkness.

'Holy cow, you're a thrillseeker, Olivia.' A figure vaults the fence, runs up to me and kneels beside me.

I look at him. What's Rosco doing here?

He touches my arm and scans my face as Joe Cocker suggests I take my coat off. 'Are you okay?'

'Madeleine ...' I look into his eyes. I wish he'd put his arms around me. 'She pushed me in.'

'The yoga instructor? But why?'

I shiver, but I'm not sure if it's from the cold. 'I think she might have killed Ajay.'

'What? Really?' He frowns, then gives a tentative smile. 'I thought maybe you'd decided to take a swim with the sharks.'

'Do I seem like a swim-with-sharks kind of person to you?'

His hand is still on my arm. 'I'm not sure if I know what kind of person you are anymore.'

We are quiet for a while and Rosco leans closer. I can feel his breath on my face. My stomach flips as he touches my hair and pulls a leaf out of it, his fingers brushing my cheek. 'You never used to be this crazy.' His voice is low.

'We should go after her.'

'Let the police pick her up.' Rosco takes off his sweatshirt. 'Here, put this on. You're shivering.'

I hesitate, then pull his sweatshirt over my head and dig my hands into the pockets. This is becoming a habit.

'We're trespassing. We should get out of here.' He stands up and puts out his hand, pulling me to my feet. He holds onto my hand for a little longer than necessary before letting go.

'What are you doing here, anyway?'

'Your grandmother was worried when you didn't get home for dinner. She called me and said you'd gone to Ocean World this afternoon. I told her I'd check it out.'

'She didn't need to do that.' James was right; there *is* something ludicrous about a private investigator living with their grandmother.

'I saw the police cars out the front and put two and two together.' Rosco glances over at the shark pool. 'It was lucky I heard you splashing around.'

I feel embarrassed now. 'It was all in hand.'

'Yeah? Well, sorry to interrupt your swim.' Rosco thrusts his hands in his jeans pockets. His eyes flicker down my legs. 'You're bleeding.'

I glance down. A red gravel rash covers my right calf, below my cargo shorts. A queasy feeling rises inside me. 'It's nothing. Let's get out of here.'

'Yeah, we'd better move.' He seems to notice the music for the first time. 'What's with Bob Marley?'

'It's sexy music for sharks.' I explain the concept.

'Huh. They have strange tastes, don't they? Not sure 'Rock Your Body' would make it onto my sexy music list. How about you?'

'Probably not.' I don't really want to talk about sexy music with Rosco. Not unless he means it.

As we walk back towards the main entrance, my legs are like spaghetti. I run my hand along the walls to steady myself. If Rosco notices, he doesn't say anything. I suppose I'm just one crisis after another as far as he's concerned.

There's no sign of police or security, but we keep to the shadows.

As we pass the penguin enclosure we hear footsteps. Rosco pulls me around the corner and we duck behind a wall. A security guard with a flashlight walks past. In front of us, a sign is illuminated in the glow of the night light.

When a pair of penguins reunite after a separation they stand breast to breast, heads thrown back, singing loudly with outstretched flippers trembling.

I read it twice while we crouch there. A rush of emotion blocks my throat at the thought of those little penguins in love. It gives me a warm glow – the flipper-trembling part, especially. I'm clearly a little overwrought after my swim with the sharks. The warmth of Rosco's shoulder next to mine and the smell of his sweatshirt around me isn't helping.

We stand up cautiously as the security guard passes.

'Romantic little critters, aren't they?' says Rosco, glancing at the penguins.

I glare at him. He sounds so offhand. 'That's like saying that Romeo and Juliet were romantic little critters.'

'Well ...' he looks puzzled, 'they were, right?'

He doesn't understand that a wildly romantic moment has completely passed him by. 'Never mind. It's stupid.'

I notice he doesn't contradict me.

A gate near the staff change room has been left unlocked. Outside, in the enormous car park, my car stands forlornly next to Rosco's.

'So, bye. Thanks for coming.' I sound like a hostess at a party. *Let's do it again some time. Your shark pool, or mine?*

Rosco fiddles with his car keys. 'You can give me back the sweatshirt later.'

'Thanks.'

'I don't suppose you've got any idea why the woman downstairs from me thinks I'm a terrorist suspect?'

'No.' I hope I sound surprised. 'Why, what's she doing?'

'She's always watching me through her window. I think she's keeping notes on my movements. Yesterday she took a photo of me as I came in with my shopping. Hope I don't get raided.'

I shuffle my feet – confession time. 'I may have accidentally given her the idea that ASIO is keeping an eye on you.'

Rosco gazes at me for some time. 'Why? No, never mind.' He holds up his hand as I open my mouth. He sighs. 'You are so infuriating sometimes.'

'I've had a hard night. If you want to pick a fight can we do it some other time?'

Rosco continues as if I hadn't spoken, gazing over my shoulder at Ocean World. 'But I think you could be a bloody good PI if you stick with it.'

'Oh.' I wait, but nothing more is forthcoming. I open my door. 'Well, I guess I'd better ...' Climbing into my car, I start the engine.

Rosco leans over and looks in the window. 'Are you feeling better?'

I stare at him.

'Your message. You said you weren't feeling well.'

'Oh. Yes. I am.'

'Are you still working for me?'

I gnaw my lip. 'I don't ... I'm not sure.'

'I'm prepared to forget the incident in the cupboard the other day if you want to come back.'

It's not exactly an effusive invitation. I suppose that hiding in your boss's cupboard is an employee performance issue. I stare at him for a while. 'Thanks. I'll give it some thought.'

'Your call.' He stands up.

As I drive away I see him standing next to his car, watching me go. I almost turn around and go back, but then I think of the expression on his face when I came out of his cupboard and I keep going. Maybe it's time to accept that Rosco and I are not a good combination.

Jacq and Nan are in bed when I get home. I lock the front door and go and stand under the shower until the water runs cold.

Wrapping a dressing gown around me, I pad to the phone. *Now for the tricky bit.* I've decided an anonymous message is the way to go. Picking up a tea towel to muffle my voice, I call the police.

'Ferris here.'

Damn. I'd been hoping for one of his underlings. He sounds like he's had a bad day. He always does though. 'I've got a tip-off into Ajay's disappearance,' I murmur in a deep voice. 'Madeleine, I don't know her second name. She's a yoga instructor at Lighthouse Bliss. She's got red hair and she wears lycra tights. You should talk to her.' Before he can ask me any questions I slam the phone down.

I check the locks before I go to bed and lie there thinking for a long time. It's not only the idea that Madeleine is out there, prowling around, that stops me sleeping. There are parallels between her situation and mine. There's been nothing but frustration since I started with Rosco. Childhood friendship is not a good basis for a professional relationship. And the Spark that may or may not exist between us has only complicated things. Rosco's not going to change and neither am I. We're always going to be butting heads. By midnight, I've made my mind up.

Crawling out of bed again, I dial. 'Welcome to Gold Star Investigations ...' I wait for the beep. 'Hi, Olivia here.' I keep my voice cheerful and matter-of-fact. 'Thanks for asking me back, but I don't think it's working out. I've decided to move on. Hope it all goes well for you. Anyway, lots to do, busy, busy, busy.' I put the phone down and shuffle back to bed.

Bunching my pillow, I press my face into it. But despite my tiredness I still can't sleep. Every time I drift off I feel the shark against my leg. I toss and turn, jumping at every sound, changing sides every five minutes. My clock clicks as it turns over to two am.

40

My tail slices the water. Through the blue, a dolphin approaches. I recognise her wise black eyes. Her sonar clicks penetrate my brain. 'Change from within. Change from within.' Bubbles follow her tail as she vanishes into the indigo depths.

I wake to a quiet house – Jacq has already gone to holiday program and Nan is out somewhere. A dream lingers at the edge of my consciousness. *Bubbles.* That's all I can remember.

I sit up. What am I going to do about Madeleine? *Nothing without a cup of coffee.*

Nan has left the *Gold Coast Times* on the kitchen table. Brandon's done his job. The front page shows the dolphin leaping, the banner behind it. **Police Seek Protesters**, reads the headline.

Bizarrely, the opening beat of 'Push it' starts on the radio. I slam my finger on the power button. I never want to listen to any of those songs again. Something occurs to me. *Luna.* I have to tell her about Madeleine. Maybe she'll know what to do. I try her phone, but it goes straight to message.

Pulling on a T-shirt and pants, I run out the door.

Downtown, cleaners are sweeping away the debris of the

night. Seiji's Outback Bar is dark, but the door is ajar. I push it and call into the shadows. 'Luna?'

There's scuffling in the darkness. I blink, getting used to the gloom. A figure is sitting on a chair in the corner. I step closer.

'Ajay?' I run towards him. He is gagged with a koala-print tea towel and his hands are tied behind his back.

'Mmm arrgra mmm.' His voice is urgent, but unintelligible.

'What?'

'He said Madeleine, I think.'

I turn.

Madeleine stands next to me. She looks different to normal, like she's had a hard night. Her lipstick is smudged, her fake eyelashes are shedding, her red hair is dishevelled and her zebra-print tights are dirty. 'We meet again.' She doesn't look pleased to see me. 'Still poking around, are you? How was your swim with the sharks?'

I glare at her.

'Shh grrr nng,' says Ajay.

'What?'

'He says I've got a knife.' Madeleine's hands drop to her sides and I see something shiny.

I stare at her and lick my lips. 'You don't need that. We're all friends here – all yoga teachers.'

Madeleine laughs. 'That fluffy koala over there is more of a yoga teacher than you are.'

I open my mouth to protest but shut it again. The main thing is to keep Madeleine talking. 'I can do headstands. I bet that koala can't do headstands.'

Madeleine raises her eyebrows. 'Really? Go on, let's see one.'

'Ss a ass aa,' says Ajay.

'Who asked you?' Madeleine's mouth twitches as she turns to him. 'I know it's called sirsasana. Just shut up and watch. I'll show you how to run a yoga class.' She looks back at me. 'Headstand.'

I have no strategy, but it's best to go with the flow. If Madeleine wants me to do a headstand, I'll do a headstand. I kneel on the ground, cup my head in my hands and slowly lift my legs into the air. I keep my face pointed towards Madeleine and Ajay so I can see what they're up to.

'Nng a ayy ack.'

Madeleine glares at Ajay. 'Who's running this class?' She looks at me. 'Keep a straight back.'

It's the first time I've done a headstand away from the wall. My feet paw at the air, my arms strain to support me.

'Salamba sirsasana activates the circulation, endocrine and lymphatic systems.' Madeleine glances at Ajay. 'See, I know my stuff.'

I wobble, stretching my legs higher, making my back as straight as it will go. I'm doing a headstand without the wall. *My signature move.* It's a miracle only I can appreciate.

'Oog.' Despite being tied and gagged Ajay still thinks he's the lead yoga instructor.

'Not bad,' Madeleine concedes. 'Oog is stretching it.' Her voice changes to a soothing chant. 'The headstand tones and cleans. It encourages deep breathing, which gently massages the internal organs. Fresh warm blood invigorates the cells.' She pauses. 'Now a dropback.'

A dropback? I don't even know what that means. I'm exceeding expectations already.

'Oooowa eg acken.'

Madeleine glares at Ajay. 'I can run a yoga class without your assistance. I'm the lead instructor at Lighthouse Bliss now. Lots of people have told me they like my classes better than yours. My adjustments are more precise.'

His eyebrows twitch.

'Lower your legs into a backbend,' Madeleine snaps.

'What?' I wobble in my headstand.

'Do it,' says Madeleine. 'The headstand dropback is an excellent shoulder stretch.'

'Oog,' agrees Ajay.

'Shut up,' says Madeleine. 'I'm the rock-star yoga instructor now.' She glares at him. 'You're not even that great. You've got inflexible hips.' She smirks. 'Your eka pada sirsasana's are a total joke. Everyone thinks so.' She turns to me. 'Don't they?'

It seems best to agree. 'Yes. Total joke,' I mumble. It's hard to talk in this position.

'See?' says Madeleine to Ajay. She obviously believes this is a crushing blow and, in fact, it does shut him up.

I wobble again.

'Mr Iyengar says you don't stop trying just because you're not perfect,' Madeleine murmurs. I'm not sure if she's speaking to me or to herself. 'Dropback,' she commands.

Bending my knees, I lower them towards the floor. My back gives a clicking sound. It's not going to work. I try to bring my knees back up again but I'm too far advanced. My feet drop to the floor, my neck twists and I scream and collapse.

'You're not trying. Yoga requires total commitment.' The knife shines in her hand as she steps towards me.

'No, no, I'm trying,' I squeak, jumping up into warrior pose.

'Ah, warrior pose. Good choice. Warrior pose strengthens the legs and opens the chest and shoulders.'

'Vv baa aa ung.'

Madeleine glares at Ajay. 'I know it's virabhadrasana one. You think I couldn't speak in Sanskrit if I wanted to? You think I haven't studied Sanskrit?'

Ajay lifts his shoulders.

Madeleine's nostrils pinch and she clenches her jaw.

'Eee ung il aa, ee ow ack.'

Madeleine gives a high-pitched wail. 'You breathe in the silver and blow out the black yourself, jerk.' She lunges towards him.

Jumping out of my warrior pose like Rakesh, the Bruce Lee yogi, I leap into action.

41

'Aaargh,' I scream as I race towards Madeleine. She half-turns, her red hair swinging out from her face.

With a leap – unlike Rakesh, mine is neither high nor catlike – I land on her back. My superior weight sends her tumbling to the ground, the knife still in her hand. We roll around on the carpet, then she throws me off as if I'm as light as a yoga blanket.

'Egg acck iffe,' yells Ajay.

I don't have time to think about what that means as Madeleine flings me onto my back. I heave and struggle, but her arms are like steel cables. All those forearm balances have really paid off.

The door bangs and someone comes in. It's Luna, wearing a kind of beige mini-kaftan, which can only be made of hemp.

'Drop the knife,' she shouts.

Madeleine lets go of me and stands up. 'Keep it down, Luna. It's just a souvenir butter knife.' She holds it up. It is indeed a harmless blunt little knife with a kangaroo picture on the handle. 'I was just trying to get Ajay to shut up for a bit. He's been driving me crazy. It didn't work though.'

'Don't trust her,' I call to Luna. 'She threw me in the shark tank.'

Luna looks at Madeleine. 'The Ocean World shark tank?'

Madeleine nods.

'Awesome. Swimming with sharks is really empowering, isn't it?' says Luna.

I blink, reliving the rasp of sandpaper against my leg. 'What?'

'Those sharks are big softies,' says Madeleine. 'They're wobbegongs. They're like labradors; they don't bite and they love a pat.'

'Is that why they were circling me?'

'Yeah, the keepers feed them by hand. You didn't think I was trying to kill you, did you?' says Madeleine.

'Um, yeah. You threw me in a shark pool.'

'I just wanted you to back off,' says Madeleine. 'Quit chasing Ajay.'

'You could have sent me a text,' I say.

'You're more likely to be killed by a falling coconut than one of those sharks. That's right, isn't it, Luna?'

'Yeah, they're cool. I would have loved to go for a night swim with the sharks,' says Luna. 'Next time, invite me.'

'No hard feelings?' Madeleine smiles at me, displaying her perfect white teeth. 'People pay big money to dive with the sharks, you know. You got it for free.'

Her chutzpah is incredible. I almost smile back.

'I think the cops might be on the way,' says Luna. 'I saw them stuck in traffic out on Cavill Avenue.'

'The cops?' Madeleine pales. She glances at Ajay. 'I suppose I'd better let him go.'

'Good thinking.' Luna does a double-take. 'What are you doing with him anyway? And why are you here in Zander's bar?'

'I had to move Ajay from my place.' Madeleine glances at me.

'I figured you'd send them after me. I didn't think there'd be anyone here in the bar at this time of day.'

This doesn't answer the main question, which is what exactly Madeleine is doing with Ajay, but there doesn't seem to be any time for that now.

Madeleine unties Ajay and he stands up, glaring at her and massaging his wrists. 'You're fired,' he says.

Madeleine glares back at him. 'What a surprise.'

'I'll be pressing charges,' he says.

'I don't think that's a good idea,' says Luna.

Ajay turns to her.

'Brandon filled me in on your starring role in *The Mystic*,' she says. 'That was naughty of you, making all that stuff up about the guru.'

Ajay's face blanches.

There's a crash and the door swings open. Three cops run in, Dan Ferris in the lead. Brooklyn, in a midriff-baring rainbow singlet and voluminous fisherman pants, is behind them. She meets Madeleine's eyes and shrugs, while the cops are all brought up short by the sight of the yoga guru.

'Ajay?' says Dan. 'Where have you been?'

Ajay's eyes flicker to Madeleine and then to Brooklyn and on to Luna. He hesitates. 'I've been on retreat in India. Just got back. Sorry if there's been a misunderstanding.'

Dan looks deeply suspicious. 'You were reported missing.'

'I was on an ashram. There was no reception,' says Ajay.

'Right.' Dan sniffs. He seems disappointed not to have a murder case on his hands. He pulls out his notebook and flicks through it. 'There are a few other issues. The rat incident at Lighthouse Bliss and the Ocean World protest last night.' He looks between all of us. 'Can you provide any information on these?'

Luna and I stare at Brooklyn and Madeleine. I'm pretty sure Luna's thinking the same thing I am. *Should we tell him about their role in the rat incident?*

Brooklyn and Madeleine stare back at us. *Shall we tell him about your role in the Ocean World incident?* their eyes flash.

A sizzle of energy passes between the four of us. Luna and Brooklyn hold each other's gaze. A bit of extra sizzle seems to be going on there.

Eventually we all shake our heads.

'Really?' Dan glances from one to the other of us. 'Nothing to add ... ladies?'

'No.' We all speak together.

His gaze comes back to me. 'We have caller ID, you know.'

I flush. I should have thought of that. What kind of idiot makes anonymous phone calls from their home phone?

'If everything's in order, I have to go,' says Ajay. 'I have a business meeting.'

Dan nods and he stalks out.

After Ajay leaves, Dan pockets his notebook. 'I've got my eye on you. All of you.'

There is silence as the cops leave. We lower ourselves into a couple of couches next to a large emu model. It feels like we four have unfinished business.

The door bangs again and Zander comes in. He eyes us from under his long fringe. 'The party's starting early today, huh? Nancy Drews all round?'

'Better make it mocktails,' says Luna. 'I haven't had breakfast yet. You haven't got any wheatgrass juice, have you?'

Zander snorts. 'As if.' He ambles over to the bar and comes

back with four glasses of pink and yellow liquid with a slice of lime on the side.

Brooklyn places her lips to the glass. 'Mm, grouse.'

We all stare at her.

She looks up. 'What? Did I say it wrong?'

'No, that was fine,' says Luna. 'Just ...'

'Surprising,' I supply.

Zander turns on the radio and starts to wipe down the camel next to the bar.

'It's a beautiful morning here in Paradise, offshore winds, three to four foot waves, five on the sets, the points are cranking ...'

So here we all are. There's just one thing I still don't understand. Apart from Madeleine kidnapping Ajay, that is. 'What was with the fake arm in the shark pool? That was pretty random. Who did that?'

Luna and Brooklyn shrug and look at Madeleine.

'That was me. I got one of those fake arms off the internet and drew Ajay's tattoo on it,' says Madeleine. 'Then I threw it in the shark pool.'

'Why?' I ask.

Madeleine looks at me like I'm stupid. 'It was a message to people like him, of course. I was hoping it would catch on ... you know, go viral or something. I Instagrammed it but it didn't take off. I don't know why.'

'You're sharkgirl?'

'Sometimes.'

'I saw the hashtag. Fake arms against harassment, right?'

'Right. I didn't mean for the shark to eat it, but whatever.'

'I'm not sure I get it,' I say.

Madeleine and Brooklyn exchange a glance.

Luna eyes them. 'I get it. He tried it on with me too.'

'Did I miss something?' I say.

'He's a creep. He's got roaming hands,' says Luna.

'That's why I had him dumped as the face of McSushi,' says Brooklyn.

'Good job,' says Luna.

Brooklyn and Luna smile at each other and their eyes linger.

'He only promotes instructors who sleep with him,' says Madeleine. 'I'd had a gutful. I guess I snapped. I figured with him out of the way, I'd be chief instructor.'

'Right, but kidnapping him? That was kind of extreme,' I say. Batshit crazy is what I mean.

Guilt flashes across Madeleine's face for a moment. 'I just wanted a chance. I knew I was the best. What else could I do?'

It sounds almost logical, the way she says it.

'Looks like I'm out of a job now though,' says Madeleine.

'They need someone at the Pink House,' says Luna.

'Cool,' says Madeleine. 'I'll chase that up.'

'Shouldn't you report him?' I say.

Madeleine, Luna and Brooklyn roll their eyes in unison.

'He makes sure there are no witnesses,' says Luna. 'When I complained, all that happened was I lost my job.' She laughs. 'I never thought of kidnapping him. That's out-of-the-box thinking. Bizarre but effective. High five to that.' She puts up her hand and Madeleine slaps it.

'Yoga teaches us to cure what need not be endured.' Madeleine smiles. 'Being chief instructor was my dream. He had it coming. Brooklyn was in on it too.'

Luna and I turn to her. 'Really?'

'Fair dinkum,' says Brooklyn.

Luna taps her glass against Brooklyn's. 'Cheers to that.'

Brooklyn consults her phone. 'The bloke is lower than a snake's belly,' she enunciates in her American drawl, as if speaking a foreign language.

I glance at her phone.

Brooklyn smiles. 'I keep notes on Australian slang. It's good public relations to master the native dialect.'

I sip my mocktail. Ajay certainly has a lot to answer for. I'm not sure that kidnapping was an appropriate response, but no-one else seems to have a problem with it.

'So, Brooklyn.' Luna tilts her head. 'Are you still trying to open a McSushi in Byron Bay?'

Brooklyn taps her glass. Her fingernails are decorated with stick-on unicorns. 'My father ... He really wants to open up the market, get the company in there.'

'You don't?' asks Luna.

Brooklyn's mouth twists. 'I've always been, like, totally on board with the whole expansion thing, but now ...' She twists her dark hair with a finger and gazes at Luna. 'The afternoon after I let the rats out, I did one of those goddess dances on Wategos Beach. I read about it in the *Lighthouse News* and thought I'd go along. Just for a laugh.' She gazes at the stuffed camel with a faraway look. 'Something happened. It was really transformational. And now, I feel like I'm metamorphosing into something new.'

We all stare at her.

'My father wants me to be like my sister – she's rising up the McSushi ranks – but I just want to find my inner goddess, you know?'

'Totally,' says Luna. Her face has gone a little pink.

'I'm going back to America soon,' says Brooklyn. 'They're not happy with my progress. Or with my methods.'

'The rats?' says Luna.

'I knew you would be the logical suspect,' says Brooklyn. 'With you out of the way it would have been easy to move in.'

'You put the rat hairs in Luna's car?' I ask.

Brooklyn nods.

'You left a McSushi wrapper behind.'

'Oh.' Brooklyn puts her hand to her mouth. 'I must have been one sausage short of a barbie that day.'

Zander perches on a seat at the bar and opens the *Gold Coast Times*.

I sort through everything that's happened in my mind. Fake arm. *Tick*. Georgia Hansen photos. *Tick*. Rats. *Tick*. Ajay's disappearance. *Tick*. 'What about the McSushi poster in Byron Bay? Who painted *stop the whale killers* on that?' I ask.

'Oh, that was me,' says Brooklyn. 'I was on my way out of town after the goddess dance when I saw the poster and, this feeling came over me, it was like an explosion. I felt compelled ...'

'The whales called to you,' says Luna.

'Exactly,' says Brooklyn.

'This is making my head hurt,' I say.

Luna cocks her head. 'I don't know why. It's all perfectly clear. The whales told her they didn't want a McSushi in Byron Bay.'

'That's right.' Brooklyn nods. 'Are you heading back to the office soon, Olivia?'

I cross my legs and sip my drink. 'I've finished at the agency.'

'You've finished?' says Luna. 'Why?'

'Rosco and I ... We don't get along.'

'That's strange,' says Brooklyn. 'He seems like a pretty cool guy.'

I stare at her. Well, she would think that, wouldn't she? 'I didn't feel like he was being honest with me. Or valuing my skills.'

Brooklyn tilts her head, then touches my arm. 'Just so you know, my relationship with Rosco is purely professional. After he dropped the McSushi contract Madeleine and I persuaded him to come back on, for a private project.'

I wait.

'We were trying to dig up dirt on Ajay,' she sips from her drink. 'To see if it was worth taking things further legally. We didn't get very far. He covers his tracks.'

So that's what she was doing at Rosco's that day. Well, it's too late now ...

'What will you do now?' she asks.

'I'm thinking of becoming a yoga teacher.'

Madeleine's eyes widen. 'You'll need to work on your dropbacks.'

'I'm joking.' I swivel towards the bar. 'Pass me the "positions vacant", will you Zander?'

Zander pulls off the back of the paper, rolls it up and throws it to me. I flick through the jobs. My finger pauses on the ad, before moving on. But something makes me come back to it. *Change from within,* says a voice in my head. Normally I'd ignore it, but my options are limited. Maybe I should take guidance in whatever form it's offered. I slide my phone out of my back pocket. 'Here's one.'

Luna, Madeleine and Brooklyn lean across the table, trying to read the ad.

'What's it for?' says Luna.

I hold up one finger and, scanning the ad, punch the number into my phone. *Looking for girls to join the iconic Surfers Paradise meter maid team. Must be enthusiastic, well-groomed, have a happy personality and a nice bikini body. Ages between 18 and 30.* 'Hello? I'm interested in the meter maid position.'

'A Queensland meter maid is a beautiful young lady dressed in an eye-catching gold bikini. She projects confidence, sophistication and independence, yet still represents the ultimate in femininity. She is sleek, classy, carefree, sassy, cheeky, but still professionally serious ...'

Charlene at the meter maid agency isn't happy to see me. She sizes up my figure, my glasses and my lack of tan.

Her leathery face puckers. 'I don't think you're suited to this job, dear.'

'My appearance doesn't affect my ability to do the job. I can still feed money into meters.'

'We don't have your size.' She gestures triumphantly at the rack of size six to eight gold bikinis.

'I've got my own.' I pull it out of my bag and brandish it at her.

She sighs. 'Why do you want to be a meter maid, anyway?'

It's a good question. Some mad whim has sent me here. Some crazy idea about changing the system from within. Clearly I'm not going to tell Charlene this. 'I need a job.' This is also true. 'It looks like it could be fun.'

She still looks dubious.

I wrack my brain for something I can offer as a counterpoint to my physical unsuitability. 'I can do a headstand. I think it would go down well with the customers.'

'A headstand, ay? Let's see it then.'

I kneel down, put my head on the carpet and raise my legs. I hardly wobble at all. Lowering my feet to the ground, I jump up, throwing my arms out. 'Ta da. What do you think?'

She shrugs. 'Got to hand it to you, you've got a bit of get-up-and-go.' She puts her hands on her hips and seems to come to a decision. 'I'm pretty short-staffed right now.' She opens a drawer and hands me a gold sash reading *Gold Coast Meter Maid* and a cowboy hat. 'You can start tomorrow. Don't suppose you'll last long, anyway.'

It's weird out on the street my first day. No one seems to know what to make of me. A chubby bloke in stubbies that display his bum cleavage elbows his mate and snickers as I pass.

'What's your problem, buddy? I'm putting money in your meter, aren't I?' I say. I saunter down the street, coming to a halt outside the newsagent.

Ajay to Launch New Yoga Centre on Gold Coast

I grind my teeth, pick up a copy of the newspaper and read the story.

> *Ajay is launching his latest Bikini Body Boot Camp Speed Yoga centre, Gold Coast Bliss. The opening will feature the famous Gold Coast meter maids ...*

Well, that's interesting. I ponder the story as I continue my beat. Madeleine and Luna have lost their jobs and here's Ajay, launching a new yoga centre. It doesn't seem fair. Minor case of kidnapping aside ...

'Hey, hey, what do you think you're doing?' A man bounds out of Paradise Real Estate and scampers after me, his white shoes flashing like twin rabbits. He has a razor-sharp line down the front of his lime-green slacks. His face is the colour of polished cedar and thick white hair sweeps off it like a wave running out to sea.

I eyeball him over the top of my glasses, sliding a one-dollar coin into the pay-and-display as I do so. 'Just doing my job, sir.'

Something flashes across his face – recognition that I might be a force to be reckoned with. 'You, you can't be a meter maid. I pay my money to have meter maids who are going to attract tourists.'

'Your point, exactly?'

'Well ...' He isn't sure how to break it to me. 'You don't look like a meter maid.'

'I don't?' I feign amazement. 'But all I've ever wanted was to be a meter maid. This job is a dream come true for me.'

'Where are you from?' he asks.

'Northcliff. You know, just down the highway.'

'I know Northcliff,' he snaps. 'What I want to know is why you've been employed as a meter maid when you are clearly unsuitable.'

'Well, sir, it's morally wrong to discriminate against generously proportioned girls with glasses. Haven't you heard of equal opportunity?'

This is clearly news to him. 'Ridiculous – why can't we have good-looking girls on the street?'

He must see the look I shoot him as his chivalrous side comes to the fore. 'Not that you're not a good-looking girl, but you don't look the part.'

I lean against a car and read the name on his badge. 'Well, Kenny, the way I see it is ...' I don't know where it all comes from – maybe it's been bottled up for too long – but words erupt like a volcanic explosion. The cultural desert of the Gold Coast, the way women's bodies are used to sell junk, the demeaning nature of some souvenirs – with these topics and more I earbash poor Kenny.

To his credit he listens. Not only does he listen, he nods at appropriate moments. 'I haven't considered that before. You could have a point there,' he says when I finish.

I'm flabbergasted. I didn't expect him to listen; I was only venting.

Kenny's face is thoughtful. 'You know, you remind me of my late wife. She used to go on like that. I never listened though – wish I had.'

We chat for an hour, Kenny and I, leaning against the meters, moving on every now and then to pop tickets on windscreens ahead of us. We should have nothing in common, except … I remind him of his wife. He'd been too busy buying real estate while she was alive to listen to her crackpot theories.

At the end of the hour he shakes my hand. 'Nice meeting you, Olivia. If you ever need anything, just ask for Kenny the King.' As my coins slide into the meter, a penny drops in my head – this is Rosco's landlord.

Over the next few days, Kenny is my staunchest ally in a battle for the hearts and minds of the Gold Coast. Whenever he sees me getting a hard time he pops out, white shoes blazing. 'Listen, mate,' he says. 'Don't you know all women are beautiful just the way they are?'

Those clients who still want to dispute my viability as a meter maid mostly back down after a lecture on the politics of body image. If things get tricky, I put my cowboy hat on the ground and do a headstand on top of it. What's the point in having a signature move if you don't use it?

The other meter maids aren't sure how to take me at first. Conversations stop as I come into the change room. I catch them eyeing my stomach. They gradually come around though. At the end of the week they invite me out for Friday night drinks.

I end up delivering my manifesto to a circle of blow-dried beauties. 'It's not you girls that are the problem, it's the system. The system that says bikini girls on the streets are good for business.' Some of them nod like they take my point.

'Right on, sister,' says Lena, a dark-haired girl with an English accent, reaching for the peanuts on the bar. A couple of others follow her lead. I'm pleased to see them developing an appetite.

'Hey,' says Lena, coming in on Monday morning and patting her flat-as-a-pancake stomach. 'I put on half a kilo, but I guess if Olivia can do it, so can I.'

Word gets around about my unusual approach to the craft of meter-maiding. Some tourists come to have their photo taken with me. The cameras go crazy when I do a headstand. Bizarrely, I become something of a cause célèbre. On Tuesday, someone from the women's studies section of the university comes to interview me.

'Did you deliberately set out to subvert the dominant paradigm?' an earnest short-haired woman asks me.

I blink. 'Yeah, I guess.'

Back at home, Nan's silence on my new occupation is hard to interpret. 'I suppose I'm going to have to get myself a new bikini,' is her only comment.

Jacq is so used to me going out the door in peculiar outfits it takes her a while to register that anything has changed. 'Why don't we see Rosco anymore?' she says eventually as I'm heading out the door in my bikini.

'I've changed jobs. I don't work for Rosco anymore.'

'That's stupid. Why not?'

'I needed a change.'

'What do you need a change for? You just had a change.'

There isn't much I can say – not without making her worry that her sister is unstable. I kiss her, fluff her hair and duck out the door.

If my beat ever takes me near Gold Star Investigations I walk quickly and don't look up at the windows. Once, I get an upside-down view of Rosco driving past while I'm posing for a photo in my headstand. His head turns, but he is past before I can register the expression on his face.

It's painful to think about the way I've stuffed things up. I'd dreamed of being a PI for so long – catching villains, hiding in dark alleyways with my collar turned up. Sure, the reality was vastly different. I'd still loved it though – the thrill of the chase, the puzzle of it all.

And it isn't only the job I've stuffed up. There's also Rosco. Sometimes I have to control an urge to burst back into Gold Star Investigations and demand to know what went wrong. But ... he knows where to find me.

On Thursday, as I feed a meter near McSushi, I notice the posters of Maya have come down. Hopefully it's a sign she's taking control of her sponsorship deals. In her place is a glamour shot of Georgia Hansen. 'Is that a nori roll in your pocket or are you just pleased to see me?' reads the caption. *Classy*.

I gaze at the poster and my heart gives a rapid pit-a-pat as I remember what's happening tomorrow.

On Friday afternoon, Madeleine, Luna, Brooklyn and I peer through the window of the exclusive Paradise Nightclub.

The party for the launch of Gold Coast Bliss is in full swing. Beautiful people, buffed, toned and tanned to within an inch of their lives, rub shoulders inside. The media is here too. I see a TV camera and a few reporters with zoom lenses. My mouth is dry and my heart thuds in my chest. Madeleine and Brooklyn look nervous too. Luna, however, is pumped.

'Let's do it.' Luna puts up her hand and we all slap it. 'All for one and one for all,' she says. 'No one gets left behind, right?'

'Right,' we echo dutifully.

Luna looks disappointed at our muted response. 'Right?' she says again.

'You got it, babe,' drawls Brooklyn.

A pink flush moves up Luna's cheeks.

Dressed in our gold bikinis, high heels and tiny white aprons, we go in the service door and head for the buffet. We stash a backpack under the table, pick up a tray of canapés each, and circulate. I've worded up the other meter maids, so they don't bat an eyelid.

I hand around oysters, ignoring the guests' double take at the sight of me in a gold bikini. Madeleine, Brooklyn and Luna raise some eyebrows too. Madeleine and Brooklyn are lily-white and Luna's legs are au naturel, a soft, golden down covering her calves. At least she hadn't insisted on a hemp bikini. We are not 'bikini-beach-body-ready', but here we are, with our bodies in bikinis nonetheless. Confusion ripples through the crowd in our wake.

After fifteen minutes or so, the microphone squawks and Ajay climbs to the stage. Luna, Madeleine and I ditch our canapés and pull out the special trays from our backpacks.

'I'm delighted to announce,' says Ajay, 'the opening of my new venture, Gold Coast Bliss. Gold Coast Bliss will continue my mission to bring Bikini Beach Body Speed Yoga Boot Camp to the world. It's an exciting—'

I press a button on my phone and 'Rebel Girl' by Bikini Kill blasts out from the little bluetooth speakers I've placed on the stage. Ajay falls silent as Luna, Brooklyn, Madeleine and I sashay up the stairs, holding our trays in front of us, as if to offer him a delicious treat.

Clearly he recognises us, but he doesn't look too concerned at first. I'm sure he assumes someone has organised a special presentation. As the music blasts, we dance on the stage next to him, our trays held in front of us. The guests watch this avant-garde performance with interest. A couple of cameras flash.

As the song reaches its chorus, we whip the tea towels off our trays and pick up the objects beneath.

'One, two, three, go,' I call.

Four rubber arms with an inked-in tattoo of a man in lotus position fly into the crowd. We put down our trays. Still dancing,

Luna whisks off her apron and strides to the front of the stage. Madeleine does the same, then Brooklyn, then me.

I look out at the sea of phones, held up to take our photos. Written across our stomachs in large, black letters are: *Ajay Keep, Your Hands, to Yourself, #fakearmsagainstharassment*. As my stomach provides a broader canvas than the other girls', I volunteered for the hashtag. We pose for a few seconds, our clenched fists raised.

A security guard has decided we are not an approved part of the program and is heading towards us. I glance at Ajay before we run off the stage. He is gazing at us with the startled expression of a rabbit caught in the headlights.

As we race for the door, I hear clapping. I pause and turn. It's the meter maids. They clap harder and harder. Lena raises her fist in a salute. I smile at them and wave.

'Come on, Olivia,' yells Luna from the door. 'No one gets left behind.'

The security guard is heading for me. I kick off my high heels and run. We race down Cavill Avenue, the security guard gaining on us. He reaches out and his fingers brush my shoulder. I accelerate, passing Zander, where he stands in front of the souvenir shop and outback bar.

He nods at me and steps in front of the security guard, holding up a life-size kangaroo soft toy to block his path. 'Special. Twenty dorrars,' I hear him say as I round the corner.

Madeleine, Brooklyn and Luna are still running ahead of me. Brooklyn and Luna are holding hands. Somehow, this is not a surprise.

We reach the car, leap in and accelerate away with the wind in our hair, laughing fit to burst.

The next morning, Jacq and I jump in the car. On the spur of the moment, I've decided to clear out of the Gold Coast for the weekend and go camping in Byron Bay. It might be best to lie low until the dust settles. I stop off at a newsagent on the way, pick up a copy of the *Gold Coast Times* and scan the headline.

Meter Maids Disrupt Gold Coast Bliss Launch.
Ajay, founder of Bikini Beach Body Speed Yoga Boot Camp, has gone into hiding as harassment complaints flood in following yesterday's surprise demonstration ...

I look at the picture below and smile. Legs apart, arms in the air, Madeleine, Brooklyn, Luna and I look like warriors. We are Princess Leia after she vanquished the giant slug. Rey after she defeated Kylo Ren. Wonder Woman after she thrashed Ares. The horse is with us. It's not a revolution, not yet, but it's a start. In some small way I've done my best to make the Gold Coast a place I can live in.

But over, I guess it's safe to assume, my meter maiding days are.

44

Jacq and I turn the radio up loud as we drive under the monorail and past the casino. Every time I leave the Gold Coast I'm reminded of a scene in that old movie *Muriel's Wedding* where she leaves Porpoise Spit. *Goodbye high rise, goodbye malls, goodbye tourists.* It's not long before we pass the *Welcome to New South Wales* sign – always an exciting moment.

'Why don't they have pictures?' Jacq asks. 'Like the Queensland sign?'

Jacq's right. New South Wales is lacking in image enhancement. On arrival in Queensland you know what you're getting – life savers, beaches, happy times. On arrival in New South Wales you know you're getting your speed checked.

I tune into Lighthouse FM as we drive towards the town. ' … chunderous fat junky mushburgers,' drawls the announcer. It must be the surf report. That's thirty-seven words for surf now. We're going to beat those Inuits, I know it.

Jacq and I attempt a surf, but the surf report is right. Or mostly right. Grovelling gutless crap would describe it better. *Forty words.* The waves are all wrong – too sweepy and sucky. I go straight down the face and crash into the shallow sandbank.

I keep expecting to see Maya carving it up and putting me to shame but there's no sign of her.

In half an hour Jacq and I are swept over a kilometre down the beach. 'Is it still surfing if you don't catch any waves?' Jacq asks as we trudge back to the car park with our boards. Despite the quality of the waves, it's still good to be out there.

I've arranged to catch up with Luna and Madeleine in a café. Brooklyn should be on her way back to LA by now.

'You sheilas are bonza,' she said as she hugged us goodbye at her motel. Her hug with Luna lasted much longer than mine.

'It was awesome riding shotgun with you,' I said.

She gave a honking laugh and high-fived me. 'Native dialect, right?'

'Right,' I said.

Jacq and I are at the café first. I haven't checked my phone since this morning, so I pull it out now. Messages pop up on the screen.

Luna and Madeleine burst in, broad grins on their faces. Luna is wearing a brown hemp jumpsuit and Madeleine's red lycra tights match her glossy hair.

'We've gone viral.' Luna holds out her phone.

'Oh yeah. Three hundred thousand views and rising,' says Madeleine. 'Fake arms against harassment is trending on Twitter.'

'Wow.' I smile at them. It's a little overwhelming.

Luna puts up her hand and Madeleine and I smack it. 'Cool protest,' she says. 'I'm pumped. I've decided protesting is my vocation. I'm thinking of joining that mob who sink whaling ships now.'

'Who, Greenpeace?' I ask.

'Nah, Greenpeace are wimps. Sea Shepherd – they've got the mojos, they just ram 'em,' says Luna.

'I'm in,' says Madeleine. 'As long as they have showers on board and somewhere to do yoga.'

'You'd both be good at that,' I say.

'You should join too. You were probably a whale in your past life,' says Luna.

I turn my snort into a sniff. 'Maybe.'

Jacq has been sipping her milkshake quietly and absorbing our conversation.

Luna turns to her now. 'You too. You have a beautiful aura. I bet you end up working with whales or dolphins. Would you like that?'

Jacq nods. 'I like dolphins,' she almost whispers.

'I knew it,' says Luna.

'Hey gang.' The voice is a loud American drawl.

We all turn.

Brooklyn is standing next to the table wearing bib and brace shorts with a red singlet and a red felt hat.

'What are you doing here?' Luna's voice is low. 'I thought you were on your way home.'

'I was, but ... I was at Gold Coast airport and I watched that video of us and, you know, I had another epiphany.'

Luna blinks.

'I love this place and I love you chicks.' Brooklyn rests her hand on Luna's shoulder. 'And I just felt like I should stay.'

Beneath Luna's tan a deep flush runs up her face. She meets Brooklyn's eyes and they smile.

On Sunday, Jacq and I climb the steep steps to the Lighthouse. A northerly wind whips at our hair and flattens the surf to whitecaps. Panting, we look over the cliff edge and see two dolphins, a mother and a calf, below us. They don't seem to be doing anything except enjoying the warm water. I imagine them as the slackers of the dolphin world. *I can't be bothered catching fish. Let's get takeaways tonight.* If I was a dolphin, that would be me.

Jacq starts back down the track, but I stand and watch the dolphins for a while. It's only two weeks now until uni starts. Abbey and Frannie will be back from Asia soon. Mum and Dad are back from Nepal on Monday. They'll be wanting to know what I'm doing.

I wish I knew.

45

Jacq and I drive back to the campsite. A guy is lying on the grass outside our tent with a cap over his face. When he sits up, my stomach feels like *it's* been put in a rocket and someone's pressed launch.

'Rosco,' squeals Jacq. She climbs out of the car, runs over and jumps on him.

I follow more cautiously. I thought I'd moved on but, no, my preposterous pounding heart tells me otherwise.

'Your grandmother said I'd find you here.' Rosco pants as he wrestles Jacq to the ground. 'I win – you've got to give me and Olivia a few minutes to talk now.'

'How many minutes?' Jacq checks her new digital watch. I bought her one at the same time as I bought a new one myself – hopefully it won't beep at inappropriate moments.

'Ten minutes,' says Rosco.

Jacq starts her stopwatch and runs away towards the playground.

Rosco sets a timer on his phone and stands, brushing off his board shorts. 'Hey.' He flicks his blond hair out of his eyes.

'Hey.' I fold my arms. 'Are you down here surfing?'

'You're joking; in that manky pissweak slop?'

I pull out my phone, consult my list and pump my fist. 'That's it – forty-three words for surf. We've beaten the Inuits at their own game.'

Rosco looks at me blankly. 'Huh?'

I drop my hand. 'It doesn't matter – it's this thing I've been doing. It's stupid.'

Rosco gazes at me for a few moments. 'I wanted to show you something.' He picks up an issue of *Tracks* from the grass next to him.

He came here to show me Tracks? It's a 'boys own' surf magazine – girls generally only feature as beach decoration.

Rosco flips it open. The page is titled **World Longboard Championships – Waikiki.**

'How'd Maya go?'

Rosco points to a tiny picture in the corner of the page – three girls lined up with surfboards. The rest of the page is devoted to huge pictures of the 'real' surfers – i.e. men. 'She came second.'

'Oh.' I wonder how Brad took that.

'That's not the main story though.' Rosco points to one of the larger pictures, a close-up of two men sitting on the beach. The caption is *Feud ended?* One of the men is Brad Cahill and the other ...

'Budgie Goldsworth?'

Rosco nods.

I peer at the photo. The men aren't smiling. It's hard to read much into their expressions – a wary acceptance seems to be the mood of the day. I read the article.

Former world champion Brad Cahill said he 'couldn't be prouder' of his daughter Maya's second place in the titles.

Asked if he and Budgie were now on speaking terms Brad commented enigmatically – 'Me and Budgie ... we've banged the drum together. Once you've done that, well, you know what's important. Maybe Budgie was right all along. Surfing isn't about chasing big sponsorship deals. Money goes, but in the end it's those surfs in the sunshine you'll remember.'

I smile. At least one thing's turned out the way it should.

'You did that,' says Rosco.

'I did nothing. James and Maya did that.' There's a long silence. I thaw a bit. It was good of him to come all the way here to show me the article. 'How's your neighbour? Does she still think you're a terrorist?'

'Yeah, she's been sorting through my rubbish. It doesn't bother me too much.' Rosco glances at his phone. 'I've only got five minutes left.' He rolls and unrolls the magazine between his hands. 'It's nice to see you again.'

'You too.' I'm not sure if it is though.

'Brad's right y'know – about finding out what's important.'

'Surfing in the sunshine? I thought you knew that already.'

'Yeah, surfing, but other things too. Getting your priorities right, that's what's important.'

I nod. 'Mm?'

'I saw you out there on the street – meter maiding.'

I flush, waiting for him to tease me.

'Every time I saw you I wanted to stop and talk, but ... your phone message – it sounded like you wanted to move on. I didn't want to get in your way. I saw what happened at Ajay's launch though. It made me laugh.'

I frown.

'Not *at* you Olivia, not at *you*,' Rosco says quickly. 'At everything, at the system, at how you brought that slimy weasel down.' He is smiling now. 'No one except you could have done that. You drive me crazy, but you're something else.' He shakes his head. 'You were like a tornado in the office.'

'Well, I guess the weather must be fine there now.'

Rosco clears his throat. 'When I saw you doing that headstand on the street...' He bites his bottom lip, like he's trying to suppress a laugh.

I wait. I'm not going to help him out.

'I'd like you to come back.' The words come out quickly.

I take off my glasses, clean them and put them on again. 'What sort of an offer is that?'

There's a long silence. 'What sort of an offer do you want?'

I take a deep breath. 'There's only one way this could work.'

He tilts his head. 'And what way is that?'

'Full partnership. I want to buy in. I don't want to be your sidekick anymore.'

'Ok-ay.' Rosco draws out the word. 'Why not? I'm prepared to give it a go.'

'You are?' I smile.

He nods. 'You'll need to get your PI license.'

'I will. Do you think we can make this work?'

'I don't know, but I think it's worth a try.' He puts out his hand. I stare at it.

'Shake.'

'Oh, right.' We shake hands.

He glances at his phone. 'One minute left.' His eyes meet mine.

There it is again – that flash, that Spark, that surge of energy. A hot flush spreads over my face and down my neck.

My flush infects Rosco. His face colours too.

We stare at each other.

In the end – *what's the worst that can happen?* – I'm the one who moves first.

And – I knew it! When you get kissed by the right person it's totally different – like an explosion racing through your body. *Zing pow zap*. It's like being on a wave that goes forever. Sixty seconds isn't long, but it's just enough time for a heart-stopping, Hollywood-style, red-hot kiss. A Notably Notable Exception.

We step apart as we hear Jacq's watch beep over at the playground. It's probably lucky; I might have gone up in flames if that kiss had gone on any longer. My heart thumps in my chest, my legs are weak, my brain's forgotten how to think. 'I didn't see that coming.' I touch my lips.

'Neither did I.' Rosco looks stunned. 'That was ... It was like ...'

'Han and Leia in *The Empire Strikes Back?*'

He smiles. 'Exactly.'

Jacq runs towards us. 'Time's up.'

'And here come the stormtroopers, right on schedule,' says Rosco.

We smile at each other, slow and dreamy. I have no idea how this is going to work, or if it's going to work at all, but right now that seems okay. I'll just have to take it day by day.

Epilogue

Rosco and I climb over the sand dunes and down to the beach with our boards under our arms. The wind has died off and the sea is glassy. The full moon casts a silver trail across the water.

We push our boards out into the water, jumping as the waves splash at us. Paddling hard, we push through the whitewash. When we get out the back, we sit up, breathing deeply. Across the bay, the hills are dark against the sky.

A wave – a ripple of silver – is coming.

'Yours,' says Rosco.

Pulling the front of my board around, I glance behind my shoulder and paddle. The wave picks me up and, jumping to my feet, I glide down the black face. My body moves like it knows what to do.

It's just like flying.

The sea is black, but beneath me an eerie green glow appears. It's like I'm trailing luminescent paint. *Phosphorescent algae*, I think, but my heart whispers *magic*.

The wave breaks with a roar, catapulting me into blackness. I come up gasping, saltwater running down my face. I fling handful after handful of water into the air, watching it fall like glowing snowflakes. Green sparks flash around me.

I'm here. I'm back. I am Olivia Grace, private investigator, and I'm not going to let the weasels get me down.

Acknowledgements

Thank you to everyone who has helped me bring *The Girl with the Gold Bikini* to publication.

Wakefield Press has been a joy to work with. Special thanks to Margot Lloyd, for her enthusiasm and skilful editing.

In its early stages, this novel was supported by a Litlink Residency from the Varuna Writers Centre, which included invaluable advice from Peter Bishop. I also received sage counsel from Marele Day, on an even earlier version, through the Byron Writers Festival's mentorship program.

The Byron Writers Festival staff past and present have been a source of support over many years.

My writing group – Helen Burns, Jane Camens, Jessie Cole, Siboney Duff, Michelle Taylor and Jane Meredith – provided support and advice over various iterations of the story.

Thank you to my agent, Jane Novak, for finding this novel such a perfect home at Wakefield Press and also for being such an insightful reader.

My family: John, Simon, Tim, Sue and all my extended family, too – thank you for your ongoing love and support.

And finally, thank you to my readers. I hope you have had as much fun reading *The Girl with the Gold Bikini* as I had writing it.

Author's note

Everyone has the right to a workplace free from discrimination and harassment. In Australia, national and state laws cover equal employment opportunity and anti-discrimination in the workplace. Discrimination on the basis of appearance is, however, currently not regulated in any of the states except Victoria.

Wakefield Press is an independent publishing and
distribution company based in Adelaide, South Australia.
We love good stories and publish beautiful books.
To see our full range of books, please visit our website at
www.wakefieldpress.com.au
where all titles are available for purchase.
To keep up with our latest releases, news and events,
subscribe to our monthly newsletter.

Find us!

Facebook: www.facebook.com/wakefield.press
Twitter: www.twitter.com/wakefieldpress
Instagram: www.instagram.com/wakefieldpress